Strange — she'd never made love to Alison in such total darkness. Even with lights off, drapes drawn and doors shut, slivers of light always seeped into their respective bedrooms at home in Berkeley. Somehow the curtains here at the hotel were designed to completely cut off any light at all, and Helen felt her headache dissipate as she moved farther down Alison's body. There was something freeing about darkness, she realized, something that allowed her to ignore Alison's halfhearted protests. Her mouth and her hands took on a life of their own, and her lover's voice faded into unimportance.

Half-shocked at her own feelings of detachment mixed with desire, Helen trailed her lips downward. Alison was silent now, save for a deep sigh as Helen gently pushed her legs apart.

It didn't take long for Alison to reach climax. "Again," Helen whispered as Alison started to roll over on her side.

She slid her hand between Alison's legs. Her fingers played with the warm wet skin she found there, and Alison's body heaved in response.

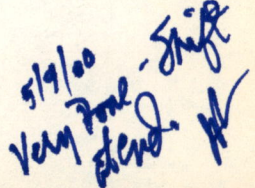

LOOKING FOR NAIAD?

Buy our books at
www.naiadpress.com

or call our toll-free number
1-800-533-1973

or by fax (24 hours a day)
1-850-539-9731

Snake Eyes

A Helen Black Mystery

by

PAT WELCH

THE NAIAD PRESS, INC.
1999

Copyright © 1999 by Pat Welch

All rights reserved. No part of this book may be reproduced or transmitted in any form or by any means, electronic or mechanical, including photocopying, without permission in writing from the publisher.

Printed in the United States of America on acid-free paper
First Edition

Editor: Christine Cassidy
Cover designer: Bonnie Liss (Phoenix Graphics)
Typesetter: Sandi Stancil

Library of Congress Cataloging-in-Publication Data

Welch, Pat, 1957 –
  Snake eyes : a Helen Black mystery / by Pat Welch.
    p.   cm.
  ISBN 1-56280-242-9 (alk. paper)
  I. Title.
PS3573.E4543S65 1999
813'.54—dc21   98-48245
                                                                 CIP

About the Author

Pat Welch was born in Japan in 1957. After returning to the states she grew up in an assortment of small towns in the South until her family relocated to Florida. Since attending college in southern California she has lived on the West Coast, moving to the San Francisco Bay Area in 1986. Pat now lives and works in Oakland. *Snake Eyes* is the seventh novel in her Helen Black mystery series, which include *Murder by the Book, Still Waters, A Proper Burial, Open House, Smoke and Mirrors* and *Fallen from Grace*. Her short stories have appeared in several Naiad anthologies.

Prologue

This time the photograph had two tiny perforations where her eyes should have been.

Last week a red felt-tip marker had slashed across her body in the picture, and the time before that her entire face was blacked out with rough strokes of a ballpoint pen that had pierced through the paper.

Carmel Kittrick forced herself to breathe slowly and deeply, and with a careful calm motion she placed the sheet of paper flat on her desk. All around her, various and sundry office minions swirled and eddied, carrying on the business of her business, completely unaware of the roiling in her stomach that threatened to leave her lunch in unsightly chunks all over the walnut desk.

As phones and pagers hummed in the background, she did the same quick study of the photograph and envelope she had before. Same details as before. It was almost boring, really — a black-and-white copy of a photograph, the kind of copy that could be made at any print shop or office supply store. Ragged edges on the original, as if whoever was sending these things to her had ripped out the picture from the newspaper and run off a stack of photocopies in great haste. Plain white business envelope anyone might have obtained from anyplace, with her name and company's address on a label that could have come from any laser printer in the country. Postmarked in Jackson, Mississippi, two days previously, with no return address. Just like the last four.

She'd almost tossed out the first one. Arriving in a huge pile of mail, consisting mostly of responses to her feelers about expanding the business on the West Coast, it had slipped down unremarked into the stack of nothings she usually let Louise sort through at the end of the day. After all, why bother with a simple photocopy of an old newspaper clipping? That one had shown no signs of cutting or marking or mutilation — just the copy in grainy black-and-white, fluttering out on the desk like a scrap of flotsam on a sea of trivia.

She still didn't know what made her pick it up and shove it into a drawer. Maybe just the fact that it made no sense. It wasn't advertising, it wasn't a bill, it wasn't even a letter from someone wanting something. Its oddity had clicked in her mind, so she kept it. And forgot it.

Until the following week, when the next one came sporting a tear in the page at the point where her neck met her head. A small, precise incision that hinted at deliberate and meticulous intent.

And the photograph torn from the *Jackson Commercial*

Register was two – no, three – years old now, dating from the time she took over the business from Old Fart. So why had these things started showing up? Why not three years ago?

Once again it had been hidden in Wednesday's shuffle of parcels and envelopes and packages directed toward her office from the mailroom in the basement.

She looked up from the desk and tuned in briefly to the bustle just beyond her office door. Did anyone out there have any idea of what she was looking at? She caught glances now and then from some of her forty employees but noted nothing in their expressions beyond the faint anxiety of worker bees keeping watch on their irritable and inscrutable queen. Did one of those blank faces hide a smug satisfaction at having successfully terrified her? Was there someone out there answering a phone or holding a meeting or scrubbing a floor who harbored intense hatred for her?

Stupid questions, really. She sighed and carefully folded the sheet along the creases left by the sender who'd originally created this ghoulish work, then she slipped it into the envelope. After all, a woman in her position was likely to get all kinds of odd things in her mail. Besides —

"Ms. Kittrick?"

"Yes, Louise."

Louise's soft drawl oozed over the intercom. She could tell, from the edge in the secretary's voice, that Louise hadn't yet had her midmorning coffee and cinnamon roll — there was just a tinge of iron beneath the molasses of that ladylike tone Louise cultivated. And Louise hated dealing with the phones before her morning coffee and cinnamon roll. "It's your father on line two."

"Thanks, Louise." She lay the envelope on her desk and reached for the phone. She put a hand on the receiver, then took it away and pushed a button on the phone and leaned back into her chair. "Yes, Daddy?"

Her father's voice bellowed out into the room. "You got me on that damned speakerphone again?" he barked.

She smiled sweetly and folded her arms over her chest as she snuggled down deep into the chair, savoring the feel of the expensive cushions Louise had found after months of searching. "Sorry, Daddy, got my hands pretty full," she lied. "What's up?"

"Seen your brother yet? Think he's s'posed to be back from Area whatdyacallem last night—"

"Area Fifty-one, Daddy," she said with a snarl. Why the hell her father insisted on keeping her idiot brother Wilbur informed of the family business, she had no idea. It didn't seem to matter to Daddy that while she ran a highly successful multimillion-dollar business, Wilbur Kittrick was off in the desert, hoping to be abducted by aliens. She couldn't imagine that, even in his drug-fogged, failing state, her father seriously believed that his son would one day take over the business. "Don't worry, he promised to be here for the Winners' Circle today."

He sighed. Even over the breaks and hums of the speaker, she could hear how his stiffening lungs, squeezed under the weight of a lifetime of cigarettes, struggled for oxygen. "Just got that little speech this morning, the one you wanted me to say when we greet the sweepstakes winners?"

"Uh-huh." She rolled her eyes. Why the hell hadn't she cut him out of it altogether? She should have known he'd make trouble for her about this. She swiveled the chair around so she could see out the picture window. Just below the office building the Mississippi River gleamed in the mid-morning sunlight as it curved around Natchez Pier. Magnolia trees loomed thick and green with lush, glossy beauty around the red brick paths circling the company grounds, and one of those restored steamboats, filled with tourists hoping to capture a glimpse of the antebellum South, trailed a graceful path of white splendor on the river. No doubt the tourists' cameras were trained on this very building as the steamboat passed by.

And here she sat, ruling the whole thing like some medieval potentate, forced to listen to Old Fart once again.

"It's all that stuff about the New South, babydoll," he wheezed. "I just don't think these folks want to hear that. I mean, they ain't interested in politics, Carmel. They just want to know what they won."

With a grimace she spun the chair back around and glared at the telephone. "Daddy, we've gone over this before. Now you know we went to a lot of trouble to hire those marketing people. Why don't you just trust me on this?"

A fit of coughing ensued. Even over the speaker she could tell it was a bad one, and she had an uncomfortable glimpse of her father shuddering and retching as his body gave way to a desperate paroxysm of pain.

As soon as the coughing passed she heard the muffled gasping that meant his oxygen mask was now clapped to his face. Good. He wouldn't be able to interrupt her.

"Now, Daddy, honey, you just rest up. You have to meet these people this afternoon, and you need to relax. I'm the one who's going to fly out to Nevada with them next week, so after today you won't be involved in any of this. You don't have to give a speech at all, okay, darlin'? You just leave all that to me."

She waited long enough to get a whispered assent from Old Fart, then cut the connection. Good God, why didn't he just go ahead and get it over with and die? She was already running the business alone. Lord knows he wasn't able to lift the proverbial finger to help her, not without hacking and wheezing, anyway.

"Louise, what time is that meeting with marketing?"

"Eleven-thirty. Then you have lunch with Haskell, Haskell and Grimes, then the Winners' Circle."

Thank heavens, Louise must have had a sip or two of coffee. "Thanks." She flipped open the maroon leather daybook resting next to the speakerphone. "Get Bill Hefley in here for me, please."

"I haven't seen him yet —"

"Then page him, Louise." She stabbed the button on the phone and cut off any further protest. Might as well get this over with, and here at the office was the best place. Much better than some restaurant or in either of their own homes. Hef wouldn't dare pull some scene on her here. Not if he valued his balls.

She eyed the white envelope still sitting on the desk next to the intercom. Quickly she got up from her chair and crossed the spacious office to close the door, then went to a small bookcase behind the desk. She ran her fingers along the top of the bookcase — the catch was just under the molding at the side, hidden beneath the lacy fronds of the enormous potted fern.

No. Wait. Why not just leave the envelope out, sitting there on her desk? That way she could see Hef's reaction to it. Then she'd know for sure it wasn't him, that her first assumption had been right all along.

Louise buzzed her within two minutes, and Bill Hefley walked in.

The smirk on his face disgusted her. She stood up, swallowing the nausea burning in her stomach at his evident pleasure in being summoned to her presence. How could she ever have let this overgrown, aging football star paw at her body for all these months? Boredom, she realized, taking in his paunch straining at the oh-so-casual Dockers, the thinning hair artfully arranged over a gleaming forehead, the piggy dark eyes nestled in a beer-bloated face that would, in just a few more years, melt into jowled flab. Boredom and the need for a good fuck — something she'd been certain that the former Ole Miss quarterback and Heisman Trophy winner would relieve.

He shut the door behind him, holding his palm against the wood to muffle the noise, then turned that big grin on her. "Hey, babe." He crossed the room quickly, his arms spread wide for a hug. "Just about got this show on the road now. Oh, by the way, your brother Wilbur is here. Wants to see you." He put one hand on the small of her back and leaned in for a kiss. She reluctantly let him peck at her cheek. "He's still trying to get me to go to one of those UFO conventions, now that he knows I'll be over in Nevada."

"So now my idiot brother is privy to business decisions? Since when?"

"Hey, back off, babe." He put his hands up in mock surrender and treated her to a goofy grin. "Your old man knew that once you put me in charge of Western Region I'd be going to Nevada to set up that chain of restaurants out there. He just wants his son to have a baby-sitter. But don't worry, sweetheart. You won't get neglected."

"Sit down, Hef." She eased back into her chair and watched his face. The tightening of his features indicated that her tone alerted him something was up. "We have to talk."

"I'm listening," he responded, all overtones of the good ol' boy abated.

She sighed and fingered the white envelope, watching him closely. "I don't know a way to do this delicately, Hef, so I'll just come to the point. When you go out to Nevada to manage the chain of restaurants, our, uh, relationship will be over."

"Over." It wasn't a question or a plea or a whine — just a word, muttered through those pouting full lips that had no doubt gotten him into quite a few beds since his Ole Miss days. And not a glance at the envelope.

"Yes. It's been fun, Hef, but it can't continue." She let the envelope fall and faced him squarely, determined to get rid of the image of his fat sweaty face heaving up and down over her prone body the last time they'd fucked. "You'll be leaving next week, of course, and I just wanted to get this taken care of —"

"Like everything else on your agenda, right?" His face

was so red it was almost purple. She watched his hands flexing on the arms of the chair.

"Oh, for God's sake, Hef, don't give me this crap." She sighed again, shaking her head. "The only reason you wanted to screw me was to get that managerial position, and we both know that. Well, you got it. So you can leave that scorned suitor bullshit back in the locker room."

He got up, his mouth working hard beneath his bushy mustache. When he spoke again, his voice was choked and harsh. "Fine, Carmel. If that's the way you want it."

"That's the way I want it."

"You weren't that good a fuck, anyhow."

"Is that the best you can do, Hef? A man of your talents?" She opened her daybook again. "Don't miss the meeting with the Winners' Circle this afternoon, Hef. I'm sure the men will want your autograph." She looked up. Hef had already made his exit and her words were directed at the closed door.

With a sigh she shut the daybook once again. Hef would pout for a while, no doubt, but at least now that he'd be overseeing the Western Division of Kittrick she wouldn't have to endure his bad behavior. Grasping the envelope, she went back to the bookcase behind the desk.

The side of the bookcase snapped outward slightly as she pressed the edge of the molding. The slender metal wedge of the small safe gave off a dull sheen when she opened it and took out the pile of plain white envelopes.

That made five, now. She placed her newest missive onto the slim heap, aligning the edges of the envelopes. Handling these fucking things somehow made her feel better — as if she were really in control of it all. They were just pieces of paper, anyway.

The sound of a motor revving rose up from the grounds. Carmel moved to the window and saw a three-man maintenance crew preparing to work on the pristine landscape. One of the men glanced up and saw her standing there. It was the one she'd noticed before, the new employee. Jeff? Or was it Jim? Something like that. Even at this distance, and in those ugly beige overalls, he looked good. She smiled to herself. With Hef out of the way, maybe she could borrow Jim-Jeff for some home maintenance. As if he'd felt her gaze, Jim-Jeff ducked his head and fiddled with the lawn mower. A nice touch, she thought, that shy awkward thing. Sort of appealing.

She turned back to her desk. So what if she'd pissed off some good ol' boy? They couldn't touch her now.

Could they?

Besides, she had a fair idea of who was sending them.

Now it was just a question of what to do about it.

Chapter One

Helen Black leaned against the wall of the elevator, then moved away with a swift intake of breath and gingerly positioned herself in a more comfortable stance. Even though the bullet had gone in a clean shot through her side, missing vital organs and veins by several inches, she still found herself favoring the right half of her body as if it were only yesterday — not just over eighteen months ago — that she'd been wounded while on her last case as a private investigator. The doctors had all agreed that she'd healed nicely, and two small scars were all she had to show for the surgery and the nightmares and the pain that had come with the fragment of metal shattering her life into unrecognizable odds and ends.

Other people crowded into the elevator at each floor, most of them carefully holding plastic containers filled with coins and tokens for the slot machines and gaming tables down on the first floor of the Silver Saddle. Cradling the containers as if they were each a remnant of some gambler's holy grail, they grinned cheerfully at Helen, including her in their delight at being here in Laughlin, Nevada's haven for geriatrics' nickel-and-dime games of chance.

Helen smiled and nodded, telling herself for the millionth time to be polite and not spoil the fun. After all, an awful lot of these people had saved for years to purchase a weekend at one of the casinos along the Colorado River. Their pleasure didn't need to be spoiled just because Helen Black, misanthropic ex-detective, was in a bad mood.

The elevator stopped at every floor, and Helen tried to distract herself by guessing the destination of the people compacted in the small chamber as it slowly made its descent. The two men in spandex and tank tops were no doubt headed for the gym that occupied half of the third floor. That woman wearing the paisley scarf twisted around her head might be going to the beauty salon across the corridor from the gym. The three women giggling and checking their tickets were probably on their way to the movie theater that sported a glittering marquee in the heart of the casino. Helen wasn't sure, but she thought the first-run flick featured this week was the latest Hollywood action flick, complete with musclebound star and lots of car crashes.

Loy and Edna had assured Helen on her arrival last night that the Silver Saddle was able, under one enormous roof, to cater to every single one of their clients' needs. Including church on Sundays, they'd exclaimed, pointing out the notice board outside the entertainment hall on the second floor. Sure enough, beneath the headliner country-and-western has-been featured for Saturday night, the Laughlin First Baptist Church announced, in smaller lettering, its Sunday morning services. Presumably they'd get the stage area cleaned up overnight before church services began.

The one thing the Silver Saddle didn't have, Helen had learned quickly, was comfortable beds. Although the twinges in her side alarmed her, she was now almost certain that they were more the result of sleeping on a terrible mattress. It was as if the Saddle's management were determined to keep their patrons out of the bedroom and down in the casinos. Heaven forbid that anyone should waste a single moment away from the tables and slot machines.

Helen fought for control over her bad mood. Unfortunately, it didn't help that the big-haired woman next to her smelled strongly of cheap flowery perfume. Helen shifted and faced away from her only to get a whiff of her companion's equally cheap aftershave.

The woman jiggled the coins in her cup. "Tonight we'll hit those machines over by the entrance. I saw someone get almost eight hundred dollars in nickels there day before yesterday," she murmured to her companion as she straightened the waistband of her orange pantsuit. "And don't you go off wandering into the bar and get drunk again. You really embarrassed me last night," she hissed in a final angry spurt.

He glanced behind him, saw Helen, looked her over quickly and apparently decided she didn't matter. His pate gleamed under the fluorescent tubes overhead as he passed a hand over artfully arranged thinning hairs. "Shut up," he muttered. "The only one you embarrass is yourself. We came here to have a good time, damn it."

By the time their exchange had ended, the elevator had reached the casino. The muted bell chimed as the doors slid open onto a softly lit scene that reminded Helen of nothing so much as the interior of a monastery she'd once visited. Same dim glow of yellowish lamps, same quiet noise in the background, even the same sense of intense concentration.

Except that at the Silver Saddle, the dim glow came from the low-hanging lamps over card tables, not votive candles. The noise in the background was not prayers but the click and clang of hundreds of slot machines. And the devoted attention offered by supplicants was focused on the acquisition of cash rather than meditation on God. Well, Helen smiled to herself, possibly on Mammon as opposed to the Holy Trinity.

Even the cigarette smoke hung in the air like a cloying incense that permeated the skin and teeth until Helen could taste its tang no matter where she went in the casino.

She strolled from the elevators, relieved to be out of the enclosure reeking of bad imitation perfume, and took her time weaving through the crowd of bettors, most of them in various stages of glazed-over intensity. Nearing the polished marble reception desk, Helen saw them again.

When they'd pulled up in their RVs in the Saddle's enormous parking area, Helen didn't even have to see the discreetly posted rainbow stickers on the bumpers. Hairstyles that would have been called "mannish," comfortable clothes, no makeup, even the way they leaned toward one another in easy familiarity — it had to be a group of older lesbians roving across the country and enjoying their retirement years together.

This evening, though, they clambered around the reception desk, talking excitedly to one another and to the pair of pretty young women behind the counter. Beneath their curls and smiles and long fingernails tapping tourist pamphlets and flyers, these two girls wore expressions of patient boredom as the older women oohed and aahed about the various sights to see in Nevada near the Saddle. Helen tried not to grin as she rea..zed these girls didn't quite get that their irritating patrons were actually flirting with them, but one of the women saw her and grinned back.

Oh, well, Helen thought. Busted.

"They come through here every year." Helen spun around and saw a security guard clad in various shades of blue leaning against a faux-marble pillar. "Saw 'em last year, and the year before that, too."

Helen stepped closer and read the bronze nametag pinned over the guard's ample bosom. "They must have a good time here, Shelley."

"Hope I have that much fun when I'm that old," Shelley said with a smile. Helen couldn't help studying the woman's garb and comparing it to the one she'd worn during the past year, when she'd had to close up her office and take a minimum wage job, after her injury, just to cover the rent on her tiny house in Berkeley. For a moment, Helen felt better. At least she hadn't looked like a rent-a-cop when she went to cover the front desk at the manufacturing plant in Oakland down at Jack London Square. At least she'd gotten to wear a decent jacket instead of this cheesy imitation police uniform. Then her spirits plummeted yet again at the realization of just how much she'd lost in the past year. "Hard to imagine being able to afford an RV on my salary, though."

Helen shrugged, reluctant to encourage Shelley in further conversation and reluctant to determine whether or not the bosomy blonde security guard was hitting on her. "You never know, Shelley," Helen responded, managing another courteous smile. "Maybe you'll get lucky at the slot machines."

The woman shook her head vigorously. "Don't let anyone hear you say that! I'd get my head handed to me if they caught me gambling here. I always go to one of the other casinos. Like the Hat, or the Spur."

"Well, good luck." Helen walked away before Shelley

could give her in any more hints about her possible location after hours.

Trying to still the voice of panic that threatened to break out in a scream, Helen plodded past rows of tables and aisles of slot machines and speakers blaring country music. Not only had she lost her career and nearly lost her health when she'd been shot, her ability to communicate with the human race had suffered, too. Jesus, the poor woman was just trying to seek out some conversation. And she probably didn't meet a lot of other dykes in a place like this.

Helen sighed, brought up short behind a line of people waiting to get into the restaurant that was also her destination this evening. A frazzled young man, pale and pimply and nearly seven feet tall, worked his way down the line to take names for tables and write up to-go orders. Seeing the determined, impatient glares and head-shakes of the people ahead of her, Helen decided to wait until the kid came to her to explain that she was expected at the Winners' Table.

Standing opposite a mirrored wall, she could see herself only too well. The extra pounds she used to mourn had dropped off swiftly during the past year, leaving her gaunt and haggard. Her hair was as thick and dark as ever, but it was limp. Her face had thinned to a pale composite of planes and angles, and her eyes stared out dark and huge and terrified. She kept staring, unable to turn away, angry at herself for believing that she was a ghost that didn't belong in the land of the living.

"It will take time, but those feelings will alter," the shrink had insisted. "Not go away, but change. You have to be patient with yourself, Helen."

And she had tried, making sure she attended therapy each week, doing the little "exercises" the psychologist had recommended to familiarize herself with life once again. Going to those interminable support group meetings and grudgingly admitting to herself that they'd helped. Having regular visits to the doctor after the second bout of surgery that cleaned out the last pieces of the bullet that had sliced her gut apart.

But, Helen thought, forcing herself to turn from the mirror, none of those things eased any of the pain that welled up in her around the day she'd had to close her office. Alison had been there with her, of course, a presence of quiet strength that Helen only now appreciated. Alison had organized the files to be safely stowed in Helen's house, worked out new terms with the landlord, found someone to sublet the office space for a year, lugged boxes and furniture down to the rental truck and then helped Helen to get everything moved into her house across town.

"Helen, you don't have to get a job. Why don't you just take things easy? We can cover rent and groceries for a few more months..."

Alison's eyes misted over as Helen refused. "I know, Alison. I know all that. But, sweetheart, don't you see, I have to do something. It will be a lot worse if I just sit around and have you wait on me."

"May I help you, ma'am?"

Startled, Helen controlled her urge to recoil as the kid towered over her, his pale face sweating around the bumps of acne spattered across his nose. "I'm expected at the Winners' Table. My name is Helen Black," she stammered.

At this his eyebrows lifted. Glancing down at the clipboard in his immense hands, he nodded. "Yes, here you are. You didn't have to wait out here, ma'am."

"Well, I didn't want to cause a fuss." She gritted her teeth and followed his red-vested back past the lines of irritated clients into Romie's Catfish House.

Immediately she was engulfed by the overpowering fragrance of frying foods. Even without taking a breath Helen would have known exactly where she was by the decor. Every single Romie's had the same look — bright red vinyl cushions on chairs and benches, blue Formica tables, white paper placemats in the shape of fish, and the telltale whiskered logo of a grinning catfish leering out at the patron from napkins, glasses and plates. Tonight, in the brand new Romie's just opened up inside the casino, every booth and table was crowded with people stuffing fried fish and hush puppies and coleslaw into their mouths, washing down each bite with enormous tankards of iced tea.

If memory served Helen correctly, going by past experience in the dozens of Romie's dotted around Mississippi she'd frequented in her youth, paper hats in the shape of the grinning catfish logo were available to all customers. She prayed, as she nudged her way behind the kid in the vest, that the Winners' Table guests wouldn't be required to wear the damn things. She'd have to refuse, although she'd hate to disappoint her aunt and uncle.

Loy and Edna McCormick waved at their niece as she rounded a booth peopled by a particularly raucous group of men who'd somehow squeezed their paunches along the narrow benches. Helen waved back, nearly upending a tray full of iced tea tankards in the process. She murmured an embarrassed apology to the waitress she'd nearly baptized and waited for a moment until she spotted the path of least resistance.

Alison was already there, and Helen saw by the look on her lover's face that Alison had nearly snapped the last nerve she had left. Not only had Alison been horrified at the tendency for the chefs at Romie's to deep-fry everything in sight, she'd been terribly nervous at meeting her in-laws.

"Are you sure they're going to be okay with this, Helen?" Alison had asked at least a million times on the drive out from San Francisco to Nevada the night before. "I mean, your family back in Mississippi pretty much disowned you, right?" Alison had squirmed around in the seat and fumbled noisily in the box of tapes they'd selected for listening to during the drive.

Helen had ignored Alison's nervous mood — there was nothing she could do about it now, and besides, they had just passed Needles and were almost to Laughlin. In the black-velvet night sky, a waxing moon swelled up across the sprinkling of stars and gleamed down on the smooth expanse of empty desert that had just hours before looked dry and dusty and dead. "Everyone but Loy and Edna. They took me in when my father kicked me out, and they've always been there for me. How could I pass up a chance to see them, when they're this close?" She shifted her position in the driver's seat, then checked her motion as Alison whipped around to study her. Helen had insisted she was strong enough for the long drive, despite Alison's worries about straining her still-fragile body. With a sigh Helen stretched her left leg as far as it would go under the dashboard, and Alison finally relaxed against the seat. "Look, honey, it's just for the holiday weekend. We'll have Thanksgiving dinner with them, just spend some time on Friday visiting — rather, I'll spend time visiting. You don't have to, really."

Alison shook her head. "I don't mean to sound so awful, Helen. I'm just kind of nervous, you know?" She picked up the box of tapes and sorted through them again.

Helen reached across the seat and patted her lover's hands. "It'll be fine, honey. And I do understand that you're sacrificing Thanksgiving with your folks to do this with me." She gripped the wheel again as the car took a curve. "I would have understood if you'd refused."

"What?" Alison gasped in mock horror. "And miss the chance of a lifetime to go to Laughlin?"

"Ah, you jest, but you have no idea what a big deal this is!" Helen wagged a finger at Alison. "Where I come from, Romie's is the epitome of gourmet dining. For Romie Kittrick to open up a few catfish emporiums out here in the West is big news for someone like me."

What had been bigger news, of course, was the fact that

Loy and Edna McCormick of Tupelo, Mississippi, had been one of two couples named as Grand Prize Winners in the Romie's Catfish Farm Sweepstakes. Not only would Romie's put them up at the Silver Saddle and feed them for their entire stay in Laughlin, but the Kittrick Corporation would also treat them to tours of local attractions, a stipend for gambling and several shows.

"Oh, darlin', y'all have just got to come out and see us!" Edna had gushed over the phone last month. "This is going to be so wonderful, and — what's that, hon? Oh, Loy says tell you we'll pay for your hotel room. We'll get you out there in the Silver Saddle with us!"

"Now, Aunt Edna, I won't let you do that."

"Don't you worry about a thing, darlin'. Y'all just get out here and we'll take care of the rest." Edna sniffled, and Helen could picture her aunt's plump body squeezed into a too-tight, too-bright dress, her hair gleaming gray with a blue tint. She was sure Loy was standing right behind her, smiling and silent as always, his John Deere cap perched on his balding scalp.

And, of course, Helen had worked hard to trade shifts with the other security guards to cover Thanksgiving weekend, even pulling some overtime herself, in spite of Alison's worried looks, so that her relatives wouldn't have to foot the hotel bill. She still hadn't told Alison about her promises to the other security guards, the promises that involved covering their graveyard shifts on weekends and at Christmas. And Alison herself had done some wheeling and dealing with her temp agency to finesse a few days off. When she finally drove Alison's late eighties Toyota station wagon into the brightly lit parking lot of the Saddle, she was actually looking forward to their stay in Laughlin.

Loy and Edna were waiting for them at the lobby entrance. "My Lord, have mercy!" Edna had squealed, trotting out in her brand-new pantsuit and gold slippers to give Helen a big hug as the valet slipped behind the wheel.

"You're looking so good, honey!" Edna wiped at her eyes. With a guilty shock Helen had realized then that they'd not known what to expect after hearing she'd been shot.

"Uncle Loy!" Helen smiled. Edna must have persuaded him to leave the John Deere cap behind. He smelled of cigarettes as he hugged her — an odor that strangely reminded Helen of her youth.

They had both been shy and anxious as Helen introduced Alison. It had been a relief to busy themselves over luggage as they entered the lobby and headed toward the elevators.

Later they'd discerned the great big saddle on the roof, a saddle that could have held an entire rodeo. Alison had stared up in horrified wonder. "I don't think I've ever stayed in a hotel where a giant saddle swung over my head."

Helen had sniffed. "Doesn't look silver to me. Let's just hope there's not an earthquake while we're here."

At least, Helen thought as she slid into the chair next to Alison, we can't see that fucking saddle from inside the restaurant.

What she could see only too clearly were the other sweepstakes winners, whom she had met briefly that morning. Heather and Bud Gilley, owners of a thriving exercise and health club who hailed from Vicksburg, still didn't seem too certain what to make of Helen and Alison. As Helen nodded to the couple, Heather's well-manicured hands fluttered to the buttons on her silk blouse as if Helen might try to rip her clothes off and violate her delicate Southern virtue. Bud kept his dark little eyes narrowed on Helen a moment too long for courtesy, twitched his pencil-thin mustache once, then went back to his catfish. His body, heavily muscled and just beginning to lean toward middle-aged fat, hunched over his plate protectively. Helen wondered if he thought she'd try to contaminate his dinner with lesbian spit. The other couple seated in the Winners'

Circle, Jack and Marla Tilson of Biloxi, smiled vacantly at Helen. The elderly African-American couple, both retired teachers, had the same distant looks on their faces Helen had noted that morning, although Jack certainly seemed more alert than his wife. Their plates were untouched, and as Helen sat down Jack was just finishing an entreaty to his wife to try to eat something. Marla turned her remote expression toward her husband and obligingly picked up a fork only to lay it down right away.

At least no one had put on a fish hat, Helen thought. Loy and Edna were in their usual polyester glory. Edna had somehow managed to find a shade of blue that matched the tint of her hair, and Loy sported an immaculate long-sleeved white shirt with cufflinks. The clip of his bow tie had loosened, threatening to drop into his iced tea at any moment.

"We was just about to send out the guard for you," Loy said around a mouthful of cole slaw.

"Did you get some rest, darlin'?" Edna asked, patting Helen on the arm. "Alison was just telling us about that last surgery you had to go through." Edna gave her arm a squeeze. "All that physical therapy, and all!"

Helen glanced at Alison, who shrugged and smiled weakly as she picked at her salad. Helen suppressed a grin, wishing she could tell Alison that gossip about operations and troubles and the ominous reports of doctors were bread and butter to her relatives. In fact, she couldn't remember a family gathering that didn't include a litany of various relations who'd suffered surgery or illness or amputation or some other bodily affliction.

"Kinda like that time your cousin Bobby ran over his toe with the lawn mower. You remember, Helen, you was there that afternoon," Edna supplied.

"Or my great-uncle on my mother's side, Rupert Wilkinson, who almost blinded himself when he was just about your age. Bad liquor, so they said."

"Was that the one who had the triplets that time? Not Rupert, I mean his daughter. Ethel something."

"No, you're thinking of Edith Mae Wilkins. Her husband's name was Robert."

Helen, as soon as she saw that Loy and Edna were taking a pleasantly ghoulish trip down memory lane, turned to Alison. "You look really good," she murmured. "I like that color green. Brings out your eyes."

"Why, thank you, Helen." Alison gave up all pretense at eating her salad and picked up her glass of water. "By the way, I thought you'd like to know that I won a few bucks at the slot machine."

Helen made a pretense of groaning. "Oh, my God! I've created a monster."

"No monsters here," Bud said with a grin. "Just a bunch of very lovely ladies with their escorts."

The only person that didn't smile politely at this chivalric comment was Bud's wife. Heather pursed her lips as if biting back words and edged away from her husband.

Just then Marla sighed and leaned forward. Jack stood up in alarm. "I believe my wife is not feeling well. Would y'all please excuse us?"

No one spoke as Jack led his wife away. As soon as they were out of view, Bud shook his head and said, "Don't know why the hell they're here, anyway. They're not even winners, like us. Kinda makes you lose your appetite, looking at her. She'll probably drop dead before the trip is over."

Heather glared at him. "Bud, please!" She looked at the others as her face burned bright pink with embarrassment.

"They're just guests. That's what Carmel called it, guests. Not winners."

"Is that what you were talking about on the flight over from Mississippi yesterday? That poor old woman?" Heather snorted and tossed her napkin on the table. "Somehow I don't think so."

"Well, dear heart, did you go to that gym this morning, like you was talking about?" Edna asked in a panicked voice. "I remember you wanted to take a look at that walker thing, what did you call it?"

"Treadmill. It's a treadmill," Heather answered through gritted teeth. "And yes, I did go to see the gym. Alone. Unaccompanied. My husband was going to go with me, but he was somehow detained."

The domestic squabble was interrupted by the arrival of Carmel Kittrick, in royal procession, accompanied by three Kittrick minions. Relieved to be distracted from the dirty laundry of the Gilleys, Helen pulled names from her memories of introductions earlier that day. Bill Hefley, the red-faced blustering football hero who had somehow found a niche in the Kittrick family enterprise, walked a deferential two paces behind Carmel, his face a study in apopleptic discomfort mingled with an embarrassing servility.

A gaunt woman who sported glasses with Coke-bottle lenses and whose frizzled hair had escaped from a plain chignon handed Carmel a cell phone as they progressed across the restaurant. The Winners' Circle's own private waitress, whose nametag identified her as Sue, took up the rear, bearing an enormous pitcher of iced tea. Sue's plain pockmarked face looked exhausted.

Carmel had the cellular phone clasped in one red-nailed hand. Helen wondered briefly if the woman had purposely designed her ensemble to match the Romie's star-spangled decor. The red suit, no doubt expensive, featured a spray of glittering sequined stars across the lapels, and the silk blouse chimed a cold blue note in the midst of so much heat. Fat white stars perched on her ears beneath the long blonde curls, and Carmel's eyes were an icy blue that matched the blouse.

"Kind of scary, huh?" Alison murmured.

Helen nodded in agreement as Carmel's bright red pumps clicked up the three steps leading to the Winners'

Circle table. "Happy Thanksgiving!" Carmel beamed at the gathered celebrants as she snapped the cell phone shut and handed it without looking to Bill Hefley. "So — do y'all agree with us that catfish is on its way to replacing turkey for Thanksgiving dinner?" Helen admired the way she had the patter down. Bud sat up straight and sucked in his gut as he stared up with adoring eyes at the heir to the Kittrick millions. Heather twisted her napkin in her hands and said nothing, but Helen saw her eyes sparkle with tears.

"I believe there's someone missing. Are the Tilsons not joining us?"

"I believe Mrs. Tilson wasn't feeling well. They were here for a little bit, though, weren't they Loy?" Edna said brightly.

A shadow passed briefly over Carmel's face. Helen wondered what on earth the Tilsons meant to the Kittrick family. If they weren't winners, why were they here? And why did their absence worry Carmel?

"Well, I know you'll agree that it couldn't have been this wonderful dinner that kept them away from the Winners' Circle!"

Everyone dutifully laughed. Helen's gazed drifted away from Carmel and over to Hefley, who had stepped away from the Winners' Circle and was talking in hushed tones to a man who hadn't come in with the original Kittrick group.

This man's resemblance to Carmel was astonishing, yet it was as if Carmel Kittrick's near-perfect all-American features had been molded from clay and then pressed and squashed into a fun-house caricature. On Carmel, the Kittrick nose was aquiline and patrician; on this man, it was too long and too fleshy. Carmel's cheekbones could have earned her thousands on a magazine cover; his dissolved into puffy red flesh. Her smile, whether natural or purchased with costly dentistry, was flawless; the man standing with Hefley had an overbite that emphasized his weak chin. He looked like a beaver in search of something to gnaw. Slung over his shoulder was a strap attached to an expensive camcorder, and at his feet rested a flightbag. Judging by his disheveled appearance, Helen decided that he must have just gotten off a plane or out of a car after a long drive.

What struck her most, though, was the way Hefley talked to him. It was clear that Hefley was furious at being interrupted by this distant member of the Kittrick clan. His clenched hands and stony expression left no doubt in her mind. When Carmel leaned over the table to talk to the Gilleys, Helen strained to hear what the two men were saying to each other.

"But this time I have film, Hef! I saw it myself — making right angles and then shooting off over the mountains like nothing man-made! You gotta see it!"

Carmel turned around briefly, and Hefley smiled up at her. He offered a gesture, arms out at his sides with palms upturned, as if to tell her that this man's appearance was not his fault. As Carmel turned back to her guests, his face iced over with barely controlled rage, but Helen wasn't sure if the anger was directed at Carmel or at this intruder.

Hefley patted the man on the shoulder. "Not now, Wilbur. Your sister and I have to set up the photoshoot for the Jackson papers."

"Don't you even want this, Hef?" Wilbur Kittrick — Carmel's brother, Helen decided — shoved something into Hef's hands. Grimacing, Hef twisted it around, then took Wilbur by the shoulders and steered him away from the Winners' Circle area.

"And this here is our niece, Helen Black, and her, ah, her friend, Alison."

"Welcome to Romie's, Helen. I'm sorry I didn't get to meet you when you first got here." Helen shook hands with Carmel, noting with surprise that the woman's palms were sweating. What the hell did a Kittrick have to sweat about? "You, too, Alison." Carmel's cold blue eyes took in the two of them as she shook Alison's hand, and Helen knew from that look that her uncle's awkward introduction hadn't fooled anyone. "I hope you're enjoying your dinner, and your stay at the Saddle?"

"Yes, thank you."

"Helen here is a private eye, Carmel!" Aunt Edna bubbled, unable to contain her pride as she squirmed in her seat.

"She lives in Berkeley, California!"

"Is that so?" Carmel said. "A private investigator?"

"That's right." Helen bit back the impulse to explain that she wasn't working now, that she hadn't had a case in over a year, then she caught Alison's watchful eye.

"Well, that's very, very interesting." Those ice-blue eyes stared at Helen for several moments, and an unreadable expression moved across Carmel's face. "I'd really like to hear more about that, Helen."

Just then Wilbur Kittrick coughed and cleared his throat in a theatrical attempt to get his sister's attention. Seemingly oblivious to everyone else in the room, he grinned and nodded at Carmel.

Helen shuddered at the look Carmel gave her brother, certain that if she herself had been at the business end of such a double whammy she would have hightailed it as far away as she could get.

Carmel took a deep breath and turned that bright smile back to the sweepstakes winners. "Don't forget, folks, we get our picture taken for the Jackson paper after dinner. You can tell all your friends to look for you in the *Lifestyles* section on Sunday!" She gave Helen a final glance, then rejoined Hefley and Wilbur a few feet away as her secretary trotted close behind.

"Well! Our pictures in the paper! Loy, we have to call up Bobby and tell him to look for us!"

"Now, honey, you know Bobby won't be lookin' at the paper," Loy said, patting Edna on the hand.

Helen watched the Kittrick crowd as Loy and Edna continued debating whether or not her cousin Bobby, long known throughout the family as "the simple-minded one," would deign to turn his limited attention to a newspaper on Sunday. She could see the bright red of Carmel's skirt flaring out at the edge of the room, near the narrow corridor that led to the restrooms. Hefley and Wilbur Kittrick both stood within her line of sight, just beyond a row of potted palms, and they appeared to be listening intently to whatever Carmel must be saying to them.

Then Helen saw one hand with red fingernails slicing the air between the two men. Helen guessed, from the way Wilbur and Hefley took a step backward, that she'd given an immutable command. Carmel then stalked out of the restaurant, with Wilbur tagging at her heels like an unloved puppy.

"Helen? What's the matter?" Alison nudged her.

"Nothing, I'm fine." Helen got one last look at Hefley before he, too, headed out of the restaurant. Did he just drop something on the floor? She saw a small black puddle on the tile beneath the rack of public phones between the men's room and the wall. Maybe it was whatever Wilbur had forced on him moments ago.

"Excuse me — be right back." Helen wedged her way out behind Alison and went toward the restrooms.

"I'll order you some pumpkin pie!" Aunt Edna's voice rang across the restaurant, followed by a shushing sound coming from her uncle.

Fortunately, no one else was in the corridor, and she reached over pick up the black gift offered by Wilbur to Hefley. It was a baseball cap.

"Helen Black?"

The voice startled her just as she was turning the cap

over in her hands, and Helen looked up to meet the worried gaze of the secretary who'd had custody of Carmel's cell phone.

"Yes?"

"Ms. Kittrick wanted to know if you could meet with her this evening."

"Excuse me?"

The woman checked off a couple of items on a notepad, then delicately pushed the heavy glasses up on her short nose. "If that's convenient." When Helen hesitated, she added, "It's a professional call. You are the private investigator, aren't you?"

"Yeah. That's me."

"Ms. Kittrick has an hour free at" — a quick look at her wristwatch followed — "it looks like nine-thirty would be the soonest we can manage."

"Okay. Uh, where?"

"We're in the Palace Suite, up in the penthouse." The secretary handed her a card. Only then did she glance around the narrow hallway and sniff in distaste. "Sorry to corral you like this, but Ms. Kittrick wants to be discreet."

"Naturally." A burly man squeezed his way past them toward the men's room, and Helen followed the secretary back into the main dining room.

"We'll be expecting you, then," and she disappeared into the casino, her sensible shoes clicking on the tiles.

Helen looked down at the card. The silvery gray background of the heavy parchment bore Carmel Kittrick's name in thick gold script. Beneath it were written the time and location of their meeting.

She slipped the business card into a pocket, then looked at the black baseball cap. Stitched onto the canvas with white thread were the letters UFORA. She folded it up and tucked it into another pocket.

"We thought you got lost," Alison murmured. "Thank

God you're back — your Aunt Edna is just about to tell me all the details of how Cousin Omer got his wooden leg."

Helen looked without appetite at the slab of pumpkin pie oozing beneath a half-frozen dollop of fake whipped cream. "Sorry — something came up."

"Wasn't that Carmel's slave you were just talking to?"

"Yes, it was." Helen picked up a fork and stabbed at the piece of pie. "It seems I have a date with Carmel this evening."

Chapter Two

"But why the heck would Carmel Kittrick want to talk to you?" Loy sat down heavily on the double bed in his room at the Silver Saddle and scratched his bald pate before replacing the baseball cap on his head. Edna stood nearby, a puzzled expression creasing her plump face, arms folded across her ample chest.

Helen leaned against the fake walnut dresser and shook her head. "Hard to say." She was certain, however, that her aunt's crow of delight in announcing her occupation explained Carmel's interest.

"Do you think it's something to do with the Winners' Circle?" Edna kept swiveling her gaze between Loy and Helen, her face growing red with consternation as she fussed, then began to pace in front of the bed. "Maybe there was something wrong with the contest?"

Concerned, Helen watched her, noting once again that their room was identical to the one Helen shared with Alison. Same inexpensive gray carpet, same uncomfortable mattress on the bed, same cheap television mounted on the wall in a metal brace to discourage theft.

"Now, darlin', you know there was no problem about that!" Loy rolled his eyes and looked helplessly at Helen, his hands outstretched in exasperation, his expression pleading with her to reason with Edna. "We won fair and square, and no one minded when we said Helen and Alison was gonna be there with us for a couple of nights!"

"Tell me about how you won, Aunt Edna," Helen asked, more to still her distress than for further information about Romie's Catfish Farm. She'd already heard enough from Carmel Kittrick and Bill Hefley, their speeches reiterating the splendors of the brand new western version of Romie's making its debut in several select locations throughout California, Nevada, and Arizona.

Once again, Edna went through the tedious story of how she'd written her name on a card and dropped the card into a giant fishtank replete with plastic grinning catfish. "Win a Trip for Two to Laughlin!" claimed the banners and posters adorning every single Romie's along Highway 49. "You Are Invited to Celebrate Thanksgiving with Us!"

"You coulda knocked me over with a feather when we got the phone call!" Edna exclaimed. "You remember, Helen, how I used to always enter those sweepstakes and kept waiting for Ed McMahon to come right up to my door with a check!"

"Of course, we just go to the one near Tupelo," Loy

interjected as Edna stopped for breath. Aunt Edna's color didn't seem too good at the moment. "Except sometimes we go to that new one out by Hattiesburg, close to the college."

Alison watched from the armchair in the corner of the room, her eyes dark and unreadable and remote. Her green suit, its color so admirably matching the deep shade of her eyes, clashed unfortunately with the orange-toned plaid of the bulky chair. Helen glanced at her guiltily. Had it been a mistake to tell them about this strange assignation with the heiress to the Kittrick millions? No, she decided, taking another surreptitious look at her lover's face. There was no sense in going behind her girlfriend's back or conniving at secret meetings without her relatives' knowledge.

"Well, we can speculate all we want," Alison said, speaking for the first time since she and Helen had entered the room. "But we won't know until Helen goes to talk to her."

"Hell, maybe she wants to offer me a job," Helen joked lamely. "I'm sure the Kittricks need a security guard now and then."

"Oh, do you think so?" Edna sat down next to Loy, a look of jubilant expectancy on her face. "Then you could come back to Mississippi with us! Oh," she added, looking toward Alison, "and you, too, sweetheart."

Better to break up this little party before it got too awkward, Helen thought. "At any rate, I need to get going if I'm going to solve this mystery." She hugged her uncle goodnight, then her aunt. At the feverish flush of Edna's skin, Helen leaned back in alarm. "Aunt Edna, are you sick?"

Edna McCormick shooed her away. Her aunt's face was flushed and streaming with perspiration. "Oh, it's nothing, hon! A woman my age has to expect a few hot flashes now and then."

Her uncle who looked away in embarrassment at this open discussion of "female troubles." He grabbed the remote from the night table and switched on the television set, moving toward the other end of the bed and staring fixedly at the screen.

Helen sank down on the bed next to her aunt. "Are you taking anything for this?" she asked. "Estrogen or something?"

"Shoot, no! I won't let those doctors give me pills," Aunt Edna protested, flapping her hands at her face in a futile attempt to cool down. "'Sides, it's nothing unusual. Every woman goes through this as she gets older." She took a deep breath, and Helen saw that the bright red flush was draining from her cheeks. "Least I'm not getting grumpy, like some women I know."

"Just forgetful," Loy muttered. "Keeps losing the key to the room."

"Now, Loy, it was just that once!"

Helen managed to steer Alison and herself out of the room before further conversation around her aunt's menopausal woes could take place. For once the small gilded chamber was empty.

Alison leaned back against the wall as the elevator door slid shut. For once the small gilded chamber was empty.

She closed her eyes and took a deep breath, then let out a sigh. "Remind me again, Helen, why we're here."

"Why?" Helen regarded Alison from the other side of the elevator, taking in the thick dark hair, pale skin and fine-boned slender hands that hung limp at her sides. "Because Aunt Edna and Uncle Loy are the only relatives I have. Because they're the only ones in my whole family who still talked to me after my dad beat me for being queer and then kicked me out of the house when I was sixteen. Because they're two of the best, most decent human beings I know, in spite of what may look like incredible naiveté and provincialism."

Alison opened her eyes and looked down at her feet. "Sorry," she whispered. "I know all that."

The elevator door slid open and they were greeted by a boisterous party of men and women carrying the inescapable plastic tubs rattling with coins for the slot machines.

By the ice machine on their floor, Alison said suddenly, "So what do your aunt and uncle think of me?"

Helen paused outside their door. "They love you. Who wouldn't?" She fumbled for the oversized brass key, her fingers brushing against the folded black baseball cap, which she stuffed back into her pocket.

"They've been sweet to me." Alison smiled ruefully. "I guess they probably don't quite know what to think of me. It's obvious, though, that they really love *you* a lot."

Helen was suddenly overcome by anger at herself for insisting that Alison accompany her to a family gathering. "I shouldn't have made you come."

"Really, there's nothing wrong. It's just a little — well, overwhelming." Alison followed her into the dark room. "Maybe I just wasn't quite ready for catfish as Thanksgiving dinner."

"Actually, you're the real reason we're here," Helen murmured, catching her lover's hand before it could reach the light switch on the wall. "I don't ever want you to think I don't know how to show a girl a good time." Before Alison could answer, Helen stopped Alison's lips with her own. "I mean, catfish and relatives — does it get any better than this, baby?"

"Is that what this is?" Alison asked. Helen's hands traveled across Alison's shoulders, tracing the seams of her blouse over her breasts. "A good time?"

"I don't know why — being in a hotel really turns me on," Helen whispered against Alison's neck. She had to find out what that perfume was — something with lavender in it, maybe. Lavender and vanilla.

"Even knowing Edna and Loy are close by?"

"Especially knowing Edna and Loy are close by."

In the darkness Alison wrestled Helen's shirt from her

pants. Her slim warm fingers stroked the flesh around Helen's waist. "Mmm, I'm feeling a little flushed. Do you think I'm experiencing some mysterious feminine complaint, like Aunt Edna?"

Helen chuckled. "I know a surefire cure. Just what the doctor ordered."

"Wait." Alison gently pushed her away and reached for the lights. "You have a date, remember?"

"Damn." Helen sighed and checked her watch beneath the bright light of the foyer. "I just have time, too."

"Don't worry. I'll keep things warm for you." Alison walked toward the bed, discarding garments as she went. She was naked by the time she slipped beneath the sheets and gave Helen a parting kiss.

Back in the hallway Helen glanced at her watch again. Damn. She doubted one could reach the lofty heights of the penthouse by means of the common elevator that the peasants used to get around the Saddle. Better to go down to the lobby and ask at the registration desk.

She found the staircase and hurried down from the fifth floor. She was completely alone in the brightly lit well reaching up fifteen stories. Her shoes clattered loudly on the unadorned metal of the stairs, and she came out facing the registration desk.

"Oh, yes, Ms. Kittrick let us know about it," the young receptionist said brightly. She looked up from card where she'd noted Helen's name and glanced around. "Gee, I'm really not supposed to leave the front desk without anyone to cover." She bit her lip and cast Helen a worried look. "I mean, it's just so much easier to show you the penthouse elevator than to tell you where it is."

"Anything I can do, Amy?"

Helen turned to see the broad blank fair features of Shelley the security guard quite close behind her. Next to Shelley a tall thin woman who seemed vaguely familiar was just turning away from Shelley. Helen recognized her as being one of the women who'd arrived earlier in the RVs. To judge by Shelley's smile, the two women had just concluded an intriguing conversation.

"Catch you later, Thea," Shelley called out over her shoulder. Thea smiled, and Helen caught a glimpse of the large silver labyris hanging on a leather cord between Thea's breasts. In spite of her hesitance to be anything but neutral with Shelley, Helen found herself looking more closely at the burly security guard — gauging the curves of the other woman's body and having a brief flash of what her fair skin would look like.

"Oh, Shel, would you mind taking — um" — a quick consultation of the card — "Ms. Black to the penthouse elevator? She has an appointment with Ms. Kittrick in the Palace Suite."

"No problem." Shelley grinned at Helen and gestured with a slight motion of her head. "Right this way."

They went through a crowd of gamblers that had noticeably thinned since dinner a couple of hours ago. Helen eyed Shelley's thickly muscled body as she followed the guard through the faint miasma of cigarette smoke from the surrounding tables. Maybe I'm just starved for the company of dykes, Helen told herself as she realized how closely she was studying the other woman.

Shelley stopped suddenly, avoiding an elderly woman hobbling by, and Helen nearly walked right into her.

"Sorry," Helen muttered.

Shelley grinned. "No problem," she said once again. "Elevator's right ahead." She indicated a passage tucked unobtrusively beside a garish mural of mythical Old West images, complete with covered wagons and feathered natives and herds of buffalo. At the end of the passage was an elevator, much smaller and grayer than the one used by the other clients of the Silver Saddle.

Shelley reached for a keypad positioned outside the elevator and, using her body to hide the code, punched in a series of numbers. The steel door slid open quietly and revealed a simply decorated elevator car that had none of the glittering trappings of the rest of the casino.

"I know. Looks different than the rest of this flea market, doesn't it?"

Helen nodded, stepping past Shelley into the elevator. It was almost elegant, offering a sense of refinement in sharp contrast to the gaudy display of the rest of the hotel and casino. In the upper right hand corner of the car a small black video camera rolled in her direction, its small vacant lens adjusting to focus on the elevator's single occupant. Helen looked back at Shelley. "I never noticed cameras here before."

Shelley gave her another grin. "Good. You aren't supposed to." Then the door slid shut with a muted thud of steel resting on steel.

It was unnerving to see that there were no indicators of location in this elevator — no numbers lighting up, no mechanized voice announcing which floor Helen was on. Startled to recognize a sensation she thought might be claustrophobia, Helen thrust her hands into her pocket. The rough canvas of the baseball cap beneath her fingers distracted her from her own distress and, ignoring the presence of the camera, she tugged it out to examine it more closely.

UFORA stood for UFO Researchers of America. She remembered seeing some flyers back home in Berkeley announcing their convention in Las Vegas. Why a member of the Kittrick family would try to force such a dubious gift on Bill Hefley, a good ol' boy who no doubt scoffed at anything as odd and sissified as a belief in alien life forms, was inexplicable. Was Kittrick one of those conspiracy theorists who haunted the fringes of military installations located in the deserts nearby, eyes and ears trained on the skies for evidence of interstellar spacecraft lighting up the night?

The elevator stopped, and she stepped out into a long

corridor. Dim lighting mounted on Parsons tables behind neutral floral arrangements and authentic English pottery pieces revealed a subtler taste than that displayed throughout the rest of the Silver Saddle. Unlike the western decor in the nether regions of the casino, here the quiet landscapes and portraits hung on the walls portrayed a less rustic temperament.

The Palace Suite, Helen remembered. The door nearest the elevator bore a brass plate engraved with the words *Presidential Suite*, and the Celebrity Suite was off to her right. That left the rooms at the end of the hallway.

Helen went quickly down the hall — she was already a couple of minutes late — and was just about to knock on the door of the Palace Suite when the door flew open, slamming into the wall behind with a loud bang.

"Fine!" Wilbur Kittrick barked, backing out of the room without seeing Helen behind him. "I'll just tell Daddy about it, and we'll see what he has to say!"

With that he swung around and slammed into Helen. She almost toppled over, struggling to regain her footing without looking too ridiculous.

"Oh, my Lord!" Wilbur grabbed her by both arms and pulled her upright before she fell on her ass next to a Grecian statue on a pedestal. "I'm sorry, ma'am. Didn't mean to hurt you — hope you're all right."

"No, I'm fine. Really, I am," Helen protested, fending him off.

He stopped and stared when he saw the cap in her hands. In her haste to be on time for the meeting with Carmel Kittrick, Helen had forgotten about the UFORA cap. "I don't think I met you at the convention last weekend," Wilbur finally stammered. "I'm Wilbur Kittrick, president of the Southeast Chapter. Which chapter are you with?"

"Helen Black," she responded, grasping his big limp hand in her own. "Mr. Kittrick, I'm afraid I don't —"

Holding a drink on one hand and a cigar in the other, Carmel Kittrick appeared in the doorway behind her brother. "I see my brother has introduced himself." She took a deep drag on the cigar and blew noxious smoke at Wilbur's neck. Wilbur turned toward his sister, and Helen watched in fascination as his flabby features flushed a dark red — whether in anger or embarrassment, she couldn't tell. Carmel smiled up at him with mock sweetness. "Excuse us, please, Wilbur. The grownups have business to discuss. Go off to bed, now."

Helen looked down at her shoes and folded the cap back into a tight bundle to fit in her pocket. Wilbur was fumbling in his own pockets. His search was rewarded by the discovery of a crumpled and stained business card. "You can reach me at the toll-free number," he muttered as he slipped it into her hand.

"Night-night, little brother," Carmel sang to his back as he shambled off down the hall to the elevator. She sighed, sending out another plume of cigar smoke. "Sorry about that, Helen. I can call you Helen, can't I?"

"Sure." Helen, hoping that Carmel hadn't had one too many shots of whatever she was drinking tonight, entered the suite as Carmel bowed and made an elaborate gesture of welcome. The Spartan simplicity of the rooms amazed Helen, and she gazed around in ill-concealed astonishment. The high ceilings allowed suitable space for the few pieces of ornate Regency furniture, and the glass-fronted bookcase held leather-bound editions.

At odds with the classic lines of the room and its furnishings, a fax machine whirred softly at the other end of the room. Carmel had also installed a telephone sporting at least twelve lines, and a red message light blinked furiously. Next to a Parsons table to Helen's right a copier clacked and hummed, sorting and stapling sheaves of paper as it spat them out into metal trays. On top of a small gray filing cabinet beside the fax machine a boxy white paper shredder squatted, ejecting a stream of confetti into a plastic garbage can.

"Please excuse me while I finish this call. I won't be a moment." Carmel didn't wait for Helen's response. She pressed a button on the telephone, and a voice barked out into the room.

"Carmel? Are you there?"

"Yes, Harold, talk to me." Carmel proceeded to stretch out on the nearest sofa while the man on the phone continued talking. "Yes, Harold, I know — no, it wasn't my idea to invite the Tilsons. Probably some scheme of my father's. You know, settling old scores before he dies."

Helen stood with her back to the door while Carmel slowly rolled her stockings off, letting the sheer hosiery drop to the floor beside the couch. She sighed luxuriously, glanced at Helen and sat up. "Fine, Harold. Handle it however you want to. Oh, by the way, can you get Wilbur out of here? He's not exactly livening up the party. Good. Talk to you tomorrow." She reached out to the telephone, and the speaker fell silent. Then she watched Helen study the room.

"I know," Carmel laughed. "It's a bit different from the rest of the Silver Saddle, isn't it?"

Helen sank into a deep cushioned armchair next to the fireplace. Yes, it was a real fire and real wood burning. She could hear the snapping and popping of the resin, smell the fragrance of hot pine permeating the hearth. "Well, I guess you get what you pay for in this life." She sighed.

Carmel smiled. "Care for a drink? I've got bourbon here, but I can fix you something else."

"No, bourbon would be perfect." And it was — a marvelous blend of gold and flame sliding over her tongue. Helen sipped slowly and appreciatively as Carmel lit another cigar.

"Well. Thank you for coming up to see me this evening.

I'm sorry I had to get Louise to corner you that way, but I didn't —"

"Ms. Kittrick — Carmel —" Helen carefully placed the glass down on a brass coaster and looked at her hostess. Carmel, curled up on the sofa with her feet tucked up on a cushion, returned her gaze calmly through a screen of smoke. "Why am I here?"

Carmel reached to a long low table in front of the sofa and with one hand sorted through a stack of papers, then pulled out a thick white envelope. Wordlessly she handed the envelope to Helen.

Helen took her time examining the envelope's contents. When she handed it back to Carmel she picked up her glass of bourbon and took another sip. "I'm sure," she said, "that I can't tell you anything you don't already know. Postmarked from Jackson, looks like once a week, a progressive expression of violence with each one, common brand of envelope."

"And paper used by any photocopier in the country. Yes, I know all that."

"So, I'll ask you again — why am I here?"

Carmel finished her bourbon and set the empty glass down on the carpet, where it left a mark for the maids to scrub out in the morning. "I want to know what kind of recourse I have."

Helen stared at her. Was it the bourbon sinking in, or was this woman really nuts? "You haven't told the police?"

"Shit, what the hell could they do? Shake their heads and whine a little, then forget it?" Carmel blew out smoke and gazed into the fire. "There's no way they could investigate this. What are they going to do, put a couple of officers in the post office? Anyway, if he saw them, he'd stop, and then I couldn't get him."

"So you know who's doing this?"

Carmel twisted on the sofa, stretched her feet out toward the warmth of the fire and sighed. "Of course I know. It's my ex-husband, Marc Landry." She wiggled her toes. "Problem is, I don't have a shred of proof." Suddenly she stood up, got Helen's glass and headed back to the bar for the decanter. "What do you think my chances are of using this against him in court?"

"I don't understand." Helen took the glass from her but set it down without tasting the liquor. "What do you mean?"

A long and convoluted monologue followed, in which Carmel explained to Helen that she was legally obligated to pay out an annuity to her ex-husband. "I'm sick of being drained by that ridiculous fuck," she said as she tapped ashes off the cigar. "If I can prove he pulled this little stunt, then maybe I can get him off my hands forever. I could threaten to take him to court and get the decision overturned."

Helen took a final sip of the bourbon, which was going to her head, fast. "Look, Carmel, I don't think you want to screw around with this. I don't want to cause you alarm when there's no need, but anyone who sends these kinds of things in the mail might try something more violent than anonymous letters."

"Him?" Her laughter sparkled high and brittle around the room. "Sweetheart, I've had him by the balls for years. My daddy basically bought him for me to marry back when I was in college. You know, a tame husband for his naughty little girl. The Kittrick family owns him, body and soul, in spite of his ridiculous job teaching English at Ole Miss. This is just a sign that he's cracking." She smiled into the fire. "One more little tug and I'll be rid of him."

Helen stood up. "Then you don't need me." With mingled feelings of contempt and confusion, she looked down at the woman lounging on the sofa. "Thanks for the drink."

"But I'm just getting to the good part!" Carmel rose from the sofa and blocked her path to the door. "I'd like to hire you to work for me. You know, come back to Mississippi, poke around a little bit, get the evidence I need to take him to court."

"Why me?" Helen folded her arms across her chest and looked into those ice blue eyes. "Why not go to someone in Mississippi, who knows the territory and the people, who could —"

"That's the point! Jesus, do I have to spell it out for you?" Carmel rolled her eyes heavenward, then plopped back down on the sofa. "Of course they know the territory! And they know me and my family." She sighed, rubbing her forehead with one hand. Helen decided that Carmel looked like a pouting loser in a childhood beauty pageant. "Do you think that any detective I could hire back home would be able to keep this out of the papers? We can't risk a story like this right now — not when we're all set to go national with the restaurants!"

Helen stepped past her. "I'm sorry, Carmel, but I can't help you. I'm not prepared to go to Mississippi. I'm sure you can find a reputable firm of investigators there."

"If it's the money, that's not an issue." Carmel sprang up again from the sofa. As if gauging the success of Helen's career by the cut of her clothes, she said, "I can pay you a lot better than most of your clients."

Your queer clients, Helen mentally finished the sentence for her. "Thanks, but no thanks, Carmel. Good luck to you."

Helen hadn't yet reached the elevator when she heard the crash from behind the closed door of the Palace Suite. She briefly wondered if Carmel had chosen the Staffordshire shepherdess to destroy in her rage. Or had it merely been the nearly empty decanter? The question ceased to puzzle her long before she reached the ground floor of the casino.

Chapter Three

Helen leaned against the concrete barrier that ringed the river behind the Saddle. She couldn't see the water in the shadow of the overhanging pedestrian walkway. Earlier that day it had rippled and sparkled in the wind, flowing ceaselessly with all the indifference of nature to the comings and goings of casino patrons intent on gambling. How far down was it, anyway, to the surface of the river? Helen listened to the soothing rush of water and felt the tension that had gripped her for the last couple of hours slowly seep out into the night.

Carmel's arrogant demand of her services had upset her beyond any appropriate response to the situation. It irked her to be so disturbed by the woman. What the hell was going on?

"Are you sure you want to go out again, honey?" Alison had asked as Helen, tired of pacing restlessly around their boxy hotel room, grabbed her jacket from the back of a chair and headed for the door. "It's after eleven."

Helen shrugged into her jacket and forced a smile for her lover. "I'm fine. Just sort of antsy. Probably from being cooped up in this place too long."

"Do you want me to come with you?" Alison had turned an eager smiling face up at Helen.

"No." Helen grimaced as she realized the refusal had come out harsher than she'd intended. She leaned over the bed, where Alison lay stretched out on the cheap floral bedspread. "I just want to walk around a little bit." She kissed her, hoping to take the sting out of her insistence on solitude. "You know, work out the kinks, get tired enough to sleep."

"Well, if you're sure." Alison yawned and closed her eyes. "Just don't get kidnapped by those lesbians in the RVs and go off to see America with them."

Helen managed a laugh, got out of the room, and took a couple of deep breaths in an effort to control her shaking. "Jesus," she muttered, looking down at her hands. Her fingers were trembling. Several people passed her by, and one or two peered nervously into her tense white face. Helen balled her hands into fists and gritted her teeth as she punched the button beside the elevator.

Her therapist's voice surfaced in her mind. "When someone has been through a traumatic, life-threatening event, it's normal to have sudden and violent reactions to perceived threats. Any number of things could be triggers for a response like that."

"So I'll just flip out at every little thing that happens? Anything that reminds me of being shot?" Helen had sneered.

Helen shook her head as she stepped into the elevator. Thank God that Dr. Garrison had been such an understanding and patient woman — Helen knew she wasn't an easy patient.

At least she had the elevator to herself. Her stomach registered the movement downward, and within moments she had strolled by the registration desk and out of the casino. With each step away from the building her mood had improved. Now, standing above the Colorado River, at a point where the states of California, Nevada and Arizona met, Helen felt almost relaxed and whole again. It was amazing how the lights and sounds of the Silver Saddle faded into a dull, insignificant murmur next to the quiet steady throb of the river. Behind her, the yellowish glow of light from the casino was engulfed in the huge darkness of a November night. Helen shifted against the concrete wall, scraping a pebble beneath her shoe. She picked it up, fingered its weathered gritty surface, then tossed the fragment out over the water. Surprising that such a carefully manicured place as the Silver Saddle would have permitted a stray bit of rock to mar the pristine surface of the walkway that ringed the casino. Helen smiled. Probably better to rescue the rock from discovery by the management and sacrifice it to the river.

Of course, she thought as she tried and failed to watch the pebble arc across the river, she had freaked out at just the thought of taking up detective work again. There was no way that Carmel Kittrick could have known or cared about Helen's recent history. The woman hadn't purposely opened up old wounds. She'd merely presented the idea as one professional to another, nothing more or less.

Helen kicked at the pavement, wondering if she'd find any more pebbles on the well-swept walkway. She barely noticed the few hardy souls out walking off their Thanksgiving dinners in the chill air. Instead, her thoughts worked back through the brief encounter with Carmel. She finally decided, as she gave up scuffing for rocks, that she was torn between equal parts fear and desire — the fear of being threatened with a violent and painful death, and the desire to get back into detective work again.

"No," she'd said, almost yelling, when Alison had last broached the subject of Helen's going back to private investigation. "How many times do I have to tell you?"

"All right. Fine." Helen could still see Alison slam down the lid on yet another box stuffed with files from Helen's office. Former office. The new tenants, a bright-eyed and bushy-tailed couple who bubbled with excitement about their mail-order business, had taken the keys from Helen just before they left for Laughlin. "Go ahead and hide behind that security guard's badge the rest of your life." Alison slapped masking tape around the box, her long dark hair swinging over her face and hiding her flush of anger.

Helen stuffed a wall calendar over the pens and ink cartridges in the carton at her feet. Alison pushed past her to the stairwell. "Are you telling me you're ashamed of my guard job?"

"Jesus, Helen! Of course I'm not!" Alison rested the box on the banisters and shoved her hair out of her face. "It's honest work. I'm proud of you for making yourself go out there and get the job when you've already been through so much."

"Then what?"

"You know what." Alison took a deep breath and heaved the box up in her arms. "We both know that being a detective is your life. It's your dream, what you've always wanted. And you won't even think about it now." Alison turned away. "You've given up. And it hurts to see it."

Helen could remember silently following Alison down the stairs that day, carting the final fragments of her career out of the office building and into oblivion. She remembered how Alison had hugged her later that night, held her close and even cried for her, mourning Helen's loss. She'd lain awake all night in Alison's arms, staring at the ceiling and replaying the final moments of locking up the office.

What Helen couldn't remember was actually feeling anything. No anger, no remorse, no fear — nothing. Blank.

A sharp click broke into her thoughts, snapping her away from her vacant stare into the dark water below. To her left, just around a curve on the pavement, Helen saw something tubular and metallic glint in the dull light filtering out from the casino. Without a moment's reflection, Helen flattened herself against the barrier, heart pounding painfully in her chest and all her instincts poised to push her into flight. She cringed against the concrete as the thing extended farther out into the night, waiting in terror for the brief bright flash from the gun barrel held at arm's length, the incongruously comical pop of a silencer. Or maybe this time it would be a full-blown roar of a rifle leveled at her.

Moments of silence and calm passed, and Helen's heart slowed to a quiet thud. "My God," she muttered, willing herself to breathe slowly in, slowly out. It wasn't a gun. Whoever stood around the corner was not a killer intent on taking Helen's life. "It's okay, it's okay," she whispered. Carmel Kittrick really had stirred something up a couple of hours ago, Helen realized. What the hell was wrong with her? Maybe it was just being in unfamiliar surroundings.

"Um, excuse me?" A round flabby face loomed before the black backdrop of the night sky. Helen recognized the features of Wilbur Kittrick. "You're the woman from UFORA, right?"

"Well, no, I'm afraid not." Helen scrambled up from the pavement and hoped she didn't appear too ridiculous crouched against the wall. "I'm sorry for the misunderstanding. I just sort of found the hat. In the restaurant," she added lamely.

"Oh." Wilbur looked down, crestfallen, then glanced back up sheepishly. "You're a friend of Carmel's, aren't you?"

"No, not really. I just met her this evening."

"Hm." He turned away suddenly and walked back around the bend. Helen shivered in the cold air. She was still shaking from her terrified reaction. Stuffing her hands back in her pockets, she felt a balled-up clump of fabric crushed in her fingers.

She followed Wilbur along the walkway. "I believe this hat is yours, Mr. Kittrick." She smoothed the canvas as best she could and offered it to Wilbur.

He was bent over a telescope — the long metallic tube she'd glimpsed moments ago — and busily fiddled at a knob set just above the tripod mount. "Why don't you just keep the damned thing? Better yet, give it to my sister. That way you can prove you're earning your pay."

"I'm sorry?" Baffled, Helen watched as he eased the scope up until it pointed out over the formless mountain range across the river and into the night sky. Pulling up a folding stool beneath him, Wilbur pointedly kept his back to her and settled his face against the scope.

"You're just another in the long line of baby-sitters that Carmel and Daddy have arranged for me. You're not even a very good one — not with that innocent act of yours." He snorted, leaning back from the telescope to glare at her. "And you can tell her that I'm right here, safe and sound, just like Daddy wanted." He turned his attention back to the sky. "Although why the hell they want me hanging around I'll never know."

"Mr. Kittrick, I'm afraid there's a misunderstanding here. I'm not employed by your sister or your father." She looked out in the direction where Wilbur had fixed his gaze.

For a brief moment, Helen wondered if Carmel's angry, frustrated brother could be the source of those mutilated photographs. It was just the sort of childish gimmick that might scare the pants off his little sister. "You know," she said, giving in to the temptation to poke and prod professionally, "I'm surprised you can see anything in the sky at all, what with all the lights from the town and the casinos." Maybe if she could get him to trust her, to open up to her, she could find out more about Carmel and Carmel's enemies.

"Shows what you know," Wilbur said. "This telescope can filter all that stuff out. It's what the military uses for watching UFOs."

"And is this a likely place to see them? Here in Laughlin?"

Wilbur shrugged. "We're not all that far from the test sites in Nevada. As if you cared."

"Look, I really am not paid by Carmel to keep an eye on you."

"Then what *is* she paying you for?" He peered up at her. "Is it something to do with those anonymous letters she's been getting?"

Before Helen could ask him how he knew about the mysterious photocopies, another male voice boomed out. "Well, here you are!" Hef nodded a greeting to Helen as he glad-handed Wilbur on the back, nearly knocking the expensive telescope off its mount and into the Colorado River. Helen could smell Hef's aftershave — something that combined mint and fruit into a rather nauseating odor — as he stood over the other man protectively. "Your sister's been looking for you. Daddy Kittrick was on the phone earlier. He wished he could have talked to his kids tonight."

With surprising force, Wilbur pushed Hef away. Even in the dim light Helen could see his face, blotched white and red with fury. "Get your fucking hands off me, you fucking ape," he hissed, spittle frothing at his lips.

Hef's face stayed stony as Wilbur proceeded to pack up his telescope and mount. Hef glanced at Helen. "Now, Wilbur, we don't want to be scaring off folks!" he said with a forced smile. "Especially our grand-prize winners!" As Wilbur arranged his equipment in a huge black case, Hef cleared his throat and took a step closer to her. "Hope old Wilbur here didn't get started on you," he said, folding his beefy arms across his chest. "He's what you might call an eccentric. Of course, he's really a great guy once you get to know him."

"You must be a very close friend of the Kittrick family," Helen said with a smile.

"Oh, we're like brothers, Wilbur and me. Hold on there, I got that." Hef grabbed Wilbur's carrying case and slung its strap over his shoulder.

With a muffled curse Wilbur took back the case, shoving Hef hard enough to slam him into the concrete barrier. Helen, standing closer to Wilbur as he struggled with the case, got a good whiff of whatever strong liquor he'd been drinking. As he tried to force Hef out of his path, she could see that his motions were vague and clumsy, even though his speech was clear. Wilbur finally managed to squeeze himself through the leather strap. "Keep your hands off me, fucking asshole," he spat out at Hef.

"All right, now, Wilbur, you've had enough fun for tonight. Let's just call it a day, okay?" Wilbur ignored them as he ambled off toward the casino entrance.

Hef sighed and shook his head, a pale film of sweat shining on his thick jowls. "He gets that way once in a while. Sorry if he troubled you, Ms. Black."

Helen cocked her head and considered him. Maybe his job covered a lot more than baby-sitting Wilbur. "Are you the one who investigated me for Carmel Kittrick?" she asked him.

His smile froze and he stared down at her icily. "I'm not sure I follow you."

She managed a laugh. "Well, the last thing I was expecting this evening was a job offer from our hostess. Someone had to do a little research to find out whether or not I'd qualify."

His smile thawed, and he looked over her head at the building. "Naturally, the Kittrick Corporation wanted to find out all it could about the contest winners. We like to feel we know our clientele, that we treat them like family."

Helen decided not to point out that she could do without being treated the way Wilbur had just been handled by his family, thank you very much. Besides, it made a kind of sense that the company wouldn't want to have any embarrassments or surprises in this much-publicized event. "Just making sure no one has a criminal record or hires illegal immigrants, I suppose," she said.

He relaxed and put on the smile again. "Exactly. That wouldn't be the image we want to project to our public. The restaurants are geared toward family — family values, good times with the family, all the old mom-and-pop ambiance that never goes out of style."

Helen nodded and they exchanged chilly farewells. So, Carmel knew ahead of time that a private investigator would be at the dinner. It would have been a chance to ask for professional help, Helen realized, without jumping through a lot of hoops for the company or digging too deeply into her own personal funds. Besides, Helen thought with a flush of shame and anger, Carmel must have been fairly certain that Helen was desperate for work — any work — and would have come cheap.

Still, there was that ugly little scene in the restaurant, when Hef had more or less told Carmel that she was a bitch. Maybe there was more to their relationship than work. Helen added his name to the brief list she was putting together of people who hated Carmel enough to send her those ugly missives each week.

Helen waited until Hef made his way back into the

lights of the Saddle, then went him inside. As she reached the wide glass doors by the valet station, she stopped in her tracks.

"I waited and waited, Hef! You never showed!"

The waitress who'd served them a few hours before had her thin arms, which were covered with bruises, flung around Hef's neck. Without the badly fitted blue vest, she looked younger and slimmer than Helen remembered. Helen stepped behind a cart loaded with expensive luggage, hoping that neither Hef nor — what was her name? Oh, yes, the tag had read "Sue" — Sue had seen her. It probably didn't matter to Sue, anyway, that she was seen and heard by half a dozen people in the valet area. Three men, all wearing the requisite magenta shirts sporting a stylized saddle emblem over the left breast, lounged against a wide information booth and watched, sniggering, as Sue kissed Hef several times on the cheek.

"Where were you, Hef?" Her plain, flat face, devoid of makeup and glowing with excitement, shone under the harsh white glare of the bank of lights overhead. She snuggled tight against him, her plump breasts flattened against his chest. "I thought I'd go nuts waiting for you."

Helen was glad that Sue couldn't see his face just then. His mouth twisted in a rictus of disgust, and he patted her lightly on the back while trying to disengage from her grip. "Now, I told you I had to go round up Wilbur, remember?" Once freed, he quickly put distance between them, heading toward the entrance. The valets continued to stare.

"But, Hef, sweetie, that was hours ago!" She trotted after him, dank dark ponytail flopping down her back. "What took you so long?" she wailed.

Hef turned on her, his face reddening with anger, then he visibly forced himself to relax and put on a stiff smile. "Why don't we go inside, Sue, and talk in there."

Sue calmed down immediately. Helen wondered if she'd borne the brunt of his rage before — those were pretty nasty bruises on her arms — and she quietly followed him into the Saddle. In her wake, the three valets guffawed at some remark made by one of the trio, and with their raucous laughter Helen felt a sudden shifting motion at her side.

"Shit. There goes my ride home." The girl, who appeared to be about twenty, was wearing the same kind of vest Helen had seen Sue wearing earlier. She took a deep drag from a cigarette and blew it out in a sigh. As she turned to flick ash down onto the pavement Helen read the name "Nick" on her nametag. "Thanks a lot, Mom." She turned and noticed Helen for the first time.

Jesus. Helen glanced back at the doors. Hef and Sue had disappeared, and the parking attendants were busy with new arrivals. One of the men who'd lounged and laughed moments before now lunged for the luggage cart where Helen and Nick stood. He hung by one arm from the brass rail along the top of the rack and grinned at Nick while his coworkers giggled and smirked behind him.

"So, Nickie baby, Mom found someplace else to stay for the night, huh?" he said, leering at the girl. "You know, I was kind of thinking. Sleeping around maybe runs in the family. Like mother like daughter, right? You want to come with me and show me what your mom taught you?" Loud guffaws erupted from the others.

Nick smiled sweetly and tossed her cigarette so that it landed on the man's arm. He yelped in surprise and pain and frantically hit it away. "Fuck you, you little cunt!"

Helen couldn't keep from staring at Nick. She looked so different from Sue it was hard to imagine they were mother and daughter. Where Sue was dark and plain, Nick was golden-haired and delicately lovely. As she moved under the light, however, Helen saw the dark circles under her eyes, the lines of tension around the corners of her mouth. Nick held herself and moved as though she were fifty, not barely old enough to work in a casino.

The two men who'd been watching from the sidelines stepped forward to join their friend, who looked up from his burned arm in fury. Helen stepped forward, ready to help if it was needed.

"Hi, guys. Well, Nick, haven't seen you here for a few days. How's it going?" Shelley came up from behind them and stood next to Nick.

"Okay, I guess." Nick didn't look too happy to have Shelley come to the rescue. She lit another cigarette while the men moved away.

"I didn't know you were working tonight," Shelley continued. "Stopped by, saw your mom. You weren't anywhere in sight." She stuffed her hands in her pockets and nervously jingled change.

"Yeah, well, they were short-staffed in the restaurant tonight, and I could sure use the extra money."

Shelley looked away from Nick and realized Helen was standing close by. "Helen Black, right?"

"That's right."

Shelley glanced at Nick and fiddled with her uniform belt. "You found your way to Ms. Kittrick all right?"

"Just fine."

Nick turned to Helen. "You know Carmel Kittrick?"

Helen shrugged. "No, not really. She just wanted to talk to me about a business proposition."

Shelley's eyes met Helen's in silent communication. "Did you see Sue go by?" Helen asked quietly while Nick stared fixedly at the carpet.

Shelley shook her head and pursed her lips. She seemed about to speak, thought better of it, then took a step closer to Nick. "Tell you what, I'll give you a lift home. I just got off my shift."

"No, thanks. I'll walk around to the front and take a cab home." Nick managed a small tight smile for Shelley, then looked at Helen. "Hell, I've been talking to that

55

butthead Hef for weeks, hoping to get a chance to see the mighty woman, and you sail in out of nowhere to spend the evening with her. Perfect."

Helen stared as Nick walked away from her. Shelley sighed and shook her head. "She's not bad, really. You shouldn't get the wrong idea."

"She has an unusual name. Is it short for something, like Nicola?"

"Nicolette. She was named for her father. Jesus, I can't believe her mom did it again, after the way Hef treats her. And after the way Nick takes care of her. Poor thing practically kills herself, trying to go to college, take care of the house, working these awful swing shifts." Shelley drew a deep breath and shook her head. "Sorry. It's been a long day."

Helen studied her shoes and wondered which was worse — to feel unrequited love or to watch someone else feel it. She couldn't resist one more question. "Why does she want to see Carmel Kittrick?"

"She's got this idea that while she's going to the junior college for her business degree maybe they could create a special assistant's job for her, or something like that. She could make a little more money, get college credit."

Helen pondered the unlikely scenario of her agreeing to work for Carmel on condition that she consider Nick's proposal. Ridiculous, really, she told herself. The last thing she needed to do was get involved in all this shit, and from the way Nick avoided Shelley she was sure Nick wouldn't appreciate the interference of two perverts, no matter how well intentioned.

Shelley, now awkward and embarrassed, mumbled goodnight and disappeared in the parking lot. Helen glanced at her watch. Just past midnight, she saw with a shock. She'd better get inside or Alison would definitely send out a posse. As she passed the reception area she heard a male voice raised in a strident tone.

"I'm sorry, sir, but no one is allowed in the Palace Suite without express permission."

"Damn it, that's my wife! I've got a right to go up there!"

He'd aged since the photograph was taken, but Helen recognized the weak, trembling chin and tiny eyes set far apart in a round face that seemed oddly unfinished. Marc Landry used his considerable height to tower over Amy in a threatening stance. His disheveled clothing and unshaved face only added to his wild appearance. Helen thought he looked as though he might have driven straight from Oxford, Mississippi, without stopping.

"I'm sorry, sir. I can't break company policy," the clerk said politely through nearly clenched teeth. "If you'd like to leave a message, I'll make sure she gets it."

"A message?" he snarled. "Yeah, I'll leave a fucking message for my fucking wife." He jabbed a finger into the air just under the girl's nose. A security guard, a middle-aged man, moved up to the counter.

"Problem, Amy?"

"No," she responded calmly. "Mr. Kittrick is just leaving a message for Mrs. Kittrick."

His piggish eyes narrowed, and he moved his gaze from Amy to the guard. "I am not Mr. Motherfucking Kittrick," he spat at them. "Look, she knows I'm coming. She told me where she'd be. She wanted to see me. Now, can your empty little blonde brain grasp that information, or is it too many words to handle all at once?"

He snapped upright suddenly as the other man grasped his upper arm. "You and I are going for a little walk, sir," he said in a sprightly voice. Helen watched as Marc, no doubt surprised at the strength of the guard's grip, bent toward the pressure on his arm. The pair ambled off toward the doors.

Helen felt pain around the scars in her side. She realized she'd seen enough dysfunctional family values for one Thanksgiving and headed for the elevators and Alison and bed.

Chapter Four

"Oh, lordy, I just know I lost it again, and your uncle will be so mad at me!" Edna rummaged one more time through her oversized bag for her room key.

Helen grinned and winked at Alison, who was rolling her eyes in exasperation. "I'm sure he won't be, Aunt Edna." It was seven-thirty Friday morning, and they were waiting for Uncle Loy to join them for breakfast. Helen stifled a yawn and promised herself a nap later to make up for the few hours of sleep she'd had last night.

"But I promised I wouldn't do it, and he was saying if I

lost it one more time he'd have to take it away —" Her face puckered like a child's on the verge of tears.

"It's okay. Look, why don't you go up to our room instead, use the bathroom up there? We'll sort all this stuff out after we've gone on the tour. The trip to prospecting country doesn't leave until nine from the lobby. We have plenty of time." Edna zipped her bag and nodded, took the key Helen offered and hurried away.

"Where's your uncle?" Alison asked.

"I'm not sure." She glanced around the casino again. "He told Aunt Edna he'd meet us for breakfast at the fish house, but apparently he took off about an hour ago." Although she didn't want to say anything to Alison, Helen had noticed the day before that Uncle Loy had acquired a habit of quietly disappearing from the scene — half an hour here, twenty minutes there, forty-five minutes sometimes. What the hell was he up to?

Helen's train of thought was arrested by the sight of three men, all heavily muscled and wearing military-style green fatigues, standing just outside the entrance and handing out flyers to people coming and going from the casino. She watched as one elderly woman, replete with blue hair and thickly rouged cheeks, had a flyer forced on her as she entered the Saddle. The woman scanned it, then flicked it away onto the carpet as she made a beeline for the nearest row of slot machines. Curious, Helen picked it up. It advertised a gun show to be held that very day in the auditorium of one of the Saddle's rival casinos. Helen crumpled the flyer and, while searching for a trash can, spotted Wilbur Kittrick studying the same flyer. He carefully folded it and tucked it into his shirt pocket, then checked his watch. He didn't notice Helen as he pushed his way outside and started talking to one of the leafleters.

"What's that?" Edna pointed at the flyer balled in Helen's hand. She gave Alison the room key

"Nothing," she said, tossing it into the garbage. Outside,

Wilbur was smiling and nodding at the three men as he ambled off through the parking lot — presumably in the direction of the show, which was scheduled to open at eight.

Alison sighed. "Well, let's go in and see what they have on the menu, get a table." Resolutely she started off for Romie's.

Helen laughed. "Hey, relax, you're not going off to an execution."

"Tell that to my arteries."

"This is a unique cultural experience for you, Alison," Helen teased as they took their place in line. "Authentic Southern cuisine."

"Yeah, I know. See it, kill it, and fry it."

But this time there was a smile on Alison's face, and Helen was relieved to see that she really was joking. The restaurant was not nearly as crowded as the evening before. At this hour, she supposed they were missing the big breakfast crowd. Lots of people were no doubt sleeping in, and sleeping off their Thanksgiving dinners.

"You look in an awfully good mood this morning, Helen," Alison remarked as they slid into a booth.

Helen, surprised, nodded in agreement. "I guess I am," she said. She couldn't quite figure out why, herself, given her late night, but she had a suspicion it had something to do with her conversation with Carmel Kittrick.

Alison was staring at her over the top of the menu. "Did you decide to take up that proposition after all?" she asked obliquely.

"No, of course not!" Helen snapped back, more vehemently than she wanted to. Why did that question bother her so much? She shot a furtive glance at Alison, but she was deep into the menu. She suddenly felt nervous and stared at her own menu, not really seeing the selections listed there. Perhaps, she reasoned as they ordered coffee, it was just the thought that she'd at least had the offer to work as a private investigator once again — an opportunity she'd never believed would come her way, not after all this time. "I have no intention of mixing myself up in that situation."

"Just as well — she'd probably pay you in catfish and coleslaw," Alison said softly in a feeble attempt at humor.

"Or a lifetime of free lunches."

"Or your very own catfish farm in Mississippi."

Helen could sense that their lighthearted banter was a fragile veneer masking stronger emotions roiling around inside both of them. She wasn't sure what Alison's feelings were about her late night visit to Carmel, but she was certain they weren't positive. She still didn't know what she herself thought, other than the fact that she'd been intrigued as well as disturbed by it.

"Uh-oh, looks like someone's honeymoon is over." Alison nodded toward the entrance of the restaurant. Through the double glass doors of Romie's, Helen saw the couple against the wall next to a bank of slot machines. Bud Gilley, his hairy chest resplendent in a shirt unbuttoned low enough to display prominent pecs, was hovering over a woman who stood in shadow just outside the entrance. His body shielded her from view, and his arm was raised up protectively over her head, his hand flat against the wall. When he moved his hand to stroke the woman's hair Helen made out the distinctive features of Carmel Kittrick, whose smile slowly lit her face, her lips parting in a simulation of lust.

Thankfully, Edna had just arrived back in the restaurant and strolled over to check out the breakfast buffet. Helen looked back at Alison and caught a glimpse of Heather Gilley in a booth opposite their own. Her eyes were wide and shining with misery, her makeup applied haphazardly and unevenly. Even in the strange unnatural light of the restaurant Helen could see smears of mascara and liner around her eyes. Heather's lip trembled as she pretended to study the menu, giving quick, nervous glances around the restaurant. Despite Heather's prettiness and obvious devotion to her husband, Helen knew there was no way that she could compete with the sophistication and power that drove Carmel Kittrick. Watching her sip a small glass of orange juice, Helen felt a wave of compassion for her.

"Here he comes. What an asshole." Alison's mouth twisted in disgust, and Helen wondered if she was reminded of her own ex-husband, who'd consistently abused her throughout their five-year marriage. "She should get on the first plane out of here, leave him and his dick in the dirt."

At that moment, Bud strode in. His hands were arranged around his pockets so that his fingers were pointing at the delights of his crotch as he joined his wife. His abrupt greeting turned into a sneer of contempt as Heather gingerly dabbed her eyes with a napkin.

"Sorry to keep you ladies waiting." Loy's voice startled her out of observation, and for a moment Helen and Alison shuffled around the booth to make room for him. "Saw Edna at the buffet." Loy finally ended up sitting alone on one side of the booth, with a space reserved for Edna beside him. Helen studied her uncle's face as the waitress came up to take his order. What the hell was he up to, sneaking off like that? Was he playing the slots? Aunt Edna must be very worried, even if she wasn't talking about it. Except for his wide grin and an air of generally being pleased with himself and the world — hell, maybe he'd won a few bucks — Helen couldn't see anything different about her usually silent and reserved relative.

Their waitress turned away only to bump headlong into another Romie's employee who was weighed down with a heavy tray of glasses headed for the dishwasher. A brief tangle ensued during which the tray landed on the floor with an earsplitting crash. Helen cringed as a few shards of glass flew in their direction.

"Oh, honey, you'll have to look where you're going! Here, let me get that."

"I'm sorry, I'm sorry." At first Helen had thought it was

Sue who'd dropped the tray, but then she realized that it was Nick, huddled over the mess on the floor, trying to round up broken glass as quickly as possible.

"Where's your mom today?" their waitress asked as she retrieved a cup that had rolled next to Helen's feet.

"She's running a little late this morning."

"Again?" Helen heard the disbelief in the older waitress's voice and caught the quick shake of her head. Sue's excuses had apparently been heard before. "And she sent you out here to cover her shift again, didn't she?"

"What the hell — I don't have classes today, and I could use the tips." Nick's face showed lines of exhaustion, and her arms, scrawny and shaking with effort, strained beneath the blue uniform as she heaved the tray up. "I had to be here anyway. I'm helping the maids clean the rooms this afternoon."

The waitress pursed her lips and glanced over at Helen's table. "Well, let's get this cleaned up. Did you get any breakfast yet, hon?"

"No, I'm all right, really. Please, don't bother." She shifted the tray onto her hip. "I'll get the broom and the mop. I'll get all the glass picked up —"

"Excuse me, could we get someone to take our order, please?" Bud Gilley's voice boomed out over the low-keyed noise in the restaurant, and the waitress grimaced. Bud peered in their direction impatiently, straining to look at the idiots who were holding up his order.

"I'll be right back." The waitress hurried off to the Gilleys' table.

As Nick turned away, holding the tray firmly, the overhead lights gleamed against the bright red splash on her hands. "Jesus, Nick, you're bleeding," Helen murmured. She glanced around the restaurant, hoping to see another member of the Romie's staff who could help, but the breakfast crowd they'd just barely avoided had suddenly arrived. The other waitress was busily pouring coffee, and the cashier was acting as hostess.

Before Nick could protest, Helen took the tray and led the way back toward the kitchen. After setting the tray down, and after a couple of inquiries to one of the cooks, who stared at her as if she'd arrived in one of Wilbur's spaceships, Helen found the first-aid kit tucked beneath one of the sinks.

"We'd better wash that out. Where's the bathroom?"

Nick led her away from the kitchen into a narrow corridor. The bathroom was barely big enough to hold the two of them. The scent of bacon wafted into the tiny chamber, battling with a faint but cloying scent of rotted food coming from the Dumpsters in the alley on the other side of the wall.

"This will sting a little," Helen warned as she drizzled a thin stream of peroxide over the slice in Nick's palm. It bubbled and fizzed as it flowed across the cut. The cut was deep and probably painful, although it probably didn't need stitches, but Nick's face was frozen in a blank mask. "Okay — that was the worst part. Now let's get it bandaged." As she fixed gauze to the wound with adhesive tape Nick muttered a thanks to Helen. "No problem. It would be nice, though, if you could not use that hand today — you know, just give it a rest."

Nick shook her head and withdrew her bandaged hand from Helen's gentle clasp. "No such luck. If Mom misses one more shift, I know she'll get canned."

As Helen debated whether or not to keep talking to the girl, the door flung open, nearly knocking her down. A young man she hadn't seen before stood in the doorway. "Can I talk to you a minute, Nick?" His pale skin stretched tight over an emaciated frame, and one shaky hand kept wandering up to his brow to wipe off beads of sweat. Baggy jeans hung loose around his waist, and his shirt flapped open, revealing his bare chest. Stubble sprouted from his cheeks and chin.

"I'm kind of busy right now, Joe."

He fidgeted around the door to the bathroom, his fingers tapping out a restless tattoo. "It's important. You know what we talked about yesterday?" His glance rested on Helen for a moment, then darted away as he shifted from one foot to the other. "Please? Just for a second."

With a sigh Nick followed him out of the bathroom and through a door at the other end of the corridor that opened to the alley. Although Joe had shut the door behind them, Helen could hear their conversation through the narrow windows set high in the kitchen walls.

"Jesus, Joe, I already told you! I'm not giving you any more money. You'll just go back out on the street and get another fix. I'm sick to death of this shit."

"Nick, you don't understand." His voice shook and he sounded close to tears. "I'm about to jump out of my skin, I got the shakes so fuckin' bad. Please, baby, just this one time."

"I said no, and I mean no! Goddamnit, Joe, get away from me!"

"Too good for me now, huh? Little bitch! You really think you're gonna get to talk to those Kittricks? You think you'll get the time of day from them?"

"Get your hands off me!"

"I swear, Nick, I'm going crazy here. I've gotta get some or I don't know what I'll do —"

Just as Helen was about to walk outside, the other waitress appeared. "Where's Nick?" she asked.

Helen busied herself with gauze and peroxide bottles. "Talking to someone outside."

"Talking to who?" The waitress didn't wait for an answer. She stomped down the corridor and out the door into the alley.

"Joe, what are you doing hanging around here? The

manager told you the day he fired you he doesn't want to see your face again. Besides, Nick has other things to do." A moment later Nick was walking back down the hall. "Now, hon," she said, steering the girl out of the bathroom with a motherly arm wrapped around Nick's shoulders, "we're just gonna let you stay up at the cash register this morning. You just sit tight up there and run that register."

Nick allowed herself to be led away, and Helen followed them out of the kitchen after stowing the first-aid kit back under the sink. She felt deflated by the whole thing. Was it sadness about Nick's apparently hopeless plight, the mother-and-daughter role reversal? Or was it dismay at her own inability to do anything about the situation? Not that Nick seemed to want things to change, or that Helen had any business at all interfering.

As she shoved the first-aid kit back under the counter where she'd found it, she saw the older waitress and Joe the bus boy having a whispered argument at the other end of the counter.

"You'd better not be pestering that girl, Joe. She's told you before, she doesn't want to see you anymore."

"That's between her and me." His eyes flashed with anger. Each word he said was punctuated by nervous gestures, and his skin was filmed with a thin sheen of perspiration.

"Yeah, just like her paycheck, right from her to you so you could get your next fix." Suddenly the waitress turned and saw Helen. Joe took advantage of the distraction to slip away. "Thanks for helping with Nick."

"No problem. I was right there."

Glum thoughts chased her as she carefully stepped around the three cooks who were busily stirring and toasting and frying in the kitchen. As she stepped back into the restaurant, the shift in sight and sound and smell briefly disoriented her. Suddenly the lack of sleep, the strange excitements of the previous night and the overwhelming scent of eggs gave her a wave of nausea. Helen caught sight of Alison and Loy and Edna in the booth, looking at her worriedly. With a wave, Helen headed for the restrooms.

A couple of seconds alone in the bathroom and a splash of cold water on her face seemed to restore her. Helen went back out only to find the narrow corridor leading from bathroom to restaurant blocked by Bud Gilley, whose hands fiddled near his crotch. Helen realized he was zipping his pants after a visit of his own to the men's room.

"Excuse me," she murmured, hoping to make a quick escape.

He seemed to have other ideas. Instead of stepping aside so she could pass, Bud moved so that she couldn't get by. What's your hurry?" He stepped closer and she caught the smell of his cologne, spicy and strong.

"I think your wife is waiting for you," Helen said as coldly as she could manage.

"Let her wait. I've been meaning to talk to you since the moment we met."

"I can't imagine why." Helen tried again to step around him, but again he blocked her path.

"Relax, would you? I'm just trying to talk to you. I'm not touching you." He put both hands up in the air, and the light shone against the thick chain that decorated his chest, a ropy gold twist of metal studded with heavy nuggets. "I just wonder if Carmel made her suggestion to you last night."

"Suggestion?" Helen found it hard to believe Carmel would have confided in this lout about anything, but after seeing their sleazy display of affection earlier she realized she might have misjudged the woman. "I don't know what you're talking about."

"You know." He leaned in closer. Had he been drinking

so early? Helen thought not, but of course there were other indulgences besides liquor. "Putting on a little show. You and your girlfriend."

"What?" Helen's jaw dropped.

"Carmel seemed really interested when I asked her about it — in fact, it made her very, very hot. I think she'd get off on it as much as I would." At this point he reached out and fiddled with the lapel of Helen's jacket. "And I know Carmel would make it worth your while."

"You think that Carmel acted on your idea for me and Alison to do some kind of live sex act? Do I have that right?"

"Just name the day, baby. It'll be terrific." He let her lapel go but moved in on her, his face inches from hers.

Helen knew he had to be on something more than a high from screwing Carmel. Unless he was on something pretty powerful, not even a Bud Gilley would be so stupid as to proposition a woman in a family restaurant, while his wife sat at a table not ten feet away.

Another man chose that moment to squeeze past them into the men's room. Helen took her chance to edge past Bud, who still leered down at her. "If you ever say anything to me again — not even so much as a hello — I promise to rip your manly balls off your body and fry them with the catfish. Do you understand me?" She punctuated her whispered comments with a sharp elbow in his midriff — not enough to do anything beyond knock the wind out of him — and hoped it conveyed a promise of more pain to come.

He hunched over his stricken abdomen and gasped a couple of times, then coughed as he stood upright again.

"I said, do you understand me?"

"Hey, hey, no offense — just a joke, you know, made a bet with someone, didn't mean a thing." He babbled after her as she left the corridor and headed back to her booth.

"Helen, what the hell happened back there?" Alison asked, concerned.

Helen looked up from the fast-cooling plate of scrambled eggs that had arrived during her absence. Bud, red-faced and still heaving, slammed himself into his chair opposite Heather. Heather sent an icy look toward Helen and started talking to Bud, who picked up a knife and fiddled with it, his head down, ignoring his wife.

"Helen? Is everything all right?" Edna asked.

Helen chewed on bacon and grinned at her aunt and uncle. "Fine. Let's eat."

Chapter Five

The guide herded the knot of tourists through a narrow hallway lined with old framed posters announcing rodeos and rewards for cattle rustlers. Her hair, a ludicrous white-gold soufflé that puffed around her pink face, shimmered in the bright sunlight that filtered through the fly-specked windowpane of the historic home.

"And this is the very room where Clark Gable and Carole Lombard stayed when they got away from it all here in Oatman!" The guide flung an arm in an arc across the narrow chamber. Everyone strained at the doorway, pushing one another in an attempt to see the Bedspread of the Stars.

"Let's hope they changed the sheets since then," Alison muttered in Helen's ear.

Helen suppressed a laugh and glanced at Edna and Loy. They were having the time of their lives — first a quick drive out to prospecting country, where they learned how to stake a claim from "a real old-time prospector" who had both a grizzled beard and a cell phone in tow. Then there was a frenzied photo session with half a dozen tired-looking mules — descendants, their guide informed them, of the original mules that worked the mines just outside the sleepy town of Oatman. And now they had the great privilege of witnessing the very spot where Hollywood royalty had conducted trysts.

Alison backed away from the shrine to Gable and Lombard and plopped down heavily on a picturesque rocking chair tucked behind the door. Helen joined her. "You okay?" she asked quietly.

Alison waved a hand in the air. "Don't mind me. Sorry I'm such a grump today. I'll keep it under control."

Helen felt a guilty twinge as she crouched down beside her. "We should have taken the morning off and let Loy and Edna do this on their own."

Alison smiled and shook her head. "They're having a great time, aren't they? Look, I'll be fine. I'll just sit here a minute until the glazed look on my face goes away."

Helen sighed and stood up. "Well, after seeing that bed in there, I don't believe there's a whole lot more to do in life. We've pretty much seen it all now."

"Except for the gunfight. Don't forget the Wild West Gunfight starting at high noon." Alison thrust a flyer at Helen. "They were handing these out downstairs."

Helen glanced through the announcement of the reenactment, then handed the flyer back to Alison. "Think we'll survive the shootout and make it back to Laughlin for another catfish dinner?"

Alison winced and began to laugh, dropping her head into her hands. "I swear I'll never touch catfish again when we get home."

Helen craned her neck and peered across a myriad of heads. She spotted Loy and Edna hunched over the rickety dresser that sported a handful of dusty framed photographs depicting famous faces posed with donkeys or cowboys or picturesque miners. Aunt Edna looked flushed, and drops of perspiration welled at her brow. Maybe she was having another hot flash.

"I think I'll go outside and scout for a nice shady spot for us to watch the shootout," Helen murmured to Alison. "Aunt Edna's looking mighty peaked right now."

Alison rolled her eyes. "Please — the last thing I need right now is for you to pick up some weird version of cowboy lingo."

"Sorry, ma'am." Helen drawled. "Reckon it's just all this authenticity, and all." With a final nod and grin to Alison, Helen turned away and prepared to squeeze back down the narrow corridor. The passageway bent to the right at the top of the stairs, and Helen almost stumbled over a woman who sat breathing harshly and heavily on the top step. "Oh, I'm sorry, Mrs. — Mrs. Tilson, isn't it?"

Mrs. Tilson's face was gray beneath a sheen of sweat. She held one hand to her side as though keeping a specific pain in place at that particular spot.

"Let me get you something. Or find your husband," Helen babbled in alarm. Then she remembered — Jack Tilson had stayed behind that morning. She hadn't seen his broad pleasant dark face on the tour bus, which had surprised her at the time since his wife was so obviously ill.

"No, no, I'm all right," Mrs. Tilson protested. A couple of people, carrying cameras armed and ready, pushed past them on the stairs. Helen waited for them to pass, then sat down next to her. Her breathing was a little steadier now. "It just got a little too warm up there."

"At least take this, then." Helen fumbled in her backpack and pulled out the bottle of water she'd tucked away that morning. As she searched she wondered if she might be in the final stages of cancer. Had the Tilsons opted for staying out of hospitals and off tubes?

"Thank you." She took the bottle with one shaking hand, then groped around on the stairs with her other hand. "My bag — it should be right here."

"Is it — oh, I see it." Helen pulled forward the big flowered carryall that the woman had with her constantly. At the sight of Helen handling her bag, Mrs. Tilson suddenly went still and quiet. Her eyes widened with an expression Helen could not identify.

"I've got it." Mrs. Tilson jerked the bag away from her. Startled, Helen let go of the canvas. The carryall swayed between them, then toppled down the stairs, tumbling over and finally disgorging its contents in small heaps on the steps.

"Oh, no." Helen sighed. She got up, almost knocking over a particularly large man smelling of coconut-scented sunblock and spicy aftershave as he ambled down the staircase with heavy steps. His size eighteen-plus feet landed neatly on a pile of newspaper clippings that had spilled from the bag onto the worn flowered runner, imprinting the shape of his tennis shoe onto the smeared black ink. "Terrific." Helen glared at the man's back as she bent over and began to gather up Mrs. Tilson's things. "No, no, I've got it. Please don't get up," she called over her shoulder as Mrs. Tilson struggled to stand and retrieve her things.

"My pills," she gasped, her face suddenly leeched pale again beneath the sheen of black skin, her fingers trembling. "Over there."

Helen spotted the small amber-shaded bottle. "Here we

go. I'll open it for you. Oh, and let me get the water." She unscrewed the cap on the water bottle as Mrs. Tilson tipped her medicine into her palm. She darted a glance at the small container of pills. She saw the name of a pharmacy in Jackson printed across the top of the label and the world *morphine* typed below that.

Mrs. Tilson leaned her head back to swallow the pills. Helen was shocked to see how thin she was, how her head bobbled on her neck as if weighted too heavily for her body to bear. She quietly placed a few stray items back into the bag as the other woman, eyes closed in exhaustion, leaned with a sigh against the wall.

"Maybe," Helen began tentatively, "maybe we should get you back to the hotel. I'm sure we could get a ride set up for you, and —"

"No." her eyes fluttered open, and Helen involuntarily cringed at the iron in her voice. "I don't want anyone to fuss over me. I'll be all right in a minute. I don't usually drink directly from a bottle," she said, softening. In fact, Helen noted, she already did look better. Her breathing was more regular, and the smooth dark planes of her thin face were less bleached.

"Okay. If you're sure."

"Yes. Thank you for your help, but I'll be all right now." Helen resisted the urge to help her as she struggled to her feet. "I believe I'll just find the restroom."

"I saw them over there." Helen gestured toward the opposite end of the first-floor corridor, in the direction of the visitors' information booth just inside the entrance.

Mrs. Tilson sighed, ran a hand across her hair, and slowly moved down the stairs. Another group of tourists, chattering to one another in a language Helen didn't recognize, swarmed around Mrs. Tilson. They were heading right for the staircase and, no doubt, the famous romantic site upstairs.

One of them, a small wizened gent with a thick head of

gray hair, suddenly stopped and scooped something up from the floor. Helen instantly recognized a newspaper clipping. She must have missed it.

"Excuse me, sir, that belongs to someone." It took a couple of minutes to persuade the gentleman that she really did in fact want the flimsy strips of paper. He stared vacantly at Helen as she tried to explain, then shrugged and handed over the clippings with a glance at his compatriots that suggested there was no accounting for the ways of these crazy Americans.

Stapled together in the top left-hand corner, the three sheets comprised a single article. Mrs. Tilson, or someone else, had cut the article out in such a way that there was no indication of what paper it had come from. There was, at least, a date on the second page. Mrs. Tilson had been carrying this around for three years, Helen saw with some surprise.

After a glance at the restroom door — no sign of Mrs. Tilson — Helen began to read. The first page, wider and shorter than the other two, was little more than a headline and a photograph, with only three lines of text beneath the picture. At the sight of the vaguely familiar face, she grinned. The young man pictured wore a high-school sweater with a big letter *H* sewn on, the kind of letter achieved in varsity sports. Helen read his name in the caption. George Tilson bore a very strong resemblance to his father, especially around the jaw. Glancing again at the date on page two, Helen decided he must have graduated about then.

It was the three lines of text below the high-school portrait that stopped her cold. George Tilson would never graduate high school. His body had been found in the parking lot of a Romie's in Biloxi. The jump page stated that the police surmised a "gang-related" murder took place after George and his fellow Hattiesburg Senior High

Hellcats celebrated a stunning victory over the Biloxi Bulldogs in the nearby town of Pass Christian. Although the local chapter of the NAACP had repeatedly registered complaints about racist incidents in assorted Romie's throughout Mississippi, officials were convinced that the brutal stabbing of the teenager was connected to gangs and drugs.

Curious as to how the youngster had ended up by himself at the restaurant, Helen was about to flip to the third and final page of the article when she heard footsteps approaching her. A soft voice said, "I believe that's mine."

"Of course." Helen refolded the yellowed sheets along their accustomed creases and handed the article back to Mrs. Tilson. "Are you feeling better now?"

"Fine. Thank you." Head held high, Mrs. Tilson slipped the pages back into her carryall and walked out into the hot sun of the late morning. Against the sillouhette of her slim form Helen saw a couple of men dressed in dusty chaps and sweat-stained hats lounging on a wooden railing that stretched the length of the hotel's verandah. When she saw the long-barreled revolvers tied in holsters at their sides, she realized the Wild West shootout was about to commence. With a guilty start Helen hurried out of the hotel and began her search for a shady spot from which Alison and Edna and Loy could watch the show.

"Sorry," Helen murmured for what seemed to her the thousandth time as, several minutes later, she finally wedged herself through a knot of people gathered by what must have once been a watering trough. It was situated at the side of a shack that Helen suspected used to house chickens but now sold a variety of high-priced cold drinks to thirsty tourists. Alongside the narrow metal trough, the ground rose slightly beneath the eaves of the ramshackle henhouse, offering some enviable shade as well as a passable view of the scene unfolding on the town's main street.

Helen spotted her party just as she'd finished paying for bottles of water while swallowing her protests at the exorbitant price of refreshment in these here parts.

She waved wildly when she saw Alison emerge from the hotel. The trio wove across the street and into the relative coolness where Helen waited. Her aunt's face was bright red — whether from heat or hormones Helen couldn't guess — and they all breathed a sigh of relief once they reached the trough.

"Thanks, hon." Aunt Edna took a bottle from Helen and tilted her head back to drink deeply. Loy and Helen exchanged glances, and Loy sighed and leaned against the shack.

"Aunt Edna, maybe we'd better go inside —" But Helen's protest was drowned out as the two men in cowboy apparel moved off the verandah and began to coax the crowd off the street onto the sidewalks in loud, twangy voices.

"Look, he's got a pager clipped to his belt," Helen heard a voice whisper.

"Kind of spoils the effect, doesn't it?"

Helen recognized two of the women from the RV gang she'd seen earlier at the Saddle. As they put their heads together to giggle, one of them glanced over her shoulder and winked at Helen. "All we need now is for him to pull out a portable fax machine from his vest."

Helen grinned in reply, then turned her attention to Loy and Edna again. Loy was finally having success in urging Edna to sit down on the edge of the trough, where a metal lip overhung the basin and provided enough room for her to perch with some ease. Her color was a bit better now, at least, Helen noted.

"Is she okay?" One of the RV women, her nose plastered with thick white sunblock, nodded at Edna.

Helen smiled. "I think so. She certainly has a bunch of us hovering over her, at least."

The street quickly filled with a variety of outlaws, gunslingers and rustlers all intent on shooting their firearms for the delight of the crowd. The sheriff, identifiable by means of the enormous silver star pinned on his chest as well as the towering white horse he rode, emerged from nowhere just in time to save the entire town from destruction by Black Bart and his Band of Outlaws.

Just when the sheriff was about to challenge Black Bart and his gang to a final showdown, one of the villains in black hats, holding his pistol high overhead, strode through the crowd. "I'll take me a hostage afore I give in to yew, yew lily-livered tea-drinkin' varmint!" he yelled. The crowd cheered wildly, applauding as he fired his pistol into the air. "Now —" He stood in the street near the shack where Helen had found refuge, his eyes gleaming as he searched the faces assembled around him. "Might as well find me a purty one, then!" With that, he beckoned to a young woman standing to his left. It was Heather Gilley. "Whaddya think, folks? Think this purty little lady could be my hostage for today?"

Heather's blonde curls glistened in the sun as she reluctantly left the anonymity of the crowd and stepped into the street. She cringed away from the ersatz outlaw but tried to smile as he gently urged her to come with him, amid wild approval from the audience. Helen glanced back to where Heather had been standing, looking for Bud, but he was nowhere to be seen.

"And what's your name, good woman?" the sheriff was asking from atop his horse.

Helen couldn't hear the whisper, but the black-hearted kidnapper shouted out her name. "Heather! That's a right purty name for a right purty little lady!"

A brief exchange followed, in which the sheriff and the outlaws flung threats and insults at each other. After a few moments of more and more colorful curses, which the crowd enjoyed thoroughly, Heather's abductor grinned and winked at her. She managed a weak smile, and Helen was surprised to see what looked like tears glittering on her cheeks.

Soon after that, the bandits and the good guys positioned themselves around the center of town for a shootout. Heather was released from captivity, and she crept back into the audience gathered around the hotel entrance. Still no sign of Bud and his intensely muscled body, although Helen would have expected him to be cradling his wife in his strong male arms after her ordeal.

"Where is Bud?" she heard Aunt Edna ask Loy. "I thought I saw him on the bus with the rest of us."

"Nope. He just got Heather on the bus, then he took off." Loy peered around the corner of the shed and looked at Heather as she wiped the tears from her cheeks. "Bet they had some kind of fight."

"Wouldn't surprise me a bit, not the way they been snapping at each other since we got here." Edna shook her head. Anything else she might have said was lost in the sudden burst of fake gunfire popping all around them as the showdown commenced. It lasted for about five very noisy minutes, replete with one man falling from a roof, another from a balcony, several dying in the arms of comely audience members, and an extraordinarily dramatic and drawn-out repentance and death scene in the middle of the street. Pretty much everyone was dead by the time it was all over.

As the crowd hooted and hollered, two cowboys sprang miraculously back to life and began to work the crowd for donations to their Living History Society. As the greasy hat passed near her, Helen fished out the change left over from her purchase of water bottles and dumped it in with a soft clink. "There — that oughta keep 'em in blanks for a while."

She found Edna chatting amiably with the white-nosed RV driver who'd been standing in front of Helen a moment ago. Uncle Loy, an awkward but pleasant smile on his face, leaned against the shed nearby as the two women discussed hormone shots. "It's the only thing that worked for me, honey," the woman was saying emphatically to Edna. And believe me, I tried everything."

"Well, I was just telling Loy here that as soon as we get back to Tupelo I'll go have a talk with that doctor of mine about it. I been reading up on it, and there's a couple of things I'd like him to try."

"Him? You have a male doctor?" The woman shook her head. "You should look for a woman doctor."

"Loy, honey, Maggie here says she can give us a ride back in her rental car." Edna smiled up at her husband. "This is my husband, Loy."

"Pleasure to meet you. Maggie Greenwald."

"Yup." Alison edged up behind Helen as the crowd dispersed. "Short no-nonsense haircut, firm handshake, sensible shoes. I think Edna is about to be abducted."

Fifteen minutes later, Loy and Edna were clambering into the backseat of Maggie Greenwald's Lexus while Helen and Alison waited in line for the tour bus that would take them back to the Saddle.

"Looks like Aunt Edna may have found a kindred spirit," Helen said.

"More kindred than she knows." Alison nudged Helen with her elbow as they settled into their seats, relaxing into the cool air that blew from vents overhead. "Look — it's our damsel in distress," she whispered.

In the seat just in front of them, Helen saw the bright blonde fluff of Heather Gilley's hair. The woman sighed and nestled back into her seat with a loud, final snuffle. No one sat next to her.

When they'd left the hotel that morning, Helen thought she'd seen Bud and Heather preparing to board. Had there been any signs of a fight between them then? Not that she would have paid too much attention to it, but Helen remembered nothing beyond Bud's usual overprotective manner toward his wife. It was odd, though, that Bud didn't accompany Heather.

Helen fell into a restless doze and didn't wake up until they pulled into the parking lot of the Silver Saddle.

In the casino lobby, Loy and Edna, minus Maggie Greenwald, were patiently waiting their turn to talk to the young woman at the long desk. A well-tanned, well-groomed couple were standing in front of her relatives, loudly complaining about the lack of service in the Silver Saddle.

"Honestly," the woman was saying as she waved her long red nails in the air, "we could have gone to a cheap motel if we wanted a room without maid service! Not a clean towel left in there!"

"Not to mention," her companion grumbled, "the bed wasn't made and the bathroom wasn't cleaned. I think we'll go for the Gold Brick next time."

"I'm sorry, sir, we'll get someone up there right away." The same young woman who'd talked to Carmel Kittrick's ex-husband Marc Landry last night was maintaining careful control of her expression as she punched numbers on the desk phone.

Helen was surprised. Their maid service had been just fine.

"Oh, hi, sweetie!" Edna looked much better — now it was Loy who looked in need of a rest, or a drink, or both. "We got here just a couple a minutes ago. That Maggie Greenwald sure is a nice lady, isn't she, Loy?" Loy smiled in silent agreement as Edna fanned out a handful of pamphlets like a deck of cards. "She had all this stuff with her about natural remedies and all. Herbs and such."

Helen glanced down at the assortment of brochures regarding various alternative approaches to medicine, everything from acupuncture to rolfing to homeopathy. "That was really nice of her, Aunt Edna."

Loy muttered something about wishing she'd had the key to her room in with all those papers.

"Uh-oh — forgot the room key again?"

Edna blushed and tucked the pamphlets into her purse. "I thought I had it right here, Loy. Hon, it must be on the dresser, that's the last place I remember it."

Helen sensed Alison behind her and realized that her partner needed a break from the folks. "I think Alison and I will go get something cold to drink. How about if we see you at dinner?"

"Catfish again, right?" Alison sipped at her whiskey sour twenty minutes later. All around them the bar buzzed with noise and activity. Helen doubted it was ever quiet and empty there, even during the Baptist church services on Sunday morning.

Helen finished her bourbon and sighed with appreciation. "Oh, I don't know." She yawned and stretched, her mood uplifted by alcohol and a few moments alone with her lover. "Maybe we should go for the prime rib dinner they have at the restaurant across the road. Just a change of pace, for one night. What do you think?"

Alison didn't have time to answer. Edna came trotting up to the bar, her face pale and drawn. Helen sprang from her chair and hurried out to meet her.

"What? Where's Uncle Loy? What happened?" she babbled.

"Oh, Helen, honey, you have to come. Come on. Right now," Edna whispered urgently. Her hands were cold and clammy on Helen's arm as the three of them rushed out of the bar and toward the elevator.

"Aunt Edna, talk to me. Tell me," Helen urged her.

Edna shook her head, staring pointedly at the other people crowded into the elevator. Helen felt her tremble, heard the stifled whimper of fear in every breath.

The ride in the elevator seemed interminable. When they reached Loy and Edna's floor, Edna scuttled them off down the hall to their room. Loy, as pale and shaken as Edna, stood guard at the door.

"We had to wait forever to get a key to the room," Edna was whispering as Loy solemnly opened the door. "Then we found her."

It took Helen a couple of moments to make out the features of Carmel Kittrick as the bloody corpse lying on the floor before her.

Chapter Six

Over the years Helen had seen quite a number of dead bodies. She'd been no stranger to death as a child in farm country in Mississippi; the regular dispatch of hogs and cattle was carried out in antiphon to mishaps from farming equipment and road accidents on the rural highways. Once she'd escaped to Berkeley there had been ten years of police work, a grim pageantry of accidents and murders and mayhem, rounded off by a long stint as a homicide detective. Not to mention the occasional body that turned up during her career as a private eye.

As she stood in the doorway of Loy and Edna's room,

however, Helen felt an odd sense of unreality fog her mind. What was it about this particular death scene that made it seem so different from all the others she'd witnessed? Perhaps it was the presence of her aunt and uncle, who huddled together in the hallway behind her. They, too, had seen death — mostly in the form of relatives or friends wasting away or tragically ripped from life in accidents — but she was almost positive they'd never experienced anything like this. Surely it wasn't on their Thanksgiving agenda at the Silver Saddle.

"Uncle Loy?" Helen glanced over her shoulder. Her uncle, who suddenly looked every one of his seventy years, slowly creaked himself up from a crouch beside Edna and moved stiffly to her side. In a quiet murmur Helen asked, "How long from the time we got back to the time you went inside the room?"

Loy glanced at his wristwatch. "Couldn't a been more'n half an hour. We got back at, what, two o'clock? Edna had left the room key behind again, and y'all went off while we got a key from the desk. Took us a while, with those people all yellin' at the clerk about the maids or something."

Helen nodded. His account agreed with her own estimate of approximately two-thirty for discovery of the body. She and Alison hadn't been in the bar for more than twenty minutes when Edna showed up. "Did you both go into the room before you came and got me?"

He shook his head and ran a hand over his balding, shiny pate in a gesture that Helen recognized as characteristic of strong emotion. "We got inside — Edna started off to shriekin', then it turned into kind of a whimper, like she's doin' right now. I don't think I made it any farther than just inside the door, here." He pointed to a spot about six feet inside the room.

"Do you remember if Aunt Edna moved anything, or touched anything, while you were both here?"

The hand moved over his head again, and he shook his

head. "I think maybe I put my hand against the wall, kinda like this" — he took a tentative step forward and charaded a hand outward without touching the wall to his left — "And then I just went right to Edna. She fell down to her knees. I remember thinking she might get sick, there on the carpet, the way she was all bent over and heaving and gasping."

"Then she didn't go anywhere else in the room?"

He frowned, then said decisively, "No. We just saw the body, and I was standing there behind her. Then I pulled her up and we went off to get you." He glanced at her sheepishly. "Of course, we had our hands all over the door, and tromped around on the carpet some. Can't get outta that one, I guess."

"Okay. That's okay. You didn't know." She patted him on the shoulder, and he went back to the relative quiet of the hall where Edna was whispering his name.

Just then Alison came in. Helen breathed a sigh of relief, grateful to have her there. It felt like hours since she'd sent her to call the police and hotel security.

"They're on their way. I saw that security guard — what's her name, who flirts with you — hanging around downstairs."

"Well, where the hell is she?" Helen snapped. "Sorry, I'm just kind of going crazy here."

"Understandable. Need me to do some baby-sitting?" Alison gestured toward Loy and Edna, who turned up their trusting pale faces toward Helen. Alison went to them.

Helen sighed. "You read my mind. Damn it, where's Shelley?" She glanced at her watch — about twenty minutes had passed since she'd arrived at the room — and prayed for the cavalry to arrive. Behind her, Alison made comforting noises to ease Loy and Edna's distress. Helen could hear the low-pitched conversations and carpet-cushioned footsteps of other Saddle residents. She knew that they must be staring at the oddly distraught tableau playing out before them in the normally quiet hallway of the hotel. How long, Helen wondered, before someone stopped to inquire if all was well here at room 505? She hoped that they would all just assume someone had just lost a bundle at the casino tables.

Still no sign of authority. Helen sighed and turned her attention back to the body stretched out by the bed. She'd been so concerned with preserving some kind of integrity at the scene, she hadn't even thought yet about the reason Carmel Kittrick had been in this particular room in the first place, or about the cause of death, or who was involved. Despite months of inertia, Helen could feel herself switching over into the hauntingly familiar work mode that had served her well as an investigator. She deliberately shut out the muffled mewls of distress coming from the hall.

Carmel was sprawled directly across the point where the room's foyer — one side leading to a bathroom, the other side opening into closet space — widened into the big square that, just like Helen and Alison's room, held two queen-size beds, a wall-mounted television and a cheap table next to the long window that overlooked the Colorado River. Two chairs, positioned so that they faced the window, stood neatly pushed under the table. The drapes were partially drawn against the late-afternoon sunlight that shone on the narrow patio outside the sliding glass door beside the table. An ashtray containing the remains of a cigarette marred the pristine appearance of the table. Was it Loy's brand? Helen fumed that she couldn't go in and take a look, but she was certain Loy hadn't been lying about staying out of the room. And surely none of the maids would have left a dirty ashtray on the table. Helen grimaced. The cigarette butt was just a bit too much — like something out of a cheesy old B-grade film noir that played on those all-night classic movie channels. The perfect clue, of course, would be Carmel's lipstick smeared on the cigarette. Still, it was too glaring to ignore.

Both beds were made, and a pile of clean white towels and sheets lay on the edge of the bed closest to Helen. She didn't dare turn on the overhead light in the bathroom, but judging from the half-dozen fresh towels stacked on the Formica counter, the bathroom had been cleaned as well. If the maids had been here, why were there still sheets stacked on the bed?

Helen focused on the corpse lying between her and the beds. There was no way to know, of course, exactly when Carmel's death had occurred. She crouched down on her haunches, wishing for better light. From the look of the victim's blonde hair, now matted and dark with blood, something had struck Carmel near her left temple. Blood streaked the carpet, and Helen could just make out a smudge in one of the dark blotches — maybe from Aunt Edna kneeling down next to the body? There was probably blood pooled beneath the body as well. And just beyond the body, closer to the beds — were those more blood streaks in the carpet? Had the body been moved? Probably, Helen thought. Etched into the thin pile of the carpet rough lines led from the bathroom to the beds. Had Carmel been struck over the head and then dragged? Could Carmel have made the marks herself, if she'd been injured in the bathroom and somehow pulled herself forward and then dropped dead on the floor? Helen realized that she'd just missed treading on the marks herself. No way of knowing right now whether or not Aunt Edna or Uncle Loy had stepped on them — that was for crime-scene people to figure out.

Fighting down a sudden desire to examine Carmel more closely, Helen studied the room. It took her a couple of moments to notice that the spread on the bed nearest Carmel was crooked; the spread on the other bed was fine. Unusual, she thought. The striped pattern of the spreads, identical to the ones Helen and Alison had in their room, made it incredibly easy for the maids to line them up evenly across the mattresses, leaving a neat, orderly and uniform — albeit maddeningly homogenous — appearance to every room in the hotel. That was, Helen was sure, no doubt the reason these spreads were used.

But the cover on this particular bed was wildly askew, barely covering the mattress on the side nearest Helen and the victim. Helen peered in the murky light of the room to see where Carmel's hand lay. No, it wasn't grasping the bedspread in some dramatic last-gasp touch of desperation. Maybe it was just the sight of the cliché cigarette in the ashtray that gave Helen the image of a clutching hand pawing at the bedspread — but no, this was just a sloppily made bed.

All that was missing was the key — presumably Edna's, although Helen couldn't begin to guess how Carmel or Carmel's killer would have gotten hold of it. Helen stood up, hoping to get a look at the carpet between the body and the bed. Sure enough, there was a glint of metal next to the dead woman's fingers, and Helen recognized the blunt square head that matched the head of her own brass key.

"This is ridiculous," she muttered to herself, crossing her arms and staring down at Carmel. Too staged, too theatrical. Dragging dead bodies, a tell-tale cigarette smoking in the ashtray, mussed beds, even the missing key gleaming on the carpet. "Now we just need the secret passage and the treasure map, then we're set."

Five more minutes passed as Helen tried to memorize all she'd seen. Surely the police would be along any moment.

With the edge of her shirt, she gingerly handled the doorknob. It was one of the newer long handles found in a lot of hotels, easier to grip and turn than round knobs, although her relatives must have left prints all over it. Odd that they still used the old brass keys, Helen thought.

Out in the hallway, Loy had his arm around a distraught Edna. They were huddled on the floor beside the door and were beginning to attract a great deal of attention from passersby, who stared curiously at them. No one had spoken; everyone seemed intent on heading back to the casinos and the promised wealth they would attain there, but Helen was certain this state of affairs couldn't last long.

"Should I take them down to our room until the police come?" Alison whispered. "Maybe we shouldn't be hanging around here right now."

Helen shook her head. "We'd better wait till the police get here. They'll want to talk to them right away. Oh, here's Shelley." Alison bent over the distraught couple as the burly security guard rushed out of the elevator, police in tow.

One of the half-dozen officers, a gaunt man of about fifty, grimaced at Shelley, who stood pale and sweating behind the cadre of police. "You didn't seal off this area as soon as you were told?"

Shelley turned a shade paler under his disapproving gaze. "No, sir," was all she said as she jutted her jaw outward.

While he was perfectly correct in his statement, Helen also thought he harbored a solid contempt for what he would have called "rent-a-cops." In all fairness, she'd despised them, too, in her days on the force. It was only in the last year, since she'd worked security in order to pay her mortgage, that she'd learned to swallow her pride and admit that it was after all a real job. The welcome sensation of mentally detailing the crime scene ebbed, and once again she felt completely useless. She hadn't even taken up Carmel's offer of detective work. Helen felt a sudden and uncomfortable surge of guilt as she remembered the offhand way Carmel had treated the subject of her own safety. Should she have accepted the offer, tried to put up some kind of screen between Carmel and whatever danger the anonymous hate mail presented? But there'd been no sense from Carmel that the sender of those mutilated photographs had meant any real harm. The offer was only an attempt on

Carmel's part, or so Helen had understood, to avoid paying out money to her ex-husband. Inwardly, Helen squirmed, uncertain of how the police would interpret the threat those missives posed to the victim — or how they'd view her own cavalier refusal of Carmel's job offer.

Besides, she reasoned, the cops couldn't possibly know that she had any experience in homicide investigations. Shelley waited quietly to one side as another officer cordoned off the area, then she took a position by the elevator so she could steer people away from the scene.

"You find them?" one of the uniforms asked.

"No." Helen pointed toward Loy and Edna. "They did. I'm their niece. I'm visiting with them. My room is down on the third floor. They came to get me when they found her. No one has been in the room since I've been here, for the last" — she glanced down at her watch — "for the last fifteen minutes." She answered his questions briefly, with no elaboration, and stood by quietly as he turned to question her relatives.

Although she'd been on both sides of this situation — first as a uniform, then a homicide detective, and later both a private eye and a witness, not to mention her recent bout as a near-victim — she still felt at a loss. Helen realized, standing in the hallway and waiting for officialdom to have its turn with her, that this was her first crime scene where she had no role to play, no hat to wear, no real function in this place. Just another bystander, she thought, saved from the appearance of ghoulish curiosity by her connection to the hotel room's residents. And it didn't help to realize that she was, at least in a professional way, associated with the cop-wannabe types represented by poor Shelley. She sighed and closed her eyes against the familiar waves of emotion that swept over her so often — grief over what she'd lost, anger at her fallen state, anxiety about her future. Although she hated to admit it, Helen was beginning to miss her weekly shrink visit.

The sight of two men not in uniform but flashing badges broke her train of thought. Shelley had abandoned her post by the elevator and was talking to them. "Yes, let me check with the clerk. I'm sure there's a room on this floor you can use." Shelley went to a white wall phone concealed behind a potted palm near the elevator to confer with one of her colleagues downstairs.

A couple of minutes later a breathless woman in a dark suit with a gold nameplate on her breast emerged from the elevator. Pallor gleamed beneath her peach-toned makeup. The two latest police arrivals turned as one to stare at her. "You the manager?" one of them asked.

As the manager dithered and fluttered around the police, waving a hefty set of keys and gesturing up and down the hallway, Helen faded back into her state of mild oblivion, conscious of the glances she was getting from the homicide detectives. Out of the corner of her eye she watched the manager fumble with keys and open the door to a room two doors down from Edna and Loy's. Alison herded Edna and Loy inside, followed by the blonde officer and one of the plainclothes duo.

When Alison came out a moment later, she stood next to Helen in the hallway. "Good God," she sighed, slumping against the wall. "At least they don't mind if your aunt and uncle get questioned together."

Helen stared at the closed door of the hotel room the police had taken over, seeing blazoned onto its polished surface the body of Carmel Kittrick. "I can't imagine they're under any suspicion."

"How the hell did this happen?" Alison murmured, turning away from the interested looks they were receiving from four elderly gentlemen, each carrying a bag of golf clubs, who were being ushered back into the elevator they'd just stepped out of.

Helen shook her head. "Not a frigging clue. I heard Loy complaining about how Edna kept losing their key, but that's all I know. Obviously either Carmel got hold of it — or someone else did, and that someone —"

"Lured the damsel to her death. Maybe with a note. Jesus, Helen, it's like a bad mystery novel. I mean, we even have an irate ex-husband lurking around the hotel." Alison shuddered, hugging herself as if she were freezing, and Helen wondered if Alison was remembering her own violent experiences with an angry ex-husband who'd nearly killed her. Helen suppressed an urge to wrap her lover in her arms — now was most definitely not the time or place.

Instead she said, "I was just thinking the same thing." They both fell silent as a couple of uniformed officers knelt nearby, pulling out tape measures and notepads. Two more men walked up, their feet swathed in plastic wrap, carrying black cases Helen recognized as scene-of-crime kits — or whatever they called them in Laughlin. Time enough for discussion later, Helen thought as a whole chorus line of technicians and police filed in and out of the room.

"I was just trying to remember," Alison went on when there was a lull in the coming and going of police, "if we saw her after breakfast this morning. I mean, after her tryst and before we went to Oatman."

"I was just trying to remember the same thing." Helen went back through the morning. She'd calmed down after her encounter with Bud and indulged in cold eggs, sausage and butter-soaked grits. Around nine they'd gathered for the tour in the parking lot. "I think," she said finally, "it was at the bus. Remember? Heather and Bud got on, and Carmel was standing right behind them, talking to the bus driver."

"I think you're right. Yeah, you are right. The driver actually said something to her about what time we'd be back from the trip."

So Carmel had gotten an assurance from the driver she'd have a free block of time — time without anyone from the Winners' Circle bothering her. And Bud Gilley stayed behind, too. Helen flashed on a memory of Heather Gilley's sniffling on the bus going home. But there was no reason to read too much into their behavior.

Her aunt and uncle emerged after what seemed like an eon. Loy was ashen-faced, his hand trembling as he rubbed his scalp again. Edna, however, seemed calmer and even cheerful. Probably just the result of having told all to official authority, Helen thought, and therefore eased any burden of responsibility she might have felt. She'd seen plenty of people react the same way after talking to the police, almost as if they'd gone to some secular version of confession and healed their souls. In a way, she supposed they had. It was a more mundane and nuts-and-bolts method of absolution, to be sure, but just as thorough and just as freeing in its own way.

That was certainly the effect it had on Edna, at least. "Alison, honey, they'll talk to you now. That nice Detective Richardson, he was so wonderful to us. He understood all about the trip and all, and how I lost the key this morning! It was like I'd known him all my life."

Helen tried to smile. She imagined Richardson and his partner quickly comparing notes on the couple they'd just interviewed. No doubt they'd dismiss Edna as a sweet-tempered but rather doddering old woman, with her ineffectual husband tagging along. And, between the trip to Oatman that morning and the fracas over the room key, Loy and Edna had rock-solid alibis, with plenty of witnesses and plenty of time-logging as corroboration. Silly old fools, she would have thought, back in the days when she did this for a living. The avuncular tone that Richardson must have used on Edna would have been softened by Helen into something more maternal and traditionally feminine — quite possibly using her technique on Loy instead of Edna.

Alison gave them all a weak smile and with a sigh knocked on the door. Edna kept babbling, "And I told them all about how you was a private investigator and all, and how Carmel wanted to talk to you last night after dinner —" Her plump face creased in concern and she looked up at her husband. "Oh, Loy, honey, I shouldn't have said that, should I? Not that it was wrong, Helen, but — oh, I did do something bad, honey! I'm so sorry," and she dissolved into tears again.

Loy, with a heavy sigh and a swift grimace, put one shaky arm around his wife. "Now, sweetheart, you just told the truth. That's all you're supposed to do. No one did a damn thing that was wrong. Least of all you, sugar."

"That's right, Aunt Edna." Helen moved to her aunt's side, sparing a glance for the four golfing gents who'd reappeared at the other end of the hallway, a good distance from the yellow crime scene tape stretched across the corridor. For their sakes, Helen was glad they'd found their way back to their rooms, but she needed to calm Edna down. "You haven't done anything I wouldn't have wanted you to. I was going to tell the police all about it anyway."

Loy looked over his wife's head at Helen. "Well, we don't know what Carmel said. Not any of our business."

Helen sighed. Her body twitched with tiredness, and her side — where she'd been shot — ached fiercely. She had a fleeting worry about the wound, just like when she had nightmares of waking up covered in blood from the reopened hole in her body. She involuntarily gripped her side; her whole body was shaking, just as it had last night when she'd been so certain that Wilbur Kittrick was about to shoot her. Maybe it was just the aftereffects of seeing death at close hand again, for the first time in many, many months.

Alison stalked out of the room, an angry look on her face. "They'll talk to you now, Helen. I'm going to take your aunt and uncle down to our room and then come back up."

Helen looked into her face. "What did they say to you in there?"

Alison shrugged, tears suddenly welling up in her eyes.

"This isn't Berkeley, Helen. I don't think they approve of the likes of you and me here."

Helen smiled ruefully and stroked one finger, swiftly and gently, down Alison's cheek, well aware that she was getting some looks from the cops lining the hall. "Don't worry. I cut my teeth on guys like this. Cake. It's cake to me."

She hoped she looked a lot braver than she felt. Without knocking, Helen entered the room.

Chapter Seven

An hour later, Helen yawned and stretched out luxuriously on the bed next to Alison, who was plying her with questions. "I did most of the talking, really." She closed her eyes and felt sleep creeping up over her dangerously, tempting her to forego dinner and turn over under the blanket and drift off. "And yes, of course I told him about Carmel's little conference with me last night."

She opened her eyes again when Alison was silent. Her lover was frowning up at the ceiling. "They didn't even say anything about your being a detective and a former homicide cop?"

Helen snuggled closer to Alison. "I didn't tell them about the cop part." And she wasn't about to tell Alison about the way they'd glanced at each other when she described herself as a security guard who'd formerly been a private investigator. Was it contempt that had flickered in their eyes, or disbelief, or weary resignation at the bizarre claims of people they dealt with? They had, however, listened to her and made many notes. The interview ended when they both slapped their notebooks shut and got up.

"Thank you, Ms. Black. We'll look into it." Richardson's partner was already out the door, and Richardson held the door for Helen. "You're the only one who kept everybody else away from the scene, right?"

"That's right." She stepped up to the door only to find her way blocked by Richardson's body. Helen was uncomfortably aware of his bulk towering over her — he had to be six-four, easy, and unlike his rather doughy partner, Richardson was clearly well-muscled beneath his cheap off-the-rack suit. His tiny dark eyes bored into her, and the marine-style haircut glistened steely gray in the soft light of the hotel room.

"Thank you for your help." Richardson had moved out of her way at last, and Helen had made herself walk slowly to the elevator under his watchful eye.

Another thing not to tell Alison about, she thought.

What had that been all about, anyway? She was used to male badgering in all its forms — from street heckling to subtle attempts to intimidate through sheer physical presence — but this was slightly different. Richardson had actually seemed — interested? Was that the right word to describe it? He hadn't really done anything beyond position himself so that she noticed him. Really noticed him. If it hadn't been for their circumstances, Helen might even have called it flirtatious.

Later, back in the room, Helen pushed herself up on her elbow, determined not to think about it for a while. "When you came out of the room, it seemed like they did or said something to upset you, she said to Alison"

Alison snuggled closer. "Well, it still makes me uncomfortable to talk about us in front of people when they so obviously hate us."

Helen looked at her. "What happened?" she asked sharply.

"It wasn't Richardson so much as the other one, Cooper." Helen hadn't even remembered the man's name, but she could clearly see his pasty, pudgy body slumped in a chair and listening intently to Richardson. "He — Cooper — just kind of smirked and raised his eyebrows when I answered Richardson's questions about who we were and what we were doing here." Alison went on, "I know, I know — I ought to be used to it by now."

"Honey, no one ever gets used to it." Helen hugged her close. "The best you can do is just learn to brace yourself for it. And even then it takes you by surprise."

They lay quietly for a few minutes longer. Helen's thoughts began to stray back to the image of Carmel dead on the floor, and she shifted so that she could look at their own room. It was all too easy to imagine the corpse there, as well, since the rooms were identical.

Alison sighed, and Helen heard faint stomach rumbling. "Awful though it sounds, I think I need to get something to eat. I'm starting to get a headache."

"No catfish tonight, I promise," Helen said as they got off the bed and straightened their clothes. "Let's get out of this place and go find something not deep fried for supper."

"What about Edna and Loy?" Alison asked. "Are they going back to Romie's?"

"I doubt it. Loy said he'd make sure they got room service. He doesn't want Aunt Edna to have to go out, once they're settled in their new room. Besides, I think you and I have earned an evening to ourselves."

Alison went to the closet and rummaged. "I don't think this town has ever seen anything approaching a bean sprout, do you?" she said. She emerged from the closet carrying a jacket. "What the hell are you doing, Helen?"

Helen looked up from where she was kneeling between the beds. "It's just weird, that's all," she muttered as she got up.

"What, your crawling around on the floor? Yeah, it's weird. Here, it's kind of chilly out there," she said as she handed Helen a sweater. "And what's weird?"

Helen brushed the lint off her knees and took the sweater. "In Loy and Edna's room, I noticed it right away. The beds." She shrugged into her sweater. Alison's face was a bit pale, but there was no sign of anger or apprehension at the subject. "One bedspread was really crooked on the bed. And the other was perfectly aligned, you know, all the stripes even. Just like here, in our room."

"And?"

"Well, the maid had obviously cleaned the room before Carmel got into it. I mean, there were those towels all over the place, right? And one bed was just as neat and tidy as could be, as if the same anal-retentive maid had fixed it up, like here."

"So? The maid got lazy."

Helen shook her head as they exited the room. "I don't think so. I think someone remade the second bed."

"Like who? Carmel?" Alison snorted. "Why the hell would she want to take a nap in your relatives' bedroom?"

Helen rolled her eyes. "There's a couple of other things you can do in bed, you know. Or have you already forgotten?" she teased Alison, patting her on the rear as they walked down the deserted hallway.

"Hey! And no, I haven't forgotten. It just doesn't make any sense." For once the elevator was empty, and they leaned on its wall close to one another as the doors slid shut. "It seems even more unlikely than Carmel Kittrick taking a little snooze up there. I mean, she has that palatial hotel suite upstairs, according to you."

Helen nodded. "Right. And the way up to that penthouse is covered with cameras. Plus, it's kind of like her office while she's here, you know?" Helen added, recalling the elaborate setup sprawled all over the suite.

"But, Helen, really! That's like something high-school kids would do. Sneak into someone else's room for a quickie? Do you really think Carmel Kittrick would do something like that?"

Helen shrugged. In the lobby they were hit with the usual wave of stale cigarette smoke and clamoring voices over a background of Muzak and clanging slot machines. "That might be fun for her. To get off on being the naughty brat." Might have been, Helen amended. Carmel wouldn't be having fun any longer, she thought, sensing a pang of regret for the dead woman.

There was quite an entourage lined up at the counter. An elderly man in a wheelchair glared up from behind an oxygen mask. He was surrounded by three — no, four — men in conservative suits who looked on anxiously as his face reddened with fury. With a start, Helen recognized Louise, Carmel's assistant, hovering in the background with her pen and clipboard. Louise's eyes flicked over Helen and Alison with confusion, as if she realized she ought to know who they were. Then she bent over the old man and whispered something in his ear.

His face was lined and weathered with pain and exhaustion. His expensive suit, rumpled by the thin cords connecting him to machines and monitoring equipment fastened to the wheelchair, seemed incongruous. There was something not right about someone so close to death in a neatly pressed suit that easily cost more than a couple months' salary. To Helen's amazement, he reached out with one trembling hand to her and wheezed something out.

On the second try his words became intelligible. "I'm Romie Kittrick. Louise tells me you found my little girl."

Helen, fighting a surge of panic — what the hell was she supposed to do now? — swallowed hard and touched the hand that clawed at her sleeve. "It — it was my aunt and uncle, not me," she stammered.

He ignored her words. His eyes, burning hot blue in deep shadowed sockets, shone out feverishly in his bony face. The oxygen mask slipped a little, and Helen stared in fascinated revulsion as spittle clouded over the clear plastic shell over his mouth. His face went from red to white as he struggled for air. One of the suited men behind him leaned over and adjusted some knob on the oxygen tank that was suspended like a fat red worm from the back of the wheelchair. Whatever he'd fiddled with on the tank seemed to help; Romie Kittrick's breathing rasped into something approaching a regular rhythm. "People lie to me all the time, never can trust them to tell me the truth," he got out. "I need to hear the truth from you, young lady."

Dreading his next words Helen waited as he replaced his face mask. Beside her Alison stood quietly, staring down at the carpet. A well of silence surrounded them, as both the Kittrick party and the clerks at the desk seemed to hold their collective breath, waiting for the next episode in their drama to begin.

"Was it fast? Did my baby girl feel anything?"

Helen's jaw dropped. Hadn't the police told him anything at all? Maybe he hadn't even had time to talk to them yet — he'd just packed up his considerable necessities, including bodyguards and medical attendants, and hauled off from wherever he'd been holed up in Laughlin. Surely he hadn't flown in from Mississippi — there hadn't been enough time for a plane to get here from Jackson.

"Well, Mr. Kittrick, I can't really say. I think the police would —"

The claw on her arm tightened, surprisingly strong in a

man so obviously weak. "People lie to me. They know I'm not going to be around much more. Like these fools." He nodded toward Louise and the four musketeers behind him, and his eyes watered with the effort of talking and moving at the same time. "Live in my own strange little world, now, see things through this damn muzzle. Need the truth. Need to know if it was fast."

Helen felt her face burn as she forced herself to look Romie Kittrick in the eye. "Sir, I really can't say. I'm not the person who found her, and I honestly think the police are the best people to talk to about this."

His hand dropped from her arm and clutched the wheelchair. Helen heard the hiss of oxygen flowing into his face mask. His breathing stilled into something approaching calm. "No one," he managed to get out. "No one tells me a damn thing, young lady. Police no good. Don't know jack."

"Mr. Kittrick —" Louise knelt down next to the wheelchair, her hornrims sliding down her nose. "I think we should just go up to our room, now, don't you agree?" She winced in ill-concealed distaste as he coughed, huge spasms wracking his body. "The police will be able to tell us everything we need to know."

"My girl!" He spat the words out in frustration and fury, and Helen felt a rush of sympathy for a man who, clearly accustomed to power and authority, was confined to infantile helplessness, at the mercy of his "assistants." His mouth worked in the mask, twisting in an agony of effort that only exhausted him. Horrified, Helen watched as his color shifted from white to red to ashen gray.

Louise stood up, shoved her glasses back up her nose and glared at Helen. "We've got to get him out of here and into bed," she barked at her.

"Fine." Helen backed away as the men moved in a kind of minuet around the wheelchair and Louise marched up to the reception desk. "It wasn't my idea to chat down here, anyway," she said to Alison.

"Hard to imagine how he convinced everyone to get him here, in his condition," Alison murmured as the Kittrick cortege maneuvered itself toward the elevators.

Helen shrugged. "Money. Maybe he threatened to write all these people out of his will. And maybe he has his own plane, too."

"He couldn't have flown in from Mississippi in so short a time, though." Alison glanced down at her wristwatch. "It's only six o'clock."

Helen tried to remember if Carmel had mentioned the whereabouts of her father last night, but her thoughts were interrupted by a crash at the other end of the registration counter, near the main entrance to the Silver Saddle. One of the big baggage carriers, the kind used by the valets in the parking lot to transport luggage from car to casino to hotel room, had toppled over and ricocheted off the counter. Coats, purses and expensive suitcases had sailed away from the carrier and landed all over the polished casino floor as well as on the unsuspecting toes of a couple of patrons.

"I knew you'd get here sooner or later!" Marc Landry, Carmel's ex-husband, pushed out from around the nearly empty carrier. He looked as though he'd gotten a bit more sleep, and maybe a shower, since Helen had last seen him ranting and railing in the very same spot he stood now, but it wasn't much improve- ment. Same disheveled clothes, same wild hair and un- shaven face. If anything, she decided, he was even more out of control than he'd appeared last night. And where the hell had he hauled himself off to, anyway? She thought of Carmel's bloody corpse and wished Richardson and his pals would show up. "Vultures like you always come in after the kill." Landry's eyes glittered as he stumbled over a stray overnight case and pushed the carrier aside. Helen laid a warning hand on Alison's arm as he reached out to grab the wrist of the clerk behind the counter. "Don't even think about it, bitch," he muttered. With a swift jerk he grabbed the telephone from the young woman's hand and ripped the receiver from the cord. Then, releasing her, he picked up the phone with both hands and yanked until it broke free. He smashed the phone into the wall behind the counter.

Helen said into Alison's ear, "Go find Shelley, or one of the guards. There's got to be someone in the casino."

"But —"

"Please." Alison slipped away while Landry turned his attention to the man in the wheelchair. The counter clerk, quivering and biting back sobs, had dropped down behind the registration desk. Helen hoped she had another phone available to her behind the counter, out of Landry's sight. A handful of curious onlookers had gathered at the edges of the commotion. Angrily she noted the presence of several burly men, any of whom could have jumped on the crazed intruder and overpowered him.

She revised her opinion of them when she saw the glint of Landry's knife. It seemed out of character. Carmel had described him as a mild-mannered professorial type, but Helen knew an amateur could be more dangerous than someone experienced with knives. Where the hell had he gotten the thing?

"She would have hated that you're here, you know," Landry was saying as he wove an uncertain path toward Kittrick. Oddly enough, the old man's color was better, and his breathing steadier, as if he'd needed a clear and present danger to confront, an enemy he could see and attack. "Don't you know how much she despised you? Your good-ol'-boy lies and bullshit? The way you always butted in and fucked up her plans." He wiped his free hand across his mouth, and Helen saw the tears on his grimy cheeks.

"No more than she hated you for being the soft pansy you are," Kittrick rattled over the soft sibilant flow of oxygen. Helen edged closer to the two men, positioning herself just a couple of steps away. Kittrick's face had paled, a sweat breaking out over his brow from the effort of speaking.

Landry's face contorted. Hate? Fear? Maybe even grief for Carmel. He raised the knife up. "Maybe so. But we're still here, old man."

"Yes, we are. And my baby girl is not. She won't ever be here — no thanks to you or to me." Kittrick's hand moved over the controls set in the arm of his wheelchair and he maneuvered it closer to his former son-in-law. Helen was close enough now to see Kittrick's eyes flick over to his bodyguards, and she realized that the old man was doing all he could to occupy Landry's attention so that one of his people could get some help.

"You old fucking hypocrite!" Landry cackled hysterically. "You never gave a fuck about her when she was alive! She was just a piece of the Kittrick empire to you! A fuckable broad you could use to make millions from that shit you call food you force down the throats of anyone in sight!" Landry wavered a moment and leaned against the counter. Helen took that opportunity to move even closer to him, staying out of his line of sight. He reeked of days-old sweat and fatigue. "You didn't give a shit that she ran the whole thing better than you or that weasel Wilbur ever would."

"Marc, son —"

Landry stiffened and stepped close enough to point the knife directly into Kittrick's face, the lethal point of metal hovering dangerously close to his oxygen mask. "Don't you ever call me that. The only son you have is out chasing aliens and flying saucers in the desert. A fitting end to the Kittrick family, don't you think? Lunatics having visions out in the middle of nowhere!"

A motion to her right caught Helen's eye, and she watched with rising panic as one of the expensively suited bodyguards withdrew a hand from his coat. The small pistol gleamed dull black in the muted casino lighting. Helen allowed herself a moment to feel fury at the way he'd just upped the stakes in this game. Landry might be on something that would ensure he wouldn't care about the gun — he'd go ahead and slice away at anything in sight — or the idiot might get a wave of testosterone flowing and decide to take matters into his own hands.

Fortunately Landry hadn't seen the gun yet. There was no more time to make decisions now. Helen stepped forward quickly and quietly, moving instinctively into a stance so she could disable Landry from behind. "Okay, Marc," she said as she grabbed his free hand and twisted his wrist around to a position that could do some damage if he struggled. "We all know you're pissed off, and we all see the knife. Let's just relax, okay?"

He surprised her by making just the right move away from her without breaking his wrist. Suddenly the slim silver blade was pointed at her chest. Landry's eyes were huge and watery as they attempted to focus on her. His dark pupils were too dilated to be uninfluenced by something. "What the fuck —"

He didn't have time to get anything else out. Without thinking, Helen swiveled and gave him a quick left to the shoulder. It had been so long since she'd attempted anything like a fight of this nature that she was surprised to see his knife hand crumple helplessly. The knife clattered to the floor, bouncing off toward the counter. One of the suits who'd come in with Kittrick snatched the knife up.

"Fucking bitch —" She could smell the results of several days' worth of drinking on his breath as he lunged forward. In another instinctive motion she jerked her knee upright. Landry doubled over and moaned.

"So he's still got some balls, then." Flushed and panting, Shelley appeared out of nowhere. She crouched over Landry huddled on the floor and looked up at Helen admiringly. "Sorry I missed most of it — I was breaking up a little family squabble in the casino."

Shelley and one of her fellow guards heaved Landry to

his feet. When flashing blue-and-red lights appeared outside the entrance, she guessed that the clerk had had access to another phone after all. A swarm of uniformed officers descended on them. Landry, still sniveling, made no resistance when he was manacled and packed away in the backseat of a black-and-white outside.

"You okay?"

"Yeah." Helen smiled at Alison, who looked shaken after having talked to the police for the second time that day. And amazingly enough, it was true. Perhaps it was just the adrenaline rush, or that the shock of the entire day hadn't worn off yet, or that she was just numb from too much input — but Helen really did feel fine. Maybe, though, it was knowing that her instincts hadn't failed her in the face of real danger. After so many months of feeling broken, a useless failure, to come up against a potentially life-threatening situation and walk away unhurt was a heady experience.

"Believe it or not, I'm starving. What time is it?"

"Almost eight." Alison sighed and rubbed her eyes. "We really had better get something to eat, I guess."

The lobby was emptying out, at last. Now that Landry had been hauled off there wasn't much to see beyond a sickly old man and his entourage. Helen tried to hide a grimace as Kittrick turned his cold glittering eyes on her and whirred his chair into life, pointing it in her direction.

"Good work, young lady." The claw touched her arm again. "Better than these fools I pay so much for." His mask slipped again as he gestured weakly to the trio behind him.

Helen shrugged and smiled. "Glad to be of help, Mr. Kittrick." She took Alison's arm and steered them away from Kittrick and company, out of the Silver Saddle. Her last glimpse of him that evening was framed against the yellow light of the casino, a lone figure hunched over in his chair.

Chapter Eight

"Well, at least it was a change from catfish," Alison said later as she and Helen made their way across the parking lot of the Branded Steer. Other restaurant patrons surged around them, coming and going from the dimly lit interior, and the scent of prime rib wafted out over them. Across the street the Silver Saddle glowed beneath its shroud of light.

"Think of it as a scientific experiment," she said. "I know you miss bean sprouts and tofu, but now you really can prove to yourself how you'd feel on a steady steak diet."

"Please — I'm trying to convince my body I don't hate it." Alison moaned in mock grief.

"Gee, Alison, let me help." Helen patted Alison on the rear as they sidled between the rows of cars packed tightly together in the parking lot. "In fact, I really like your body a whole lot. In fact —"

"Helen! I'm shocked!" Alison playfully slapped Helen's hand away while she glanced around, as if to reassure herself they weren't being observed.

"Why? Can't believe I'd be so bold?" Helen whispered in Alison's ear as she embraced her, pulling her away from the harsh glare of an overhead light further into the shadows at the edge of the lot. "Then you won't believe what else I have in mind." In the safety of the darkness Helen kissed her.

"It's not that," Alison said breathlessly.

"What, then?"

"It's amazement that you have *any* energy after eating half a cow in there." Alison chuckled. "Not to mention the two baked potatoes, extra bread and the chocolate cake."

"It is amazing," Helen agreed. "I can't believe I was so damned hungry after everything that happened today." She looked at Alison. "You hardly ate anything, I noticed."

Alison shrugged and tried to laugh. "Oh, I probably just need some rest. Maybe I'll be hungry in the morning."

Helen let Alison lead the way back to their hotel room. It did seem odd, on reflection, that she'd been so ravenous in the wake of death, violence and the fallout from her aunt and uncle's emotional trauma. Was it a sign of an unbelievably callous person? Helen hated to think so, but perhaps the events of the past year — losing her business, dog-paddling desperately to stay afloat in the midst of financial troubles, almost losing her life — perhaps all this had hardened her so thoroughly that she couldn't be moved by death or violence any longer. Maybe she was experiencing the same kind of burnout she used to worry about as a cop, when senseless pain and slaughter were as normal and everyday as a cup of coffee.

Then again, the way she'd kept her head at the crime scene, switching quickly and easily into that place in her mind that noticed details, had felt enormously reassuring. Not to mention being able to take control of a potentially violent situation with Marc Landry, disarming him without any harm to anyone. For many months now, she'd been determined to let her dreams die a decent death, to bury the vision of herself as a successful investigator along with the bullet the doctors had removed from her body. That part of her life, she'd been certain, was finished and done. Time to bury the corpse before it started to stink, she used to tell herself with what she supposed was brutal honesty.

But was it really dead? Was her behavior today that of a ghost, without life or substance? Remembering the heady flush of adrenaline that had enabled her to overpower Landry and get the knife away from him, Helen felt an unwelcome twinge of hope. And it was unwelcome, she realized, because she was afraid to hope she might get her old life back, afraid the Helen Black that had been shot and nearly died might just be more than a specter.

She realized with a start that she and Alison had reached the entrance to the Saddle, and that Alison was saying something to her. "I'm sorry," Helen said as they dodged a pair of sweating valets trundling a baggage cart between them. "What did you say?"

Alison peered at her. "Are you okay? Maybe we shouldn't have gone to that restaurant, after all. I mean, it was a really heavy meal —"

"No, no, I'm fine. I just didn't catch what you said."

"Well . . ." Alison glanced at her watch. "I was just wondering if we ought to check on Loy and Edna. It's almost eleven-thirty, though."

Helen pursed her lips and cursed inwardly. "I guess it's a little late, isn't it? Damn it, I should have thought of that earlier."

"Well, it's not as if you had anything else to think about, right?" Alison said as the elevator door closed. "I mean, just knives and dying old millionaires and dead bodies turning up in hotel rooms. Is that all you've done today?" she teased.

For the second time that day they had the elevator to themselves. Helen pulled Alison closer. "It's amazing I have the energy left to touch you," she murmured, stroking Alison's long black hair. She leaned forward to kiss her throat. "Think I'll just go to sleep right here, if you don't mind." She slipped her arms around Alison's waist.

"What if Shelley finds us like this? She'll probably get really jealous," Alison whispered.

"Maybe she'll ask to join us."

Alison backed away, her face darkening to a deep pink. "You've got to be kidding."

"You think so?" Helen's hands traveled over Alison's back, and she gently rubbed the nape of her neck. "Wanna try?"

"Jesus, Helen, of course not!" Alison pushed away from her and stared in consternation. "I hope you're just kidding around, although it's not really very funny."

Helen smiled in apology. "Sorry. Maybe it's mad cow syndrome, or something. I just feel kind of sorry for Shelley, you know? Especially the way the cops talked to her earlier today."

"Well, maybe she really did screw up."

Helen nodded, deciding to say nothing more about it for now. What had made her say such a bizarre thing, suggesting a threesome with the security guard? It was so unlike her. And to Alison, no less, who was still very new to living as a lesbian.

Her thoughts were distracted by the opening of the elevator doors. No one else was in sight. "Now, this is really odd," Helen muttered. "We haven't seen a soul in the elevators or in the hallways. What the hell is going on? There are usually people around every hour of the day and night."

"I know." Alison followed her out into the hall. "I guess the discovery of a body in the hotel has kind of put a damper on things."

"Maybe you're right, but —" Helen broke off her comments as they rounded the corner to the stretch of hallway that led to their room. Alison froze behind her. The man who was bent over the door to their room hadn't heard them yet. At his feet, a heavy black duffel bag lay open, and some assortment of small instruments spilled out of the bag onto the carpet. For just a couple of seconds, Helen and Alison watched as Wilbur Kittrick sighed and swore, fumbling at the lock on their door.

Kittrick stole a look over his shoulder and struggled with the zipper on the bag. "Shit, shit, shit," they heard him mutter. He must have heard them chattering away in the hallway, Helen thought. Had they interrupted him breaking in or making his getaway?

His face, the mouth a perfect O of astonishment, loomed up into the light as he straightened and peered down the hallway. With a startled cry he dropped his tools and took off for the other end of the hallway, where an exit sign glared red above the stairwell door.

"Shit." Helen took off behind him. "Get Shelley up here, but don't let her call the cops," she called to Alison. She barreled through the door to the stairs. She'd be damned if she let Richardson get his hands on Wilbur before she did.

Although what help the guard would be, Helen had no idea. And it would be running up the stairs, not down, Helen thought angrily as she listened to Wilbur heaving and panting his way upward. Although he certainly couldn't be in very good condition, judging by his physical appearance, Helen knew what fear could do to push the unathletic to new heights of ability. She managed to take the steps two at a time, then caught up with him just as he reached the landing at the fifth floor.

"Okay, okay! I'm stopping, I'm not doing anything!" He sniveled at her, and Helen glanced in disgust at his tear-stained face. Out of breath herself, Helen had enough energy to slam him up against the wall, wrenching the neck of his black T-shirt in both hands. She tightened her grip on the fabric at his throat and watched his face go from a blotchy red to a terrified gray. "Please don't tell my father," he whimpered.

"What about the police? Don't you think they'd be interested in your extracurricular activities? Or are you going to tell me you saw little guys with gray skin and big eyes going through the wall into my room?" She tugged a bit on his shirt and felt him tremble beneath her. "I should think, with what happened to your own sister this morning, you'd be a little more concerned about the cops than about your old man."

"Are you fucking crazy? Ugh," he wheezed as she pushed him none too gently back against the concrete wall. "My father is just about to have me locked up again in the home in Jackson," he managed to get out.

Helen stared at him and loosened her grip. "The state hospital? Is that what you're talking about?" She dropped her hands but remained standing very close, blocking his attempts to move away from the wall. She fought down her revulsion at the odor of sweat and unwashed flesh and clothing he exuded.

"I'd rather take my chances with the police," he moaned, wiping his runny nose with the back of his hand. "I'm not crazy, no matter what he thinks."

"Maybe not. But you broke into my room. No, look at me, you son of a bitch." She grabbed his shirt again. Tears streamed down his quivering cheeks. "I just might not push this —"

"Oh, God, please! Please, I'll do anything you want!"

The abject terror in his eyes both repelled and fascinated her. Romie Kittrick, limp and fragile and wasted as he was, still wielded considerable power over his minions. "I said, I might."

Wilbur stilled. "What do you want?"

"I want to know what the fuck you were doing up there. What made you try a life of crime tonight?"

He glanced past her, his face suddenly a pale mask without expression. "You wouldn't believe me."

"Well, Wilbur, I don't think you have a choice. It's talk to me or we get old Romie out of bed and let him see what his firstborn has been up to. Right now." Helen smiled and cocked her head to one side. "Your call, Wilbur."

Ten minutes later, with a chastened Wilbur Kittrick in tow, Helen was in the hallway on the third floor talking to Alison and Shelley.

"Are you sure you don't want to press charges?" Shelley was asking, eyeing Wilbur with a dubious expression on her round face.

Alison stifled a noise that might have been protest, and Helen glanced warningly at her. "I'm sure. Wilbur and I are going to have a discussion about — about things. Right, Wilbur?"

He grunted some kind of assent and nodded. Alison watched Shelley go back to the elevator before turning to glare at Helen.

"Why don't you pick up your stuff, Wilbur? We can take it with us back to your place."

"Helen!" Alison hissed as they took a couple of steps away from Wilbur, who hurriedly stuffed picklocks and flashlights into the duffel bag. "What the fucking hell are you up to?"

Helen smiled and nodded at a couple — the first plucky

pair of gamblers they'd laid eyes on in some time now — who emerged from the elevators and ducked quickly into their own room. "Alison, Wilbur is the only real way I'm going to get any information about Carmel. Yes, I know he's out of his mind, but he's the only lead I've got right now."

"Lead? Wait a minute. Did I just hear the late, great private eye say she was following a *lead?*" Alison shook her head. "I thought that was all dead and gone, Helen. And only last night you refused to help Carmel. What happened?"

Helen glanced back at Wilbur, who was just zipping up his bag. "Alison, I can't explain right now. Please, please trust me on this. I have to go with him."

"Not without me."

"No! He's already scared to death of me. It will just make it worse if we both go."

Alison folded her arms and looked away as Wilbur approached them. Through stiff lips she said, "You aren't just going to disappear with him into the desert, right? You're coming back tonight?"

"Promise. Don't we, Wilbur?"

"I'll wait up." And with that Alison marched past Wilbur and into the room, slamming the door behind her.

A few minutes later, Helen was in Alison's car following Wilbur's Jeep out onto the highway toward Las Vegas. She was beginning to doubt the wisdom of leaving Alison behind. For one thing, she had absolutely no idea where Wilbur was taking her. Although it was hard to imagine the plump, weak man as a formidable opponent, Helen knew there was no way to tell what would happen. And now here she was, rattling down some deserted two-lane road behind a maniac who saw hidden government agendas and infiltration by alien spaceships all around him. It was worse than something out of Nancy Drew — and she didn't even have a sidekick with her.

She did, however, have a tire iron. Helen glanced down

to make sure the unwieldy tool was still sitting safely on the floor, where she'd placed it before driving off behind Wilbur. Now all she had to worry about was one very pissed- off girlfriend at the hotel.

Still, Helen had been afraid that Wilbur wouldn't talk if anyone else was around — and chances were he was completely harmless. "Fuck," she said aloud as the two vehicles sped past her, well over the limit. For a few seconds Helen was distracted by the sight of the ghostly white disc of the almost full moon hanging in a completely black sky to her right. Its silvery pale light gleamed down on the shapeless, colorless desert landscape around them, bleaching the hills that rose dull brown by day into mysterious peaks and valleys that seemed to hold intrigue in every crevice.

To her right, in the glare from the car's headlights, Helen saw something big, bulky and oddly shaped suddenly loom up from the ground. Her heart caught in her throat as her gaze was torn away from Wilbur's taillights. The misshapen hulk seemed to be lurching off the field and toward the highway. Her pulse racing, she realized she was looking at an old automobile graveyard. What appeared to be two huge eyes on a beast prowling for prey turned out to be broken headlights on one particularly large dead vehicle pointed in such a way that it faced her lane.

"Great. Next thing you know I'll see a spaceship hovering over the highway."

What she did see next, however, was the turn signal on Wilbur's Jeep. He made a left in the middle of the highway onto a dusty side road. With a sense of unease, she wondered what the hell could be out here in the middle of nowhere, anyway.

The side road inclined sharply downward, and soon Helen was driving through a steep ravine. And it wasn't just some graveled path they were using. The smoothness of the ride indicated long-term use and maintenance. A private road, financed by some of the Kittrick millions? It had to be, she reasoned, when she pulled up behind the Jeep in front of a long, low house nestled in the midst of scruffy desert greenery at the base of nondescript hills. An enormous satellite dish, similar to the one used by the Saddle to feed cable signals to its rooms, seemed to teeter precariously on the front lawn, and a squat water tank stood nearby. From what she could see of the house, it reminded Helen of temporary barracks used by the military.

The moment Wilbur stepped out of the Jeep, floodlights switched on with blinding sharpness. At the sight of him standing in front of his barracks Helen wished passionately she was still able to afford her cell phone.

Wilbur walked over and tapped on her window. Helen got out of the car, realizing she looked ridiculous with the tire iron in her hand. But she was determined to be ready for anything. Wilbur didn't seem to notice. He was heading toward the building. Now that her eyes had become more accustomed to the light, Helen saw that his lair did indeed have a sort of makeshift, prefabricated look. In size it was little more than a cabin. Wilbur snapped and clicked a bunch of locks, then held the door for her. Silently, Helen entered.

Immediately she was reminded of Carmel's hotel room — Wilbur's place had an equally impressive setup of equipment, although Helen doubted he used these devices to conduct ordinary business. Some of it she recognized as extremely sensitive and expensive recording equipment. Then there was an elaborate array of cameras and lenses, one of which she'd seen the night before. And that system occupying an entire wall opposite the door resembled the "wolf ears" used by police around the country as a highly sophisticated means of listening to all kinds of broadcasts. Wilbur's version was certainly a lot better than any Helen had seen or used herself in her time as a cop.

Most of the space, except for a rather unappealingly rumpled bed and a galley littered with open cans and dirty dishes, was taken up with filing cabinets. Charts and maps blanketed the wall space around the windows, which were covered tightly with blackout curtains.

"Quite a hideout, Wilbur." Helen stood in the middle of the room, listening to the various beeps and whirrs from the different machines. As soon as the words were out of her mouth, the wolf ears squawked and buzzed. Wilbur grabbed a headset and fussed with a dial, listening through one earpiece. Then he shrugged and placed the headset down carefully.

"Fire department." He looked around his home with an odd expression on his face. It took Helen a moment to realize that he was proud of his hillside getaway. "Nothing unusual tonight. But I did get a recording, just last week, of some strange activity out in one of the dry lake beds."

"Wilbur." Helen took a couple of steps toward him. "We're here to talk about Carmel, remember? If you don't want to do that, I'm heading right back to Laughlin and Romie."

"Okay, okay! Jesus, give me a break!" He scowled and went to a filing cabinet next to the bed. With a heavy sigh he pulled open a drawer and fished out a fat folder bulging with an assortment of papers that threatened to spill out onto the cheap linoleum.

He plopped down on the bed, and Helen scraped a metal folding chair across the floor to join him. He flipped open the folder and grabbed a thick sheaf of black-and-white photographs.

"Here." He thrust the pile at her sullenly, then stared at her to see her expression. When Helen simply sorted through the pictures without comment, he went on. "I've been collecting these for almost a year. I was gonna show 'em to Daddy right after Carmel came back from Nevada — you know, let the old fart know what his precious perfect little daughter was up to."

Helen didn't want to ask Wilbur how he'd managed to

get these pictures of Hef and Carmel in such intimate detail. The camera setup she'd seen last night was no doubt sensitive and sophisticated enough to capture the gleam on a bug's behind, to borrow a phrase from Uncle Loy. She winced at one particularly revealing shot of Hef standing proudly before a kneeling Carmel, whose hands and mouth were quite plainly occupied. "Wilbur, why the hell were you doing this?"

He shrugged, his expression puzzled. "What do you mean, why? Carmel was a first-class bitch. Has been all her fucking life. She pulled Daddy around by the short hairs, even got him to lock me up that time." He slammed the folder down into Helen's lap. "Look for yourself. She fucks anything on two legs." He leered at her. "Except I never saw her with a woman. Unless you did that last night."

Helen moved one hand to feel the reassuring pressure of the tire iron resting against her leg. "You said before you thought I was spying on you for Carmel. Is that why you broke into my room, Wilbur?"

He looked away, clearly pained at the memory of his humiliating failure. "Those picklocks worked like a charm when me and some of the guys broke into that Air Force colonel's house last year. It took too much time for me to get in and take a look around. That's the only reason you caught me on my way out, because I had faulty equipment."

"So you thought maybe Carmel and I were hatching a plot to . . . what? Get you locked up again?"

With a snort he got up from the bed and prowled the room. "Between the bitch and you and Hef, it wouldn't have taken much for the old fart to call up the guys in white suits! Daddy's going to be dead meat any day now — I needed to show him what a liar and a cunt she was." Suddenly he became thoughtful. "Except now she's dead, and he has nobody else to leave the money to but me," he mused, smiling.

Helen froze, her hand gripping the tire iron. Obviously

she'd made a very, very big mistake in coming here tonight. All her high-energy sense of well-being from coping with the day had now drained into fear. Was all of this an act, put on by Wilbur to convince Helen that he hadn't killed his own sister? Helen quickly fanned through Wilbur's pictures, but saw no sign of mutilated photographs resembling the ones Carmel had shown her last night.

There was a thick brown envelope at the bottom of his Carmel collection. Helen opened the envelope and saw Wilbur flinch as she looked through the pictures inside. These were smaller, taken by a different camera. "Special set here from the family album?" she asked him.

"Those have nothing to do with my sister," he said nervously. "I didn't take them, anyhow."

"Then why do you have them?" They showed a younger Romie, before the days he was confined to a wheelchair, standing in what looked like a lush tropical setting. He was shaking hands with a small swarthy man in military garb, and a group of men dressed in similar fashion were looking on in the background. In the distance behind the group she made out a plane sitting on a runway. "Putting together a family history?" She turned the picture over and saw a date penciled on the back. "May nineteen-eighty-three. Interesting."

He licked his lips. Sweat beaded his brow. "I am doing some research. A friend of mine dug those up. Just leave them alone, okay?"

She glanced down at the folder. "Are you going to show this to your father? Now that Carmel is dead?"

He looked at her as if surprised to see her there. "Damn straight I am! I mean, that is, you're not going to tell him about tonight, are you?" The fierce, brooding look he'd had a moment ago was replaced by the more familiar aggrieved and frightened expression Helen was used to. "I brought you here and all, just like you said," he whined.

Helen gave him a hard look, then turned her attention

to the folder in her lap. There were more photographs of Carmel with an assortment of beefy men — her taste ran to the type that had once been well-muscled but were just beginning to turn to fat — and a few notes about her romantic assignations in what Helen supposed was Wilbur's oddly childish print.

After a long silence, Helen dropped the folder and the photographs on the bed and stood up. "No, Wilbur." She sighed, "I'm not going to tell your father about tonight. I think."

"You think?" He walked closer to her, and she gripped the tire iron with both hands.

"I have to see how you behave for the next couple of days before I decide."

He nodded vigorously. "Oh, sure, absolutely. I understand and all. I mean, you know" — he laughed weakly as she headed for the door — "kind of a surprise to see someone breaking into your room, right? Not that you'd expect that, right?"

His clumsy attempts at gaining assurances followed her all the way out to the car. She locked her car door and backed down the road to the highway, the two photographs she'd slipped beneath her sweater resting on the seat beside her.

Chapter Nine

"So I managed to get these two photographs out." Helen sat cross-legged on the bed next to Alison and laid the black-and-white pictures out before her. She'd turned on all the lights in their hotel room so as to be able to examine every detail. "Whatever else you could say about Wilbur Kittrick, he is a decent photographer."

Alison sat silent and motionless, backed up against the pillows, her arms folded across her chest. Helen glanced at her briefly, then went back to the picture. She couldn't make out Alison's expression, hidden as it was in the shadows cast by the bedside lamp.

"This one is weird. I mean, why would he want this? So his dad is standing in the jungle with soldiers. What the hell does that mean?"

"I was thinking about that on the way home. The way he's got his place rigged up, he seems like one of those types who believe the entire government is one big conspiracy waiting to take over."

"Jesus, you mean like black helicopters and star wars secrets?"

"Hey, they're out there. Especially around here, with all the UFO nuts." Helen picked up the picture and studied Romie's face. "Maybe he thinks his father uses his money to front some private army out in the jungle or something. Or he fell for some con artist who showed him these and sold him a bunch of faked photographs for a chunk of Kittrick money."

"Terrific. I'm surprised he didn't have a grainy photo of the shooter on the grassy knoll in Dallas."

Helen chuckled and put the photograph on the bedside table. "Actually, this one interests me a lot more." She peered down at the image of Carmel and Hef. "You know, I think this was taken here at the Silver Saddle," she said into the silence. "Look, you can see the ceiling light in the room — it's that same ridiculous mock chandelier thing we have, and Uncle Loy and Aunt Edna have, too."

When Alison didn't respond, Helen did her best to ignore her by examining details of the portrait of Hef and Carmel she'd pilfered from Wilbur. How the hell had he taken the picture, anyway? Some kind of zoom lens apparatus, although Helen had very little knowledge of sophisticated camera equipment. There was a slight upward angle to the photo, showing the lovers' faces against the backdrop of the ceiling and the telltale chandelier. Had Wilbur taken it from the spot where Helen had seen him last night, standing on the ledge by the river? No, she decided, that would have been too sharp an angle. She stretched and yawned. Where he'd been standing was not the issue, of course. More important was the fact that Wilbur's obsession with photography made him a likely candidate for the sender of the mutilated pictures. But what on earth would be his motive for such a threatening gesture? Especially when his intention seemed to be to expose his sister's nefarious activities to their father and thus secure his own place in the Kittrick empire at her expense? It was difficult to credit a weak and paranoid man like Wilbur with plotting murder, yet a man desperate enough to attempt breaking and entering in a crowded, busy hotel was perhaps just foolish and desperate enough to kill in haste and violent emotion, if not careful planning.

In this example of Wilbur's artistry, Carmel and Hef were standing close together in the middle of the room. Only the sheer curtains were drawn, and their faces were surprised, both looking toward a point in the room that was not included in the photograph. Hef's face, plump and round, looked like a doughnut with his mouth open in shock. Carmel's eyes were slitted in a bestial wariness. Hef's hand was arrested in the act of plunging deep into Carmel's cleavage through her half-open blouse. Helen was struck by the fact that they hadn't even drawn the drapes on their illicit behavior. Were they that sure of themselves, or had their passion caused them to throw caution to the winds? Maybe they thought the floor had been high enough to protect them from cameras. Or they'd gotten off in the risk of being watched.

Then Helen stared harder. Yes, Hef and Carmel were standing directly in front of a mirror. That explained the odd double image she kept seeing — it wasn't a trick of light or poor camera work on Wilbur's part, but rather the close reflection in front of the wide mirror set atop the dresser. It was identical to the dresser in front of the bed where she sat now.

"Damn." Helen picked up the picture and carried it with

her into the bathroom, where the light was stronger. Now she could see how the mirror showed the faint outline of the door to the hotel room. That explained the startled expression on the lovers' faces — the hotel room door was open, and a figure stood in the entrance, watching the two of them as they fondled each other.

"What?" Alison asked as she roused herself and followed Helen.

"Look." Helen held the photograph up to the light. "See how they're standing in front of the mirror? Just like the one in our room, and in all the hotel rooms."

"Right, you can see their reflection."

"Not only that." Helen traced the dim outline of the door in the mirror. "There's someone at the door, watching them. See that dark line in the mirror, then the light right next to it? The door is open, and someone's there."

Alison peered at the photograph and shook her head. "I can't make it out. I mean, I can see what you're talking about, but there's no way you can make out features from that."

Helen shrugged. "Maybe not. But at least Wilbur isn't the only one who knows about their affair."

"So?" Alison left the bathroom and went back to bed, where she lay down on the edge, arms folded and legs crossed. "So what if the whole state of Nevada knew? I don't understand what difference that makes."

Helen set the photograph on the dresser and sat down next to Alison, who edged further away from Helen. "All right. You're pissed off. Want to talk about it?"

"What the hell is there to say?" Alison got up and began to turn off lights around the room. "When have you ever listened to what I have to say?"

Helen felt weariness steal over her. What time was it, anyway? With a groan Helen looked at her watch — two-thirty. She'd been back from Wilbur's mountain command center for only half an hour, and she needed to get some sleep. "Alison, both of us are too tired to get into it now. And we've had a hell of a day. Let's sleep on it, all right?"

"Fine. Sure. Whatever." Alison busied herself turning down the bed while Helen clicked off the last of the lamps and lay down in darkness. Although she really was exhausted, a part of her nagged and fretted at Alison's anger until she couldn't stay silent anymore.

"Okay. Say what you have to say, Alison. Alison?"

The bed shook with Alison's sobs. "I'm not really angry, Helen. I just — I just hate it when you go off that way, tearing off into God knows what, and leave me standing in the dust with a stupid look on my face."

"What else did you expect me to do? He might have been able to really tell me something, and there was no way he would have trusted both of us together." Helen turned the lamp back on, blinking her sore eyes. "I wasn't in any danger from the likes of Wilbur Kittrick."

"It isn't that."

"Well, what then?"

"I thought you were finished with all that. Done with chasing down some lead in the middle of the night, running around after people who would kill you —" Alison stopped abruptly, sighing heavily. "I thought you were finally going to be safe, and here we are in the middle of some murder that doesn't even have anything to do with us. I mean, I don't know these fucking Kittricks from a hole in the ground, and here one turns up dead in your aunt and uncle's hotel room." They both laughed in spite of themselves. "We shouldn't laugh about it. It's awful," Alison said at last. "But you know what I mean.".

Helen felt a headache coming on. "For over a year now," she began, "I've been running scared. It's like that bullet is still chasing me down. I can hear the gun go off and I feel the pain where it hit me. All this time, giving up because I was so afraid. But today, today was like before. For the first time since I was shot, I feel like maybe it's possible to have my old life back. Do you have any idea what that's like? Can you ever understand how it feels to get your life ripped up right in front of your eyes and then have a chance to get it back again?" Helen's voice took on an edge of impatience. How dare Alison reproach her for feeling alive and well again? Then she remembered, and with a sinking feeling she opened her eyes to see Alison staring down at her with a stony expression chiseled on her face. "Sorry," she whispered.

"In case you've forgotten, I have a pretty fucking good idea what that's like. I distinctly remember having my face rearranged by my husband several times. The same husband, by the way, who got killed in front of my eyes. And you might recall that I was the one who sat by your bed in the hospital, scared shitless you would die in front of me, just like he did."

"Alison, I'm sorry —"

"For what?" She rolled over, her back turned to Helen. Her voice was muffled from under the sheets. "For letting me know how unimportant I am to you?"

"Jesus, don't start that one with me." Helen pressed her hand to her forehead as her headache suddenly threatened to break out of her skull. "Just because I take an interest in a case again you have to go through this melodrama, complete with tears and whining and God knows what."

"Fuck you, Helen." Alison flung herself out of the bed and in the darkness began to gather her clothing.

"Where are you going?"

"Hopefully there's a room left in this fucking hotel I can stay in before I get a flight out of here in the morning."

"Alison. Please stop. Look, we're both exhausted and feeling like shit." Helen felt panic rising up in her and struggled to fight it down. She forced a conciliatory tone and willed the pain in her head to recede.

"Stop what? Stop talking about what I feel? Stop letting you know that it scares me to face losing you?" She was slipping on her shoes. Helen could feel her stare in the gloom. "Or maybe just stop getting in your way with my childish emotionalism? Yeah, that sounds about right."

"No, please, Alison. Please just wait." Helen reached out and touched Alison's back. To her surprise Alison did not flinch. "Don't go. I'm sorry. This is all so hard for me."

"What's so hard for you?"

Helen lay down, pulling Alison down with her. Alison lay very still next to Helen, who kept her hands on Alison's back. "Everything. All of it. You. My work, or my nonwork, as it turns out. My aunt and uncle. This place."

Alison edged closer to her. "I know that, but you're not the only one dealing with it. I'm here, too."

They lay quietly for several minutes. Helen's hands traveled across Alison's shoulders. "You didn't button your shirt."

"Not yet." Alison lay quiet and yielding as Helen pulled the shirt off, then she sighed when Helen stroked her breasts. Helen wondered how Alison's ex-husband had made love to his wife. To banish that thought, Helen slipped her hands inside the waistband of Alison's jeans. In a moment they too were on the floor.

"I don't know if I want to, Helen." Alison's murmur was soft in her ear. Helen kissed her neck. "I'm really kind of confused right now."

Helen didn't answer. Strange — she'd never made love to Alison in such total darkness. Even with lights off, drapes drawn and doors shut, slivers of light always seeped into their respective bedrooms at home in Berkeley. Somehow the curtains here at the hotel were designed to completely cut off any light at all, and Helen felt her headache dissipate as she moved farther down Alison's body. There was something freeing about darkness, she realized, something that allowed her to ignore Alison's halfhearted protests. Her mouth and

130

her hands took on a life of their own, and her lover's voice faded into unimportance.

Half-shocked at her own feelings of detachment mixed with desire, Helen trailed her lips downward. Alison was silent now, save for a deep sigh as Helen gently pushed her legs apart.

It didn't take long for Alison to reach climax. "Again," Helen whispered as Alison started to roll over on her side.

"No, I don't think I can."

"Oh, I know you can." She slid her hand between Alison's legs. Her fingers played with the warm wet skin she found there, and Alison's body heaved in response. With each slow thrust, Helen felt further and further away, as if she were watching it all through a camera. It wasn't just the darkness. As Alison moaned and shuddered beneath her, Helen felt a momentary fear at the way she'd removed herself from it all. Odd how what should be so intimate between lovers felt for her tonight like an interesting intellectual event. Not clinical, exactly, but certainly cerebral.

Perhaps, Helen thought as she slid next to her under the sheets, the darkness and the anger surging around the room previously had turned Alison on as well. She held Alison close.

"What about you?" Alison murmured as she moved in Helen's arms.

"Go to sleep." Helen kissed the back of her head, and Alison subsided.

The scene suddenly shifted from the dark hotel room to the golden-lit casino of the Silver Saddle. Helen knew she was dreaming, but the sensation of floating just beneath the domed ceiling, awash with gilt splendor and festooned with glitzy chandeliers, was novel. She didn't think she'd had a flying dream since childhood, when all she did during long lonely nights was sail through the sky away from the heat, humidity and hatred that festered throughout her youth. Now, however, it was with heightened senses that she looked down on the gamblers and tourists roaming the floor. One or two pointed up at her — what the hell did she look like, anyway, careening off the ceiling? — but the spectators merely acknowledged her presence and quickly returned to the gaming tables and slot machines.

Looking down at her body, Helen was neither surprised nor dismayed by her nakedness. She did note, with a momentary wonder, that the scar at her side from the bullet's entry had completely disappeared. Idly she rubbed a hand over it — yes, she could still feel it, but it was no longer visible. Her curiosity faded as she moved slowly, gracefully, through the air above the light fog of cigarette smoke.

There were Loy and Edna. Uncle Loy glanced up briefly, then pulled his cap down over his weather-beaten features and averted his face. He furtively bent over the cards and pointedly turned away from Helen, hiding himself and what he was doing. At his side, Aunt Edna's body smoldered in flames, bright red flickers that reached the contours of her body and strayed no farther. Through the orange-red fire Helen saw her grin and wave, then she poked Loy with a flaming hand, gesturing up at Helen as if to urge him to look at his niece floating naked on the ceiling. He hunched down, shaking his head vehemently.

Puzzled, Helen moved on, drifting toward another aisle of slot machines. With one deft kick she steered safely around a chandelier, missing its carved and fluted sharp edges with the ease of long hours of practice. When the hell did she get so good at this, anyway? It was as if she'd been soaring away from the crowd her whole life, steering herself safely away from both danger and involvement with the ease of a professional.

Then she spotted Alison sitting cross-legged in a corner, observing the activity surging all around her. Helen tried shouting, she tried waving, she even tried pushing herself down closer to the floor. Nothing worked. Alison didn't look up or notice her presence, and for some reason Helen couldn't seem to make herself come down from the ceiling. Kicking the walls, flailing frantically in swimming motions, even yelling at the top of her lungs were all useless. She barely noticed the fact that Alison, too, was completely naked; what struck her more was the way blood welled up from the welts that covered her arms and shoulders.

With one last effort Helen shoved herself away from the ceiling in Alison's direction only to find herself standing in one of the hotel rooms. Fully clothed again, Helen blinked in the bright light illuminating every corner of the room. It might have been her own room — hard to say, because as far as she could tell every room was the same in the casino — but a glance at the dresser told her this one belonged to her aunt and uncle. There was Edna's handbag and Loy's John Deere cap resting next to it.

"This place is a mess." Carmel Kittrick stood next to Helen. With the usual logic of dreams, Helen didn't question how she could be standing there with half her head caved in. Blood matted her shiny blonde hair, and the dead woman's voice gurgled up as they were under- water. "I'm a mess, too."

Helen regarded her curiously. "What happened to you?" she asked, hoping she wasn't being too inquisitive.

But Carmel ignored her question. "I've got to get cleaned up." She sighed, and with that she lay down on the floor, taking the position Helen had last seen her in — arms and legs splayed, skirt tugged up over thighs, one shoe kicked off. Carmel lifted her head and turned to look with her one good eye at Helen. "Better call room service."

Helen knelt beside the body. She touched it but felt nothing, not even the cold skin she expected. Giving up, she stood again and surveyed the room, noticing for the first time the stack of towels on the end of the bed. "Carmel, room service has already been here," she said aloud. Would she be able to get them back up to take the body away?

At that moment she felt a tug on her leg. Looking down she saw Carmel's hand, blackened and bloodstained, gripping her ankle and pulling Helen closer.

"Helen? Helen, wake up."

Alison perched on the end of the bed, her hand still touching Helen's leg.

Helen bolted upright, her heart pounding. "What time is it?" she asked with a cough. Soaked with sweat, she shivered beneath the thin sheets. As her eyes cleared she saw with surprise that Aunt Edna was peering around the door into the room.

"It's just after eleven." Alison handed her a T-shirt and jeans. Conscious of her aunt's presence, Helen got dressed as quickly as she could while tussling with sheets.

"Morning or evening?"

Alison sighed and rolled her eyes. "Morning. Come on, your aunt is waiting for you."

"I can see that." Helen zipped the jeans and got up, still blinking and dazed from her strange dream. "Hey, Aunt Edna, what's going on?"

Edna stepped into the room and closed the door behind her, her face puckered in anxiety. For one wild moment, Helen expected to see her burst into flames. "Oh, Helen, honey, you've got to help me find your uncle."

Helen cleared her throat, wishing for a cup of coffee. "What do you mean? He's not with you?"

Two fat tears squeezed from her tight-shut eyes and coursed down the folds of her cheeks. "Sweetheart, I didn't want to tell you, it's just so embarrassing." Fist clutched against plump chest in a gesture reminiscent of penitence, Edna plopped down on the disheveled bed. Alison stood next to the elderly woman and awkwardly placed a hand on her shoulder, which trembled from suppressed tears. "I've been so careful to keep the credit cards away from him, and the banking machine card, but somehow he sneaked them out."

"Aunt Edna, what are you trying to say?" Helen sat next to her with growing alarm.

Edna sniffled and wiped her eyes. "Well, this morning I went to have a cup of tea with those nice ladies who gave me a ride home yesterday. Now, I thought I'd put all those cards in my purse, but doggone if he didn't go through my bag last night and get them out."

Alison glanced over Edna's head at Helen. "I'll get you a glass of water," she said, leaving Helen alone with her aunt.

"He's already taken all our money and put it into those awful noisy slot machines, the ones with the lemons and apples on them," Edna babbled on. "Lord above knows why he likes those ones so much. But now I'm afraid he went on to another casino, since he knows I'm watching him."

Realization, as well as the memory of her uncle's furtive behavior, dawned on Helen as Alison came back, glass of water in hand, to the bed. "How much has Uncle Loy gambled away so far, Aunt Edna?" she asked, taking her aunt's hand.

"Oh, lordy, I don't know." She drank the water down in one gulp. From her flushed face Helen thought she must be having another hot flash on top of everything else. "I only got all the cards rounded up last night — he may have run up a terrible bill. Helen, what if he's thrown away the mortgage payment for next month? We didn't have that much saved — we just have his pension, and my social security..."

"It's all right, Aunt Edna. We'll go find him. He doesn't have the car, so he can't be too far." Already Helen was thinking hard, trying to recall the different casinos that lined the river.

"Honey, I feel just awful about everything," Edna said. "I didn't know Loy would do this — he never even buys any lotto tickets when we go into Jackson. Even in Biloxi he wouldn't go into those riverboat gambling dens. And now he's off lost with a credit card in his hand!"

Alison and Helen managed between them to keep Edna calm as they left the room a few minutes later. Helen stopped to grab a cup of coffee in one of the cafés dotted here and there throughout the Saddle's casino, and they sat down to work out a search plan.

"Does he have a game he prefers, or does he pretty much stick to the slot machines?" Helen asked.

Edna sighed and shook her head, staring down at the coffee swirling around in her cup. "Well, I used to think it was just those machines. They make it so easy, you know, without having to know any lingo or to follow cards or dice or anything — kind of private-like. But now —" Her voice broke and she dabbed at her eyes with a napkin. "Now I don't know what he's been doing. Brother Naylor — that's our pastor, back at First Church of God in Tupelo — Brother Naylor warned us this might happen."

"Aunt Edna, I really don't think —"

"Just like it says in the Good Book about avoiding all appearances of evil." She nodded vigorously. Helen forced herself to avoid Alison's glances and fixed her attention on her aunt. "This might just be the first step to worse things. He could be watching some of those shows where the women dance around with nothing on." Terror shone in her eyes. "Oh, Helen, honey, do you think he might be doing that?"

Helen's mind boggled at the image of her uncle staring with lewd fascination at an exotic dancer strutting her stuff, but if Uncle Loy was capable of throwing away the mortgage money, anything was possible. Still, Laughlin ran more to a sedate senior crowd than Vegas did. None of the casinos advertised anything more risqué than a few aging, miniskirted waitresses at Bingo night.

"I think I should make one more quick walk through this place," Helen said. "Will you be okay here for a few minutes, Aunt Edna?" When she nodded, Helen went on. "Alison and I could start at opposite ends and work our way back here."

"I'll be fine, sweetie." She pursed her lips and glanced at Alison. "And I'm so awfully sorry to have dragged you into our family business, dear."

"It's okay, Edna." Alison gave her a squeeze. "I'm just so sorry your trip has turned out this way."

As soon as they were out of earshot, Alison stopped Helen. "Did you know this about your uncle?"

Helen shook her head. "Not a clue. Loy is — or was — straight as an arrow. I don't know what snapped for him."

"Well, let's get this over with. How about if I start by the elevators and work my way back to the coffee shop?"

"Fine. I'll take the other end and meet you there." Helen walked past the potted palms and toward the large gaming room. Several card games were already in progress. She could hear the racketing of roulette and the patter of croupiers as she searched the crowd for her uncle's face. On her way across the casino she passed by the familiar facade of Romie's and got a glimpse of Joe at one of the slot machines near the entrance of the restaurant. He stared down at the display on the machine, his hands beating out a nervous tattoo on the metal. He didn't look any better than he had the last time Helen saw him. She quickly scanned the crowd outside the restaurant, and when she looked back in his direction he had disappeared.

She didn't see Loy, but two other familiar faces appeared standing outside the bar next to the blackjack tables.

Bill Hefley and Sue seemed to be having an argument. Helen saw him grab her arm. Sue flinched and tried to pull away. The bartender edged closer to the couple, and Hef smiled broadly at him. He steered Sue out of the bar and toward one of the tiny tables on the raised platform overlooking the gaming room.

Helen circled back around the card players so that her path took her past Sue and Hef. He spoke in low, soothing tones, trying to calm Sue. "I've told you, Carmel Kittrick meant nothing to me. Nothing at all."

"Then why are you leaving me?"

"Babe, this is not the time or place, now, is it?"

"What do you care?" Sue sounded on the verge of tears. "Afraid someone from Kittrick Enterprises will know you've been sleeping with a waitress? Is that it?"

"Now, honey, you know that's not true."

Helen stood with her back to them, her eyes scanning a group of middle-aged men leaving a poker game. No sign of Loy yet. She turned around when she heard a chair push away from the table. Sue was standing, gathering up her bag.

"There's never a good time or place, is there, Hef? You're just like Nicholas. He left me before my daughter was even born. You're all the same, every damn one of you."

"Baby, come on, now."

"Go to hell." Sue pulled on her blue vest and wiped her cheeks. "I've got to go to work now." She walked past Helen and disappeared into the crowd. Hef stayed behind. Helen got a glimpse of him staring down at the table as she left the gaming room and headed back to Romie's.

Just as she spotted Alison outside the restaurant, a familiar figure appeared at the entrance. Loy twisted his baseball cap between his fingers, and Helen could see how his gaunt face was shadowed with burgeoning whiskers. He glanced their way, then saw Edna sitting in the café.

"I'll go wait over here, Helen." Alison melted into the crowd and made her way to the newsstand.

Loy wouldn't look at her. "How's she taking it?" he mumbled.

"Not too well, Uncle Loy. I think it was kind of a shock for her, to find out just how much you like to gamble."

"Haven't lost the house, or nothing near that," he said with a grimace. "She's carrying on so over nothing at all, Helen. I haven't spent one red cent over the limit we talked about before we left."

"Maybe," Helen said gently, "it's just that you went out to play the slot machines without telling her."

He snorted. "More likely Brother Naylor got in her head too deep before we left. Not to mention the, uh, you know, the change," he added. His face burned deep red beneath his tan.

Helen fought back a smile as he struggled with the concept of female troubles. "Well, I think she was more worried about you disappearing on her than anything else. Why don't you go talk to her?"

"Guess so. Sorry you got dragged into this foolishness, Helen." He set his jaw and headed for the café. Edna watched him, then turned away huffily as he sat down.

Carrying a *San Francisco Examiner*, Alison strolled to Helen's side. "How much damage do you think was done last night?"

Helen shook her head. "Hard to say. Doesn't look good, though, does it?"

Loy wordlessly tossed two credit cards on the table in front of Edna, who picked them up with shaking hands. He said something, then Edna spoke.

Helen sighed and turned away. "I think we should go. They don't need witnesses to this, and we're sure to get the lowdown from Edna later on."

But a sudden onslaught of people rushing through the casino prevented them from leaving. "What the hell is going on now?" Alison groaned.

Helen heard sirens approaching. "You know, I've had just about enough of the Silver Saddle's hospitality, haven't you? Maybe we should get my aunt and uncle on a plane for Mississippi and get back to Berkeley —"

"You forget, we have the police to contend with."

"Speaking of police, take a look out there." Helen pointed past the café to the registration desk at the other end of the lobby. Flashing red-and-blue lights blinked through the huge glass entrance doors. There were three black-and-whites pulled up outside the valet station. She saw one of the maroon-vested valets gesturing wildly and pointing to the casino. Shouts echoed throughout the building, punctuated by screams coming from the direction of Romie's. Helen struggled to get a better look. Half a dozen police officers, garbed in black bulletproof vests equipped with shoulder mikes, darted into the crowd.

"All right, people, out! Everyone out of the area!" One man barked orders at the crowd. He waved the onlookers behind him, and another set of policemen filed inside. They formed a tight circle as their leader gave them orders, then split into teams of two and spread around the rectangular area that had just been cleared. Weaving their way through rows of slot machines, they quietly positioned themselves and their weapons. Helen nudged her way as far to the front of the crowd as she could and got a glimpse of Romie's. She was too far away to see what was going on, but she heard a scream that she was certain came from the restaurant.

"Helen, look." Alison nudged her, and she turned to see the young girl darting through the crowd with a panicked expression on her face. Nick's maroon tunic, the kind worn by the housekeeping staff of the Saddle, flapped around her as she ran, pushing people aside with rough shoves. Helen fought her way across the crowd to reach Nick.

"Nick! What are you doing here?" Helen grabbed the girl's arm and pulled her out of the throng.

"Let go of me, bitch! It's my mother in there!" She tore away from them and wove a path amongst the people gathering at the edge of the police line.

"Damn it, Nick, this isn't helping!" Helen grabbed her again, but she broke away. Now they were both standing near one of the police officers keeping the crowd in check. He looked just as frightened as everyone else. When a woman in the crowd in front of Helen screamed, he was distracted long enough to give Nick the time she needed to slip around him and past the long line of slot machines that led right to the restaurant entrance.

"Shit," Helen muttered. She went in after Nick.

Chapter Ten

Joe had a pistol pointed at one of his hostages when Helen reached Nick. "Do you have any idea how stupid this is?" Helen asked her. They huddled together near the wall, halfway down the row of slot machines.

"He's crazy, he'll kill somebody," Nick whispered. Helen felt her body quiver as she gasped for air. "I knew he was strung out, but I didn't think he'd do something like this."

"Yeah, well, people do crazy things when they're desperate." The cops hadn't seen them yet, but Helen knew it was only a matter of time. Nick was too agitated to be still for long.

Suddenly Nick froze. "There she is! I see my mother!"

Sue knelt on the floor near the cash register, a stunned look on her face. The other people in the restaurant blurred into a sea of pale, terrified faces.

"Omigod, omigod, omigod," Nick murmured. Helen had pulled her down roughly onto the parquet floor of the casino behind a row of slot machines. The aisle stretched the length of the restaurant's front windows. Helen and Nick were crouched near the wall along the left side of the gambling area. If she kept her back to the wall, Helen could see the whole scene play out before her. Just beyond the aisle a SWAT team had formed a line, keeping the crowd away. Newspeople had hurried into the casino and fought their way to the edge of the crowd. Helen heard the crackle of radios as the team sorted out who had the best shot.

"Nick, stay down. It's not going to help if you get in the way."

"You don't understand. Oh, fuck, I should have just given him the fucking money," Nick moaned.

Helen grabbed the girl's arm. "How long has he been supporting his habit through you? Who the hell is he to you, anyway?"

"I'm not dating him. Not anymore." She wiped a trembling hand on her shirt and fought down racking sobs. "All I want to do is get me and my mom out of here. Joe would have just dragged us down, deeper into this hellhole than we already are. But he wouldn't leave me alone. He didn't want me, he just wanted money now and then. I just can't believe he'd do this."

"Just calm down. The police will take care of it," Helen said absently as she noted the two marksmen positioning themselves for a good shot. She hoped Nick hadn't seen that.

She turned a tear-stained face to Helen. "You don't understand," she repeated. "He must have gone to my house to get money. He blames me for not helping him."

Before Helen could say anything else, she heard a phone ringing in the distance. Joe, still pointing the gun at the temple of a man who was kneeling on the floor, took a step to the register and grabbed the telephone. Even at this distance, she could tell the boy was twitchy as hell. Whatever he was on had him jumping and ready to pull the trigger at the slightest provocation. Off to her right a plainclothes officer spoke quietly into a cell phone. Behind him stood three men in uniform who spoke amongst themselves in harsh whispers. And just past the uniforms Helen saw Bill Hefley. He stared across the empty expanse of the casino that stretched before them, down the gleaming rows of slot machines, into the picture windows of Romie's. Tie loosened, jacket nowhere in sight, dark sweat stains under his arms. In spite of all this, his face was impassive. Maybe it was just shock. After all, he'd seen his boss and ex-lover killed yesterday, and his current girlfriend might possibly be dead before this day was over.

Joe listened only for a moment before slamming the receiver down so hard Helen could hear a faint jangle from the restaurant. Nick was crying without a sound, and only Helen's restraining hand kept her from springing up and running for the restaurant.

"Damn it, Nick, the cops will get this under control. If you jump out now you'll just endanger your mother more than she is already."

"Fuck you, you stupid dyke!" Nick whirled away, wriggling out of Helen's grasp, and flung herself around the end of the aisle. She plowed right into the arms of the police.

Two uniformed cops grabbed Nick just as Joe fired. Helen swallowed hard, took a deep breath, and peered over the slot machine into the restaurant. She didn't see anyone down. But Sue had moved away from the cash register and now stood directly in front of Joe.

"Mom!" Nick screamed. The cops struggled to hold her

back. Joe was distracted at the sight of Nick, and his attention wavered from Sue. He swayed and wiped his free hand over his face.

Sue kept talking. She took a couple of uncertain steps closer to Joe, and Helen saw her lips move continuously. She reached out a tentative hand. Joe looked away from Nick back to Sue, then his body stilled. In thinking about it later, Helen decided that at that moment he'd finally realized what was going down all around him. The row of black-suited SWAT people must have looked to Joe like an army.

"Oh, God, Mom, he'll do it, he'll shoot you!"

"This the woman's daughter? Get her the hell out of here!" The plainclothes officer growled at his minions, and Nick was forcibly carried away from Helen's view. "You too!" he called to Helen. She nodded, kept her hands at her sides, and hurried away under his justifiably angry gaze.

Things happened quickly after that. When she'd been in similar situations before as a cop, Helen had always been amazed at the way things seemed both speeded up and slowed down at the same time, as if reality went on some strange space and time warp that bent and shaped events to its will. It was probably, she reasoned, just a function of the human mind, so that those who witnessed terrible things could distance from them.

That feeling set in when she heard another muffled shot. Helen knew it must have come from the restaurant, and she stopped just as she reached the lines of news cameras. Turning around she was able to wedge herself into the crowd enough to maneuver back into the rows of slot machines. It was the same aisle she and Nick had hidden in, but much farther back. She couldn't see Nick any longer and wondered briefly where they'd taken her.

That was when the marksman fired. She never knew where that shot came from, but she was close enough to the restaurant's glass walls to see Joe drop like a rock. Screams broke out from all over the casino, and in the chaos that followed Helen saw another body lying next to Joe. This body wore a blue vest and had long dark hair pulled back in a ponytail.

An hour later, after a brief talk with the police, Helen and Alison sat on the steps outside that led down to a walkway next to the Colorado River. The length of shadows falling on the path indicated that it was now late afternoon. People still noisily milled about, and they were even approached by a tall redhead with a microphone and a cameraman trotting behind. One look from Helen was all it took to discourage the local reporter, and she went off in search of willing interviewees.

Alison sighed and flung a pebble across the fence into the water. "From what you say, then, Sue seemed to be trying to talk Joe out of it."

"That's certainly what it looked like. Nick saw it too. She was screaming, trying to tell her mom not to try, that Joe would kill her. Jesus." Helen closed her eyes only to see the image of Joe being killed replay in her mind. "I saw him hanging around before. He was really strung out. I should have done something, damn it."

"Like what? There's no way you could have known he'd do this."

"Right."

"And?"

"I know, I know. I couldn't have predicted this. No one could." Helen opened her eyes and looked out at the river. "Wonder where Nick is, by the way?"

"Mind if I talk to you for a minute?" It must have been Shelley's day off. Jeans and a faded blue work shirt replaced the security guard's uniform. "You guys okay?"

"All right. How are you doing?"

"Okay, I guess. Better than some people. Damn, I wasn't too crazy about Sue, but this is unbelievable."

"I know." Helen briefly introduced Alison, then asked, "Do you know where Nick is?"

Shelley shook her head, and worry creased her round face. "I was going to ask you the same thing. Some of the people who work in the casino were saying they saw you in there with her. Do you know if she saw it happen? Saw her mother get shot, I mean?"

"I don't think so, but she saw a lot. Maybe Bill Hefley knows where she went."

Shelley spat on the ground. "That asshole? He's probably glad Sue is dead so she's off his hands, the fucking bastard. You should have seen her face a couple of months ago."

"What do you mean?"

"She couldn't get enough makeup on to cover the bruises he gave her. Shit, makes me sick just talking about it. Look, I'm going to see if I can find Nick. Talk to you later." She disappeared into the crowd.

Helen stood and stretched. "I don't know about you, but I think I need to get out of here tonight. Let's round up my relatives and find someplace else to go."

"Oh, that's right, you couldn't have known"

"Known what?"

Alison smiled. "Kittrick told us — well, he sent one of his people, you know the ones, they look like they could either be Mafia or secret service. Anyway, he's arranged for his grand prize winners to be put up at a different hotel for the night."

"Just for tonight?"

"Hard to say. Maybe more than one. All the guy said was about tonight, though."

"Do you know where?"

She shook her head. "A van is supposed to meet us and take us there. Oh, I told Loy and Edna to go on across the street and wait for us in the restaurant there."

"Christ." Helen leaned against the rail and squinted up at the sun. "Welcome to the family, Alison. Let's see, what have we left out? Nothing, I think. We've covered murder, suicide, gambling, UFOs, and prospecting."

"Your typical American family." They both smiled at the lame joke and began to walk toward the casino.

Three hours later, after lengthy negotiations with various officials to gather their belongings and lengthier planned escape routes to avoid reporters and casino patrons alike, the entire Winners' Circle entourage sat packed closely together in a dark blue van. With Kittrick security at the wheel, they sped in cushioned splendor along the highway that fronted the river, the early evening sun shining through tinted windows on the silent, shaken passengers.

Chapter Eleven

"How convenient it would be if that waitress had been the murderer." John Tilson gave up toying with his food and stared down listlessly at his plate. Beside him, his wife sat with her usual detachment. Helen, seated opposite the Tilsons, watched her worriedly. Tonight Mrs. Tilson seemed quite different — her silence came not so much from indifference to the world around her as it did from a strange inner peace, almost a glow. Her husband, however, looked wasted and weary. In fact, the rest of the Romie's group turned toward him when he spoke, startled to hear him contributing to the conversation.

Not that it was much of a conversation. All around them the diners at the Branded Steer talked and laughed, downing their slabs of prime rib and heaps of potatoes with gusto. The Romie's table, by contrast, was silent and gloomy. Food cooled as quickly as conversation.

This particular restaurant, situated so close to the Saddle, hadn't been Helen's first choice, especially because she and Alison had just eaten there. It took the assembled Winners' Circle nearly half an hour to decide, so she silently went along, not wanting to draw attention to herself, when they crammed back into the dark blue van to be transported down the strip. Too bad the hotel — motel, really — that Kittrick had chosen for them didn't offer dining facilities. The fact that it was small and tasteful and quiet, and removed from the long shimmering line of casino hotels, more than made up for its lack of glamour as far as Helen was concerned.

They'd all been visibly relieved when the burly driver — a new face, a bodyguard Helen hadn't spotted before — drove off with a promise of coming back and waiting outside in an hour. Helen was certain that anything they said or did around this man would be directly reported back to Kittrick at the first opportunity.

They'd been expected at the restaurant and were shown to a table that was discreetly tucked behind a partition concealing a view of the Saddle. While she'd downed her bourbon, Uncle Loy and Aunt Edna sat like weathered statues, not speaking to each other, and avoided their niece's eyes. Loy kept glancing at his wife, but Edna determinedly tore up bits of bread onto her plate. Mrs. Tilson was smiling beatifically while her husband stared off into space. Next to them, Heather Gilley gave off invisible sparks as she squirmed next to her husband. The tears and distress Helen had seen the day before had somehow evolved into a tightly wound rage. She was the only member of the group who had any appetite. Watching her shovel forkful after forkful of salad into her little red mouth, Helen doubted Heather was tasting any of it. Beside her, Bud Gilley devoted himself with the same intensity to several beers. He'd emptied a second bottle and asked the waitress for a third when the miniskirted woman began handing plates of beef around the table. He slouched down, bumping into his wife who kept pushing him away with a sharp jab of her elbow. From the look of him, Helen was certain he'd begun drinking before they'd left the motel.

Helen cleared her throat and leaned forward to get a better look at the Tilsons. "What do you mean, Mr. Tilson?" she asked. Alison shifted in her chair nervously.

"I mean, if that woman had killed Carmel Kittrick, then died today, defending the lives of others, it would work out things to everyone's satisfaction." He shrugged and reached for his glass of water. "Then the cops could wrap this thing up and we could get the hell out of here. I've had more than enough of this place."

Everyone around the table recoiled from his blunt remark. Tilson stabbed a piece of meat with his fork and swished it around in the pool of gravy on his plate. His speech was, Helen thought, an indication of how close everyone, even the cool and collected Tilsons, were ready to snap at the least pressure. And it was only Saturday night, too.

"But Carmel wasn't shot, was she? I heard she got hit in the head, or something." Bud took another swig of beer, stifled a belch, and looked around blearily for the waitress.

"How do you know that, Bud Gilley?" Heather spat out. "You were supposedly in bed with a headache all that morning."

He looked over at her as if seeing a stranger for the first time. "That bulldyke security guard, Sheila, or whatever the hell her name is. I heard her talking about it to the desk clerk. Oops, sorry." He nodded at Helen, who stared back at him in a mixture of contempt and amusement.

Helen had had just enough bourbon and just enough unusual excitement over the last couple of days to want to indulge her curiosity. "So you were at the Saddle when it happened, Mr. Gilley."

He winked at her. "Call me Bud. Yeah, I didn't want to go stare at a bunch of mules yesterday."

"No, you wanted to stare at something else. Like Carmel Kittrick," Heather burst out. "And don't try to lie about it. I know exactly what was going on that morning."

Everyone else at the table turned to their plates again and busied themselves with cold food. Bud slammed his beer bottle down on the table, and Helen was startled to see his face go bright red. "Why don't you keep your mouth shut and quit embarrassing me?" he muttered, putting his face close to Heather's.

"Me embarrassing you? That's a good one! You, sitting there getting drunk and acting ugly all the time and making a fool of yourself over that, that bitch!" Tears streamed down Heather's cheeks, and her pretty face twisted in grief and rage. Although she spoke just above a whisper, diners nearby studiously avoided them, and a couple of waitresses glanced their way.

"You're the one making a scene, stupid!" Bud slurred. He turned to the others at the table. "And what the hell are you staring at?" he snapped. "So what if I decided to have a morning to myself, away from the little woman here?" His gaze leveled on John Tilson. "You didn't go, either. Maybe *you* killed her. Yeah, you might have done it. You're just the type."

Helen froze at the sight of Mr. Tilson's face. Beneath the dark, skin muscles worked in fury as he pushed himself back from the table and regarded Bud with contempt. "The type? You better explain yourself, son."

"Look who's calling me 'son'! I mean, the quiet kind that don't say much and causes a lot of trouble behind the scenes." He shoved aside empty bottles. "I saw how you looked at her, Tilson. You hated her."

"And we all saw how you looked at her too," Heather sniffed.

"But now she's dead." Mrs. Tilson's first words for the entire evening. Helen was chilled to the bone by the glowing smile on her lips, the overt pleasure the ailing woman took in making the statement. "She's gone forever."

Like your son, Helen thought to herself.

"I happened to be getting medicine for my wife that morning," Mr. Tilson was saying through clenched teeth as his gaze moved around the table. "The police know about it. And I think my trip to the pharmacy is a hell of a lot better alibi than anything this asshole could come up with."

Bud began to lurch out of his seat just as their waitress, sensing a bad situation erupting, arrived. Bud subsided as she began to gather plates, stacking them expertly in her arms. "You done with that, hon? Want to take that with you? How 'bout some dessert?" Mercifully she kept her comments to a minimum, and Helen was fairly certain she'd conveniently forgotten Bud's request for another beer.

As soon as the waitress left, Edna looked up. "Excuse me, please," she whispered. Helen and Alison got up to let her out. Loy glanced after her, then looked with helpless appeal at Helen. With a sigh, wishing she could just finish another drink in peace, Helen went after her aunt.

She found Edna in the ladies' room, sobbing into a paper towel. "Oh, Aunt Edna, I know it's been horrible for you," Helen said, patting her back.

"Look at this!" Edna whirled on her, one hand clenched in a fist and thrust out, holding something for Helen to see. "Not only is he lying about his gambling and his women, he's taken to stealing, too!" The thick gold chain swung from her fingers as Edna opened her hand.

"Where did you get this?" Helen asked, taking it from her.

Edna wiped her eyes. "I found it in the bathroom, that afternoon when they let us go in to get our things. It was sitting there with my other jewelry — you know, those pearls Grandma left me, and the little diamond earrings. And my good wedding band."

"Didn't you tell the police it wasn't yours?"

She shook her head and a fresh burst of tears welled down her cheeks. "I've been so scared, Helen. I know he didn't do anything to that poor woman, but I was so sure the police would arrest him for murder if they knew he'd been stealing." Her wet eyes were round with horror. "I mean, after all the other awful things he's done, now this." She put both her hands over her face.

Helen put an arm around her aunt's shoulders and squeezed, glancing back at the door. Fortunately no one had followed them in yet. "In the first place, I don't think Uncle Loy has done anything so awful. He hasn't gone and sold the house, he's just played a few nickel and dime slot machines, right?"

Edna nodded, but Helen could still feel her shaking.

"And I really don't think he's chasing other women —"

"But I'm so fat and old and I feel so bad all the time," she wailed, burying her face in Helen's shoulder. "Why wouldn't he be looking at other women?" Another woman chose that moment to enter the bathroom, and Helen spent the next few minutes coaxing Edna outside into the cool night air, away from everyone else.

"I think," she said, looking out over the parking lot,

"that Uncle Loy loves you more than anything on this earth. I think you know that too, don't you?"

"I don't know much of anything anymore." Edna sighed. She pointed at the gold chain still in Helen's hand. "Not since I saw that."

"Aunt Edna, you should have told the police right away. I don't think Uncle Loy stole it to finance his bad habits, but anything unusual in your room should have been brought to their attention." Her mind raced, cataloguing possible explanations they could offer to the authorities — perhaps Edna had scooped up her jewelry in a hurry to be out of the room, not noticing the chain until she'd gone through her belongings the next day.

Funny thing, Helen thought, she sort of recognized this chain, too. She held it up to the light for examination. It was fairly thick, almost like a rope, with small nuggets of gold twisted into the chain at regular intervals. One of the nuggets had almost worked loose of the chain. It dangled precariously, tethered at one uneven edge to the strand of gold, threatening to drop off with even slight pressure.

"Edna?" Loy cleared his throat behind them, close to the door of the restaurant, a glass of water in his hand. "Are you doing okay now?"

Before Helen could stop her, Edna grabbed the necklace and marched over to her husband. "I will be, once you tell me you didn't steal this so you could pay your gambling debts."

Speechless, Loy stared at her. "I never saw that thing before in my life," he sputtered. "And how many times do I have to tell you that I don't have gambling debts?"

Helen looked down at the asphalt, knowing that her uncle would be mortified if she saw him close to tears. "Aunt Edna, he's telling the truth."

"I'm not lying to you, honey. Please? Believe me?"

Edna took the glass of water and had a small sip. Helen

grabbed the necklace from her fingers before she could protest. "I think I'll keep this tonight. Tomorrow morning, Aunt Edna, you and me and Uncle Loy are going to the police and tell them you found the necklace with your things, all right?"

"But — but they'll think we stole it!" she whispered, horrified.

"No, they won't. They'll think you're fine, upstanding citizens for coming to them with evidence."

"This is evidence?" Loy scratched at his bald pate and watched anxiously as Helen carefully looped the necklace into a neat pile and put it in her jacket pocket.

Helen shrugged. "Maybe. Maybe this belonged to Carmel Kittrick, and she left it in your bathroom right before she died. Or maybe it belonged to the killer." As soon as she'd said the words she regretted them, observing the shock on her relatives' faces. But the police would not be nearly so gentle and patient with them. She might as well prepare them.

Chapter Twelve

The next morning, Helen stood at the picture window overlooking the Colorado River and sipped the excellent coffee provided by Mr. Kittrick for his party's enjoyment. Although Romie Kittrick was in another room of the suite, she swore she could hear the hiss of oxygen as it seeped through coiled plastic tubes into Kittrick's decaying lungs. There was a dull murmur coming from assorted Kittrick minions as they arranged breakfast on the walnut table of the Saddle's Commodore Suite, which was located around the corner from the penthouse suite formerly occupied by Carmel Kittrick. This set of rooms, however, didn't contain a fax machine or pair of laptops or an elaborate phone system, as far as Helen could see. Instead, a metal cart held an assortment of pills and syringes arrayed neatly in order, she supposed, of either importance or necessity. The lower shelf of the cart sported two bright red oxygen tanks, ready for use, and a small plastic face mask. It was an incongruous display, given the suite's somewhat naval tinge of decoration. Seascapes lined the walls, and there was even a ship in a bottle on the mahogany dresser. Perhaps, Helen reasoned, the designer had heard what they were calling this suite, thrown up his or her hands in despair at the thought of evoking the ocean in the middle of the desert, and settled for throw pillows printed with sailing ships and deep blue sofas and chairs. Helen couldn't believe she'd ended up in this hotel one more time.

Even during the phone call late last night, when to her surprise Romie Kittrick issued an invitation to breakfast in his suite at the Saddle, she swore she could hear the whisper of that slender connection between life itself and the old man. It might, of course, have been the phone line sending out that sibilant hum, but Helen could have sworn that even the scent of medicine, old man and death clung to his voice.

"It was my baby girl's last wish to hire you," he'd wheezed at her. "I'd like to find out what she had to say to you, Ms. Black."

Helen squirmed uncomfortably, well aware of Alison's careful attention to luggage and toiletries, overtly indifferent to whatever Helen might be saying. Helen had positioned herself on the bed, phone in hand, so she wouldn't have to witness Alison's pretense.

"Ms. Black?" Kittrick had stretched out the honorific.

"Yes, I'm here," Helen had responded. "Mr. Kittrick, I honestly don't know what I can tell you —"

"Just be here at eight-thirty. I'll have breakfast ready."

"But —" She thought of her aunt and uncle, who were

counting on her to accompany them to the police station. "I've got an appointment downtown at ten-thirty."

He repeated assurances that she'd be out in plenty of time, and Helen had found herself giving in. When she hung up the phone Alison had given her only one brief glare, then switched on the television to the local news. That hadn't lasted long, since the biggest story in town was the dramatic events that had taken place at the Saddle that afternoon, so the two women went to bed in silence.

Alison had barely acknowledged Helen's departure that morning. "You will show up at the police station, then?" she'd said as Helen shrugged on a jacket.

"Of course." Helen decided against any further exclamations or assurances. Instead, she'd headed out to the parking lot where the now-familiar dark blue van waited, its waxed finish gleaming under the early morning sun.

Soft clinking noises and the scent of sausage indicated that food was now ready. Helen reluctantly turned away from the long glittering expanse of water below; compared to what she was about to experience, she was sure, the river provided a calm, peaceful contrast. As she seated herself at the table and glanced over the copious display of edibles, she wondered once again why the hell she'd taken Kittrick up on his offer of a breakfast meeting. She finished her coffee, not sure she'd be up for anything more. One of the well-muscled men who provided security for Kittrick was immediately at her side, pouring her a fresh cup from a delicately engraved silver pot. Another man, her chauffeur, placed one more chafing dish on the table and then left the room. Helen took a piece of perfectly toasted and buttered wheat bread and stole a glance at the other guest seated across from her.

Marc Landry looked just as uncomfortable as Helen felt. His plate contained only a slice of melon. Perhaps, Helen mused, he also thought that food didn't seem to go well with a meeting like this. Just what exactly was going on, anyway? Helen thought. She took a bite of toast that might have been cardboard, for all she could taste it, and deliberately met Landry's sullen stare. Was he too stoned the other night to remember her as the woman who'd disarmed him and handed him over to the police? Probably not, she thought, observing his flush and the way he quickly turned his attention to his melon. She puzzled again over why he was sitting here, having breakfast in a palatial hotel suite, when he should have been enjoying a meal over at the local jail, after his performance two nights ago.

The silence was unbearable. Annoyed at her own discomfort, as well as her decision to come to Kittrick's suite, Helen pulled a couple of silver dishes toward her just to have something to do. One held scrambled eggs, beaten together with mushrooms and some lightly scented cheese. The other held bacon that was a bit too well done but still smelled delicious. As she contemplated the contents of the platters, Landry spoke.

"Guess you're kind of surprised to see me here." When Helen glanced up he was carving a thin sliver of melon. "Not as surprised as I am, though."

"He didn't press charges?"

Landry shook his head, tasted the melon, and set down his knife and fork. "Somehow he managed to talk the casino people into letting it go too. Well, I guess his wallet talked." He sneered.

"I don't know that you have any right to complain about it, seeing as you're free. For the moment." Helen pushed the bacon away and reached for the eggs, her curiosity piqued. What the hell did Kittrick have in mind, bringing them together like this? "That may change, in time."

Landry snorted. "What are you saying? That I killed my wife? I can prove I wasn't here when she died."

"That's good, Landry. I'm happy for you."

As though she hadn't spoken, he went on. "I was at the

airport in Las Vegas, renting a car, and I have papers to prove it. Just like I told the cops, and like I told Romie." He shoved himself away from the table in sudden anger. "I don't know why the hell I'm here, or why you're here. I got out of control Thursday night — that's all," he said as he prowled the room.

Just as Helen realized she might, in spite of her misgivings, be hungry after all, she heard the smooth rush of Kittrick's wheelchair making its way across the thick pile carpet. He pivoted around a corner that she assumed led to a bedchamber. The mechanism that propelled the chair was virtually silent, and the old man's fingers manipulated the controls with practiced ease. Hovering behind him was a third bodyguard, and the everpresent Louise came next, bringing up the rear with a clipboard in hand. She shoved thick glasses back up the bridge of her nose and peered myopically and indifferently at the other occupants of the room.

Kittrick maneuvered himself to the head of the table. Helen spooned scrambled eggs onto her plate. Landry, she noted, had abandoned his melon and stared fixedly out the window. Kittrick looked at them both for several moments before attempting to speak. His eyes shone large and watery in a wasted, pale face. Helen found herself studying those withered features for some resemblance to Carmel or even Wilbur — maybe the nose, or the shape of his head — she couldn't be sure, now. Wilbur buried himself in his UFO obsessions and behind growing layers of fat. Carmel had chiseled out a hard, mean facade. And Romie Kittrick's physical appearance was so shadowed by illness and age Helen had no clue what he used to look like. Except, she remembered, for that strange photograph taken in the jungle.

"Mr. Kittrick — I mean, Romie — I just want to say —" Landry coughed, cleared his throat.

"Shut up, idiot." Kittrick wheezed the words out, as if

blowing through blades of grass pressed together. His face darkened, but he waved away the proffered plastic mask and managed to go on. "You say nothing until I finish. Understand?"

"Yes, sir," Landry said meekly.

Kittrick looked at her, then, and a ghost of a smile wandered across his lips. "No, this old geezer hasn't lost his mind yet. I do have a reason for getting both of you in here." His gaze swiveled back to Landry. "Just remember, you young fool, that I can buy and sell you and that university you work for a dozen times over."

"Now, Mr. Kittrick, Ole Miss has nothing to do with anything here." He subsided again and fiddled with his melon.

Helen took a bite of her eggs as she watched the two men sparring, then said, "Mr. Kittrick, while I certainly appreciate your hospitality, especially in light of your recent loss, I can't say I understand this meeting."

Kittrick struggled with a handkerchief from his coat pocket, wiped at his eyes and handed the square of cloth to Louise. "I wanted you to get a good look at the man who killed my daughter."

Landry nearly spit out his food. With a choked sound he struggled up from the table, while two of Kittrick's men positioned themselves behind him. "You old sick fuck!" he gasped. "How the hell can you say such a thing? I wasn't even in Laughlin at the time!" The two men took a step closer to Landry but didn't touch him.

"Marc, I'm well aware of your alibi," Kittrick went on in a quiet voice. "I'm also aware of how much you hated my baby girl. Ms. Black, take a good look at this pup standing here," he said, moving his chair around the table until he was next to Landry. "My daughter decided, long ago, that she loved this little worm. Kittrick money put him through college, Kittrick money bought them their house, and Kittrick money set him up after the divorce." The old man seemed to gather strength from his own anger, his voice growing louder and clearer as he glared up at Landry. "My money, goddamn it."

"What makes you think I'd kill Carmel? Jesus, I wanted to talk her into seeing me again, trying to work things out between us!" Landry's plaintive cries turned into a frightened whine. Kittrick's bodyguards hovered close behind him. "Look, the knife, the way I was acting that night — I admit, I went a little crazy. But, but just listen! I'd just gotten into town and I'd been trying like hell to get Carmel to talk to me. I — well, I just went crazy." He looked from Kittrick to the bodyguards to Helen, his hands clenching and unclenching at his side, sweat beading on his forehead. "It didn't mean anything."

Without taking his eyes from Landry's face, Kittrick pulled a white envelope from a side pocket on his wheelchair. How the hell did he get it from the police? Helen wondered. He emptied the threatening missives out onto the table amidst the lace and coffee cups and silverware.

"I suppose these didn't mean anything, either," Kittrick said as Landry stared down in puzzlement at the sheaf of mutilated photographs. "Neither does your protesting that you still loved Carmel. What you loved — what you always loved — was the money. So do your little bimbos."

Landry paled. "You're not making sense," he mumbled.

"Oh, on the contrary, I think I'm making a lot of sense," Kittrick shifted with eagerness in his chair, his voice straining with excitement. Behind him, Louise made a mute gesture of concern. Like Helen, she'd heard the rasp in his voice. "Those pretty blonde debutantes who listen to you ramble on about Faulkner and Eudora Welty and all the rest of those literary monuments to laziness, then fall starry-eyed into your bed when you talk about how your ex-wife and her horrible family abused you and misunderstood you! What's the latest one — Sharon, is it? The one you call 'my rose of Sharon' when you fuck her?"

Landry, breathing heavily, slumped down into his chair. "How do you know about Sharon?"

Kittrick grinned and reached for his face mask. He took several breaths while Landry fidgeted in his chair. Finally he said, through the plastic, "Oxford is one of those small towns Mississippi is famous for, Marc. People often forget to lock their doors in a little college town like that. Don't they, boys?" The bodyguards remained frozen, expressionless, behind Landry's chair. Kittrick let the mask fall back down beside the oxygen tank. "Not to mention the way your little girlfriends like to talk. They're worse than football players in a locker room, long as they can find someone to listen to them."

Landry stood up, hands shaking, eyes deliberately averted from the ugly evidence spread out on the table. "I don't have to listen to this. I don't know what this little show is all about, old man, but I didn't kill your daughter." He shoved his chair away, knocking into one of the burly men behind him. Kittrick's bodyguard stepped aside just enough to allow Landry to move away from the table. "Why you dragged this — this woman into it, I don't know. My advice," he said to Helen, "is to get the hell away from the Kittricks. As fast as you can."

Romie Kittrick's chair whirred into life as he propelled it forward, blocking Landry's exit. "Just remember, pup. I can destroy you with one word. I'll destroy this alibi of yours, and then I'll ruin you. Remember that."

Landry's mouth quivered as though he would retort. Finally, with a feeble push at the wheelchair, he lumbered out of the suite, slamming the door behind him.

Helen waited until Kittrick made his way back to the head of the table and the bodyguards had dispersed before she asked, "Is this a normal breakfast with the Kittricks?" She helped herself to more eggs.

Kittrick wheezed mightily, but Helen's alarm disappeared when she realized he was laughing. Against all reason, against all logic, she too was enjoying herself hugely. Later she'd try to figure out why. For now, she was determined to find out why she'd been invited in the first place.

"Forgive me if I don't join you. My doctors have advised me against any food that tastes good." His face darkened again, and he reached for the mask. "Although right now there doesn't seem much point," he said after a couple of deep breaths of pure oxygen. "I have a son who's insane, believing every damn conspiracy theory you care to invent. I have a daughter — had a daughter — who's being shipped back in a box to Mississippi as soon as the police let her body go."

Helen's appetite disappeared. "Mr. Kittrick, I'm so very sorry for your loss." He waved his hand dismissively and she went on, "I really don't understand, though, why I'm here."

"I just told you. I wanted you to see my baby's murderer. And I want you to break that alibi and see that he gets what he deserves."

Helen's jaw nearly dropped. Did the old man think she'd agreed to work for Carmel? "Mr. Kittrick, I had no understanding with your daughter. I wasn't employed by her at any time."

"It was my baby's final wish. I'm going to honor that." He sighed, and the dangerously raspy noise rattled in his throat. "Ms. Black, in the last few weeks I have left to me, I have got to do something. Can you understand that?" He fumbled at the chair's controls again, and Helen inwardly cringed as he wheeled closer to her. "Carmel was a deeply unhappy woman. Always was. No matter how I tried to love her, she wouldn't let me. Wouldn't let Marc Landry, either. Or any of her other men. I've — I've got to do something for her, now, before I'm gone too." He leaned toward Helen, and she fought to keep from backing away from the tang of medicine and decay he exuded. "If she wouldn't let me when she was alive, then I'll do it now that she's dead."

He suddenly snapped his fingers. Louise reappeared, gathered up the photographs into the envelope and handed them to Kittrick. He gazed solemnly down at the package, then handed it to Helen. "The police have decided I could have these. Now I want to give them to you." He reverently placed the envelope in Helen's lap. Not sure what to say, Helen grasped the white envelope with both hands, wondering how he'd convinced the cops to let this go. He leaned back, his fingers tapping on the armrests of his wheelchair. "I know what it's like, to live under a cloud, feeling certain that death is near. I do have some idea, Ms. Black, of what you've gone through in the past year. Of how much you've lost."

Suddenly furious, Helen almost threw the envelope at him. "Did your little friends here" — she waved a hand at the two men lounging in the next room — "come to my house in Berkeley, too? What the hell do you know about my life?"

He went on as though she hadn't spoken. "I'm offering you a chance to go back to work. Real work, doing what you want to do, not this ridiculous cop-for-hire job you've been doing now for — what is it — eight, nine months? I have more than enough money to get you your office back. I can even send you some cases."

"In exchange for what?"

His lips worked furiously, and Helen feared for an intense moment that he would weep. "Just break that son of a bitch's alibi and put my daughter's murderer in jail. That's all you have to do." He pushed himself back, his face turned away, perhaps to hide his emotion.

All appetite gone, Helen stood up, still clutching the envelope. "Why me?" she asked, walking around the table until she stood next to Kittrick. "Why the hell didn't you find someone more — more reputable? I really want to know."

"Because you're here." His emotions in check again, he gave her a wry smile. "And because I'm certain you want to get back into investigative work very, very badly. All the more reason for you to bust your ass cracking this case open."

"I think you've got the wrong person, Mr. Kittrick." She dropped the envelope onto the table and pulled on her jacket. "Unlike Marc Landry, I'm not that easily bought and sold. Money isn't what's keeping me from going back to detective work." Immediately she cursed herself for even letting that much out. Kittrick wasn't the type of man you could make such remarks to without expecting consequences. Would he persist in following up on what she'd just said?

He shook with silent laughter. "No, no, you keep those." Without letting herself think about what she was doing, Helen took the envelope from him and slipped it into her shoulder bag. "Just do me the favor of keeping them and thinking it over for a couple of nights. Just until Tuesday, when you leave Laughlin. Let's just say you're humoring a dying man. How about that?"

Helen stared down at him and thought about the picture she'd taken from Wilbur, the picture that showed Romie Kittrick smiling with a bunch of soldiers in the jungle. "Gee, everyone has been showing me their photo albums since I got here. Your son had some pictures too. Did you know that?"

He snorted. "Unidentified flying objects, no doubt."

"And a few identified ones. Like a picture of you, for example. Early nineteen-eighties. It was an interesting setting, too. Looked kind of like a jungle. And it was a party, I think. Yes, lots of happy smiling soldiers. Do you remember that, Mr. Kittrick?"

By the time she let herself out of the suite a moment

later, Kittrick was choking for air and surrounded by his staff. Helen closed the door on the sound of oxygen being released from one of the red tanks and headed for the police station downtown.

Chapter Thirteen

Heather and Bud sat silently in uncomfortable looking chairs in the hallway. Helen assumed Richardson had required their presence. They both glared at Helen and Edna as the two women emerged from the room where Richardson had talked to them. Alison had seated herself on a padded bench on the other side of the room and was trying to look interested in the newspaper. She sighed, visibly relieved, and tossed the newspaper down on the bench

"Thank God you're out of there," she muttered. "I thought those two would lynch me for sure."

Helen glanced their way then smiled at Alison. "They're the ones who need to be afraid, actually," Helen said. "That gold chain most likely puts Bud in the room at the time of the murder. And Heather was gone all morning watching the fake gunfight, same as you and me and Aunt Edna and Uncle Loy. She can't provide him with any kind of alibi — not that she necessarily wants to, anyway."

"So you don't think they suspect me of anything, Helen?" Edna's hands twisted around the clutch of her handbag, and her voice trembled. Her eyes were red-rimmed and teary, with smeared makeup ringing the dark circles under her eyes. "Or your uncle?"

Helen thoughts strayed again to the conversation she'd had the night before with Uncle Loy. As Aunt Edna had slept on the bed behind them, she and Loy and Alison had talked quietly at the small table in the motel room for several hours, putting all the pieces together.

"The cops will be mad as hornets, I bet." Loy had folded and refolded his cap in his hands as he spoke just above a whisper, not wanting to wake Edna. "Why on earth didn't she talk to me about it?"

Helen smiled. "Let's face it, she was sure you were off chasing wine, women and song — not to mention the gambling — and were now stealing to indulge your vices."

"Goldurn it!" Alison and Helen had glanced at each other, amused in spite of the serious situation — it was the only thing approaching a curse she'd ever heard from her uncle. "We've been married almost forty years. You'd think she could trust me by now. Do I look to you like the kind of lowlife who'd behave like that?"

"Of course not, Uncle Loy. But right now we have to be ready to answer some tough questions tomorrow — at least, Aunt Edna will. Like how Bud and Carmel got into the room in the first place."

Loy shrugged. "Guess he just saw her drop that key and grabbed it up. You heard how she couldn't seem to keep her mind on things, kept losing it all the time, how we kept having to go back down to the desk and ask for the spare. She didn't make any secret of the room number, either." With a sigh he dropped the much-worn cap onto the table and folded his hands in front of him. "Wouldn't have been all that hard, all the fuss made over it."

"Although," Alison had interjected, "with the kind of pull Carmel seemed to have at the casino, I doubt she would have done it that way. I'll bet you it was Bud's idea, sneaking around and breaking into other peoples' rooms. Sounds about his speed, after all."

"So he killed that poor woman?" Loy asked.

Helen couldn't help a small, sad smile. Aside from Kittrick family members, and maybe not even those, she doubted seriously if anyone who'd known Carmel would have described her in such a way. She said, "I just don't know, Uncle Loy. Bud Gilley seemed to wear this necklace constantly, so it doesn't make sense it would have been in your room unless he put it there, or unless Carmel had it. But that doesn't mean he's the killer — it just means he was in your room on that day."

Loy glanced back over his shoulder at his sleeping wife. "And all this time she's thinking I stole it. I wish she'd come and talked to me about it. Now she's going to have to tell the police, and I don't think they'll be too pleased she kept this to herself."

"I think," Alison said then, "that we can guess why they were in your room. I mean, Bud made no secret of his affair with Carmel, not to his wife or to anyone else. Although I don't understand why they'd sneak into someone else's room."

"Convenience, maybe," Helen suggested, avoiding Loy's disgusted face. "And a sense of intrigue, although it is pretty immature. Maybe that's what Carmel liked about it, though — made her feel like a naughty high-school girl again."

She wondered if she should mention the photo obtained from Wilbur Kittrick, but decided against it. For now, they all had plenty to deal with.

"Does this Bud Gilley know you have the necklace, Helen?" Loy asked, looking at her fearfully.

"No. I'm certain he had no idea what I was talking about." And she'd said nothing that would lead him to Aunt Edna, either. Helen remembered glancing over at the sleeping woman, relieved that she'd revealed nothing. She could still see Bud's burly chest, his heavily muscled arms threatening to encircle her in the dark smoky hallway, the permeating odor of sweat mingled with liquor emanating from his body. "He'll know soon enough. Tomorrow morning."

She snapped back to the present and to Aunt Edna's round worried face. "I can't imagine," she was saying, "that the police would ever suspect Loy of harming a bug, even, let alone another person. What do you think?"

"I'm sure of it," Helen said, giving her aunt a comforting squeeze around the shoulders. "Didn't Lieutenant Richardson say you were free to go now?" For herself, Helen tried to shut out the flickers of anger and amusement she'd seen across Richardson's plain, expressionless face when Aunt Edna had begun her halting and confusing explanation of events leading up to this statement. Of course, Helen had known he'd be angry at the concealment, and that potentially Edna was in a huge amount of trouble — and she'd been both surprised and pleased at how gentle Richardson had been with her elderly aunt. Forced himself to be, really, she thought.

"I should have let Loy come with us." Edna sighed, passing her hand over her face and rubbing at her eyes. "Now he has to come all by himself, to make another statement to that nice young officer."

Not only that, Helen knew. Her relatives' plans of

leaving soon would now be put on hold while the police checked everything out, questioned Bud and Heather, waited for Loy to make his appearance at the station. Fortunately neither she nor Alison had finalized their departure time, although Helen was certain that Alison's patience was at an end. If she hadn't wanted to come in the first place, by now she was absolutely determined never to set foot in the town of Laughlin, Nevada, for the rest of her life.

"Why don't we wait for Uncle Loy to get here?" Helen said, steeling herself against the knife-edged stares of the Gilleys. She guided her aunt to a chair as far away from them as possible. "Richardson said he was on his way over."

Alison didn't join them. Instead, she slung her bag over her shoulder and cleared her throat. "Can we talk for a second, Helen?" she asked in a light, sweet tone — too sweet, Helen knew. Helen took a few steps away from her aunt, making sure Edna couldn't hear their whispered conversation. "I'm going back to the motel," Alison said, averting her eyes. "I've — well, to be honest, I've just got to get away from all this for a little while."

"Of course." Helen tentatively reached out to touch Alison, but she shied away. "Damn it, Alison, no one here gives a shit if I touch you."

"It's not that," Alison said angrily. She lowered her voice, glancing around the hall, then added, "I need some space right now, that's all."

"Space from me."

"A little breathing room. I mean, we're up to our necks in death and destruction and dysfunction right now — not to mention how you're behaving."

"How I'm behaving?" Helen almost laughed aloud, incredulous. "I'm trying to be here for my family. They've always been there for me, and now it's my turn. What the hell is wrong with that?"

"Mr. Gilley?" One of Richardson's underlings stuck his

head out from the office. Bud, his face blotched and sweating, even in the overly air-conditioned police station, pushed himself up from the chair and took a couple of wavering steps toward the room. His hand went protectively to his belly for a moment — maybe he was feeling a bit queasy. Not surprising, Helen thought, considering the weekend he'd had and his fear of the police. Helen guessed he probably had a hell of a hangover from all the beer he'd consumed last night, and perhaps he wasn't even too sure what had transpired between the two of them by the cigarette machine in the restaurant.

A broad flat circle wiped of all expression, Richardson's face appeared briefly behind the man who'd called for Bud. Not for the first time she admired Richardson's control and found herself wondering how he'd handle Gilley.

Heather, clutching her oversized shoulder bag tightly, made as if to follow him. "Just Mr. Gilley for right now, ma'am," the officer said as he put out a hand to stop her. The door closed quietly but firmly behind Bud, and Heather sat down with a plop.

"Hello? Earth to Helen?" Alison shook her head as Helen dragged her attention back to their conversation.

"I'm sorry."

"Yeah. Right." Alison smiled briefly, then adjusted the shoulder strap of her bag. "Is it some kind of addiction with you, Helen? You didn't get a fix of the usual drama for the last year or so, so now you're making up for lost time?"

"Alison, this isn't the time or place —"

"No, it never is." With that she turned and strode away.

"Is everything okay, Helen?" Edna asked, picking up her handbag to make room for her niece on the chair next to her.

"Yes," Helen said with a finality that discouraged any further discussion. She slumped down in the chair only to be roused up almost immediately by a cluster of people who burst in noisily from the street outside. They looked very much like anxious parents, Helen decided, making a hasty and embarrassing trip to the police station to bail out kids who were no doubt in for the whaling of a lifetime. After a few minutes of the newcomers' hovering and chatting nervously amongst themselves — they all seemed to know one another, perhaps from the same neighborhood — Helen realized that they weren't going to be separated, and she and Edna were in the way

That left the three chairs next to Heather Gilley. "I think we'll need to move, Aunt Edna." Helen got up and beckoned her aunt away. The moment they'd vacated, one of the couples slid into the empty seats with a grateful glance at Helen.

"You mean — oh, over there." Edna's face colored, and she pursed her lips in a frown. "I think I'll just go outside to wait for your uncle."

"It's going to be really hot out there," Helen called after her, but Edna simply waved back at Helen and scurried out of the building into the sunshine.

Great. She got to deal with Heather Gilley all by herself. At least Aunt Edna's presence might have restrained the other woman's fury, out of the ingrained respect for the elderly that seemed to be part and parcel of Southern ladylike behavior.

"All I want to know is if you fucked him."

Helen looked around in surprise. So much for ladylike, she thought. Heather seemed completely calm, her voice cool and rational in spite of the rather crude words coming out of her little pink mouth. Her face, devoid of makeup and strained from lack of sleep, showed no sign of emotion. Helen wondered if perhaps she'd already been drained of feeling when confronted with the truth of her husband's behavior.

"I beg your pardon?" she finally asked, stalling for time.

"You heard me, you fucking queer. Did you, or didn't you? That's all I need to know right now."

"I think you ought to be worrying more about Bud than about me, Heather."

"Don't you dare call me by my first name." Helen glanced over at the recent arrivals to the police station, but they were far too absorbed in their own troubles to take any notice of her conversation with Heather. "Just answer the question."

"Of course I didn't do anything with your husband. And you ought to be calling a lawyer right now, not worrying about what I did or didn't do last night."

Heather smirked. "Mr. Kittrick already took care of that. He promised me a lawyer would get here before the cops were done talking to us. Least he could do, I think. If that bitch was still alive, she could call him one. She's the one he wanted, after all." A single tear leaked down her cheek. Helen doubted she even knew it was there. "I know they're in there talking to him about his affair with Carmel Kittrick."

Shit. She really didn't know about the necklace, Helen realized. Hadn't she noticed it gone since the day of the murder? Probably too wrapped up in misery to think about details like tacky jewelry. "How long have you known about it?"

"Ever since the day we first met those damned Kittricks," Heather muttered. Suddenly she looked about to faint, then recovered and batted Helen's hand away. "That press conference — the way she flirted with him. And how she was with him on the plane. She kept getting him drinks and talking to him like I wasn't even there, sitting next to my own husband. She knew how to do it just right too. She knew when to back off and when to make the next entrance. I knew right then they were going to have an affair. I can always tell when he's ready."

"So it's not the first time," Helen said hesitantly, unsure if Heather would confide any further in her.

Heather barked out a short, sharp laugh, gaining the attention of one of the nervous parents across the hall for a moment. "Not by a long shot," she said. "Although I must say Carmel Kittrick was the only one who wasn't a complete empty-headed bimbo." She leaned back in the chair, her head softly bumping against the wall, her eyes closed. "So my husband is a complete shit. Big fucking deal. It's still better than what I left when I married him." She opened her eyes and looked at Helen as if daring her to contradict. "Better than making minimum wage at the grocery store and getting pawed over by a bunch of grease monkeys. That's all there was in my town. And now we have our own business, and a nice house with a pool." A smile crept over her lips. "I did that, you know. I'm the one who got the idea to start the fitness center, and now we have six locations. Bud is nothing without me, and he knows it."

"Friday morning, the morning we went to Oatman —"

"Of course I knew he'd be meeting her. Why else would he make such an elaborate thing out of not going with me? It's all part of the game, for him."

"Heather — sorry, Mrs. Gilley —" It felt ridiculous to be so formal, after what she knew about her husband. "Bud is in a great deal of trouble right now. I don't think you understand what's going on." How the hell was she supposed to explain it to her? Helen wondered.

The big blue eyes flew open, and she looked at Helen contemptuously. "Look, Bud didn't kill her. Why would he want to? She was rich, beautiful, and for some reason she wanted to fuck him. I guess she was bored. Why else would she put up with the way he makes love?" Heather shuddered, and Helen had a brief, disturbing image of the Gilleys in bed. "Assuming he could get it up and keep it up long enough for her."

Commotion at the other end of the hallway distracted them. "That must be the lawyer." Heather got up, wiped her cheeks and smoothed her dress. The lawyer strode purposefully down the corridor, trailing a couple of uniforms behind him. His tan was sunlamp perfect, and his hair was neatly tied back in a ponytail. He carried a slim attaché case under his arm. Heather shook his hand, and she pointed out the room where the police had taken Bud for questioning. One of the uniforms let him into the interrogation room, and Heather stood in the hallway, looking after him like a lost puppy.

At that moment Loy and Edna entered the station. They blinked, going from bright hot sunlight to the dim interior of the building, then looked around for their niece. Not wanting to break the momentum of conversation, Helen didn't signal them. Quickly she turned back to Heather. "How the hell did he get the key to my aunt and uncle's room? And why meet her there?"

Heather shrugged. "How the fuck should I know? Your aunt was always going around talking about her lost key. Bud probably just thought it would be a kick in the ass to screw in someone else's room — maybe that made it more fun. Besides, the Kittrick bitch probably needed some excitement in the relationship. Bud tends to get pretty boring pretty fast." She moved as far away in her seat from Helen as she could and fixed her gaze on the door as if she could see her husband through the walls.

"There you are, darlin'," Edna said with relief. Helen was pleased to see her clutching her husband's arm as if it were an anchor in a rough sea. Exposing Bud Gilley as the owner of the infamous gold chain had magically restored Loy back to pristine purity in his wife's eyes, and he beamed down at her from under the John Deere cap. "We thought we'd lost you."

Heather deliberately turned away from them, and Helen

gave up. No point in dragging out this interchange any longer — she wasn't likely to give Helen any further information, not with the aging couple standing right next to them. And nothing Heather said indicated she had any clue yet why the police wanted to talk to Bud, other than the fact he'd been cheating on her, hardly an offense the police were likely to bother themselves about.

An uncomfortable silence ensued. Edna opened her mouth once or twice, then closed it again. Loy carefully studied his shoes as if they'd become the most interesting objects in the universe. Heather finally grabbed her bag and moved to the end of the hallway, near Detective Richardson's office. Another officer came out from the depths of the station to confer with the group of frightened parents who followed him down the hall and around a corner.

Once the area was quiet again, Helen cleared her throat and stood up. "I think now that Uncle Loy is here I'll go back to the motel and see if I can find Alison."

"What? Oh my goodness, in all the excitement I clean forgot about her." Edna took Helen's hand in both of hers, effectively preventing her from leaving. "You tell that young lady I'm sorry to have pulled her into all this nonsense. She's been wonderful to me, absolutely the sweetest thing in the world."

"I will, Aunt Edna." Helen made a few other parting remarks, but her departure was interrupted when the door to Richardson's office swung open.

The lawyer emerged. He didn't look happy. "Mrs. Gilley, I'm afraid I have some bad news," he began.

"What, what?" Heather stood up. "Where's my husband?"

Bud came out next. His face was suffused with what she could only guess was enormous surprise. He stood awkwardly, his bulk framed in the doorway, and it took another moment for Helen to see that his arms were manacled behind him. Richardson gently pushed Bud along the hallway, while the other unnamed officer closed the door behind them. Bud Gilley's stunned gaze roved the hall, and Helen was certain that nothing he saw was registering. He even stared at Helen as though he were seeing a stranger. Helen wondered, as Bud shambled off down the hall, why they'd cuffed him. Had he tried to put up some sort of protest? He looked too sick and too shocked to argue, let alone physically arrest.

"Mrs. Gilley, they've charged your husband with murder. Mrs. Gilley, please wait —"

Richardson must have started reciting Miranda inside the room. Helen caught his words referring to obtaining legal representation right before Heather started to scream.

"Oh, God, no! Bud, please —" Heather reached out in a vain attempt to grab her husband's arm as he passed. Helen watched as her long nails clutched and pulled, leaving a small rip on the sleeve.

"Ma'am, we have to take him downstairs. You can talk to him later." Richardson neatly stepped between Heather and Bud, forcing her out of the way. "He'll be able to talk to his attorney in just a little while, but there are some procedures we have to follow right now."

"Does that include putting handcuffs on him?" Heather snarled at Richardson. She turned to the lawyer next and shoved him hard in the chest. He gazed down at her in surprise as he straightened his tie. "What kind of lawyer are you, anyway? I thought the Kittricks could afford the best!"

"Where they gonna take me?" Bud whimpered. His eyes leaked tears and his nose ran freely as he wept.

"He didn't do it, I know he didn't! Oh, Bud, don't leave me!" she wailed. Richardson steered Gilley quickly down the hall. Throughout this loud exchange, he'd stared at her blankly, blinking now and then at the woman screaming into his face. As the men moved away, he looked down in surprise at his torn shirt, as if wondering how that had happened.

Heather sank into a chair. A female officer, her face set in careful indifference, hurried over to where she sat. Heather looked up as she tried to help her to her feet, then pushed the other woman away. "Get away from me, you bitch!"

Helen winced, certain that Heather wasn't mourning the plight of her husband so much as her own helplessness. Going back to old and painful childhood memories, Helen could easily conjure up an image of what Heather's life must have been like before Bud Gilley came along. Pretty, uneducated and poor — nothing going for her but looks — Heather would have learned early on that her best bet, if she stayed in Mississippi, was to marry a man who could take care of her. Helen wondered if she'd met Bud at the grocery store she'd mentioned earlier.

"Oh, Loy, we have to help that poor woman," she heard her aunt say.

"Now, Aunt Edna, I think the last thing Heather Gilley wants is our assistance," Helen protested, laying a restraining hand on her aunt's arm. Now that her own marital troubles seemed cured, Edna clearly had nothing but good intentions toward Heather and the rest of the universe. How much of Helen's explanation of the origin of that gold chain had really sunk into her aunt's consciousness, anyway? Heather would know soon enough why the police had arrested her husband, and she wouldn't thank Edna or Helen for the information, either.

Uncle Loy took over. "Whyn't you go on back, Helen? We'll just sit and wait our turn with the police." He skillfully guided his wife to a seat, and Helen left them with a final promise of catching up later at the motel.

The lawyer was now sitting next to Heather and speaking softly to her, putting on his best bedside manner.

Heather was now icily calm as if her outburst at the police had drained her hysteria. She gave the lawyer a cold stare. "I don't care what you do, or how much money you get out of the Kittricks. You get my husband out or you'll regret it. Do you understand me?"

"Of course, Mrs. Gilley. That's why I'm here."

Helen gave her relatives one last glance before leaving the station. From where she stood, her aunt and uncle seemed a perfect portrait of marital bliss. With a pang she thought of Alison, whose fury had probably reached terminal status by now. Helen shoved the door open and nearly collided with someone coming into the station.

"Oops, sorry. Hey, Helen!"

"Shelley! What on earth are you doing here?" She stepped back inside and let the door shut on the hot air.

"I, uh, well —" Shelley's voice trailed off, and Helen saw her fair skin redden with shame. "I've got to talk to the police."

"Something else happen at the Saddle?"

Shelley shook her head and pursed her lips. For a startled moment Helen wondered if she was about to cry. Then it came out in a rush. "It's Nick. She's — she's disappeared."

Chapter Fourteen

"I'm sorry, ma'am, room twenty-three doesn't answer. Would you like to use our voice mail service to leave a message?"

Helen sighed and pressed her cheek against the glass of the phone booth. It felt unpleasantly warm, and her sweat broke out on her forehead. There had been no answer when she called from the police station, either, although she knew that Alison had caught a cab back to the motel at least half an hour ago. And the police station wasn't all that far from the motel — perhaps a ten-minute leisurely ride, at most.

"Yes, please." What the hell should she say? After

witnessing Alison's fury at her involvement in all that had happened since Carmel's death? After waiting for all the appropriate tones and beeps, Helen simply said she'd be back later than she'd expected.

The line went dead, with Helen still holding the receiver to her ear. Shelley, nervously tapping her hands on the steering wheel of the car, kept trying not to look at her. The guard finally gave up and turned impatiently toward her, reflecting twin phone booths in her opaque sunglasses.

Helen shoved the phone booth door aside and got into the car, closing herself in with a slam.

"Trouble in paradise?" Shelley asked as she started her truck.

Helen squirmed, ready with a sharp retort, but decided against it. There'd been no undertone of sarcasm in Shelley's voice, and she was clearly too worried about Nick to be trying to stir up trouble with Helen. "No," Helen answered simply. "How far to Sue's place?"

"Just a couple of blocks now." Staring in the side mirror, Shelley swerved the truck back into the street. Now that they were away from Laughlin's main street and its casinos, Helen saw that the town could have been any small suburb in the Southwest. "Damn, I wish those cops had just listened to me."

"There's generally a forty-eight hour wait required before they'll file a missing persons report. It hasn't been that long yet. Nick is probably just spending some time alone. She's been through hell the last couple of days."

Shelley's hands flexed on the steering wheel. Her knuckles were white. "That's exactly why she needs me right now. I know she does, Helen." She looked over at Helen as if daring her to challenge that assertion. "I can take care of her. She's never had anyone to do that her whole life."

Helen decided it was best not to respond, and she looked out the window. Afternoon heat bathed her arm as it rested in the open window, and they passed house after house fronted with bright green manicured lawns. It finally occurred to Helen what was missing.

"Where the hell is everyone?"

Shelley looked at her, her expression wiped flat by the sunglasses. "It's still Thanksgiving weekend. They're watching football games, or something."

"My God." It was hard to believe it was already Sunday and that two days ago she had been eating catfish instead of turkey. "Alison and I were going to leave tomorrow to avoid the traffic."

"Some vacation."

Helen thought briefly of how hard she'd had to work to make this trip — all the overtime, the protests from Alison, the schedule arrangements. "Shelley, Nick is not a minor. If she's been taking care of her mother all these years, like you say, she can take care of herself. She might just want to be alone right now."

Shelley made a face. "I just want to know she's okay. Don't you start laughing at me too."

"Never, Shelley." Helen subsided in the seat, uncomfortable with the realization that she, too, was curious where Nick was. It had nothing to do with altruism. She was worried about where Nick had gotten a gun, as well as where both Nick and Sue had been when Carmel was killed.

"We're almost there." Shelley turned the truck off the main road onto a side street.

Helen climbed out of the truck and surveyed the house. They'd left the neat, well cared for houses on the last right turn Shelley had taken. While this neighborhood was by no means lined with hovels, it definitely had a used look to it. The paint was older, muddier. Older cars sat in driveways instead of garages. There were people sitting on porches and kids playing in the street. And the houses themselves weren't all mirror images of each other, built along the same model lines in block after block after block.

Shelley sighed and took her glasses off. Her eyes were red from recent crying, although she'd been careful to remain cool around Helen.

Together they approached the front door. Sue's house was no better and no worse than any of the others, but Helen saw signs of creeping neglect. All the curtains were drawn. A couple of plants hanging from the front porch were shriveling to brown, and some of the newspapers piled near the front door had already faded into yellow under the Nevada sun. A single lawn chair, rusting and peeling, sat crookedly near the steps. A broom handle poked out from under it, nearly tripping Helen as she made her way up the steps. When she pulled it out of the way, cobwebs floated off the straw into a stray breeze. Shelley pulled open the screen door and knocked, softly at first, then several loud raps. "Nick? Nick?"

Helen went to the end of the porch. Behind the house sat a late-model sports car under a sleek gray vinyl cover. Helen wasn't sure of the make, but it was probably foreign and costly.

Shelley kept pounding. With her last effort, the door swayed open a thin crack.

The two women looked at each other. "Well?" Shelley asked, a ghost of a smile crossing her lips and breaking the tension in her face.

Helen smiled back. "Someone might be hurt, or sick, or in need of medical attention. You never know."

"True. We'd be neglecting our civic duty if we didn't go in."

The house smelled musty and stale. Helen left the front door cracked open, both to get air in and to facilitate a quick getaway, if necessary. Dust motes swirled in the sunlight as they moved through the foyer into the living room. While it was too murky for Helen to see much of the house, she noted how bare it seemed, the walls naked of any adornment or hangings. A room that opened off to her right — the dining room, maybe — was completely empty. Beyond that room she could see through to a kitchen, barren except for a refrigerator.

The living room at their left held a sofa and a television set. The TV screen buzzed a grayish white at them, lighting the rest of the room with an eerie glow. Shelley saw him first. Hef lay sprawled on the couch, snoring. One foot was bare, and the other bore a dirty sock. His pants were unzipped but still hung decently over his hips. He wore no shirt, and Helen saw the shallow rise and fall of his chest with relief. She was surprised to realize that she'd expected much worse. Maybe not so strange, considering all she'd witnessed over the past couple of days.

Shelley stepped closer to the sofa. A soft clinking by her feet came from bottles and cans strewn around the floor. "Well, he's out of it," Shelley muttered. "We could empty the place, and he'd never know what hit him."

But Hef startled them both by jerking awake. "What — who —" He tried to get up only to slip back down awkwardly on the cushions. "Shelley? What the fuck is going on?" He wiped both hands over his face, coughed twice and squinted up at them, blinking hard and wincing as Helen found a wall switch and flooded the room with light. "Jesus, why'd you do that?"

"What are you doing here, Hef?" Shelley crouched down next to him, shoving debris aside. Helen stayed in the background. She was the outsider here, and Shelley was more likely than she was to get information from him. "This is Sue's house. You shouldn't be here."

"I have a key. She gave it to me." His voice came out in a plaintive whine, and he cleared his throat again. "I've been practically living with her, anyway." He looked at

Helen. "You're from the, the, what the fuck was it? The Winners' Circle, right? Shelley, either tell me what the fuck is happening or get the hell out."

Shelley straightened up with a glance at Helen. "We're looking for Nick. We thought she might be here."

Hef lay down again, covering his eyes with his arm. "Ask the cops. They'll know where she is."

"Damn it, you big fuck, don't you give a shit about her?" Shelley's patience broke, and she grabbed Hef by the arms and pulled him upright. Hef pushed away from her into the cushions. Helen stood ready to jump in — at any moment Hef would shake out of it enough to do some damage.

But Shelley had rage on her side. She leaned in close, glaring and breathing hard. "Nick is gone," she said quietly, enunciating each word with excruciating care. "Got it? She ran away. I don't know where the hell she is."

"So how am I supposed to know? Nick and Sue both, they're both totally nuts. Nick'll probably do herself in one day. Sue probably would have done herself in eventually. If she hadn't tried to play hero yesterday."

Helen flinched at the sharp crack of Shelley's palm hitting Hef's face. A couple of drops of blood stretched into a thin trickle of red that formed and spilled from the corner of his mouth. He put a finger to his lips and grinned. "That'll cost you your job, bitch," he muttered.

"Like hell! Just because you're some has-been football star that screwed his way to being the Kittrick whipping boy doesn't make you God. Besides, high-and-mighty Carmel stuck you out here in the desert to run her little show because you couldn't cut it with the big boys in the office." She took a step closer to him. "Probably couldn't cut it in bed with her anymore, either. Is that why you beat on Sue once in a while? Can't get it up so good now?"

The grin faded from his face. "That'll cost you too."

Helen stepped forward. "It's not going to cost anyone

anything. If you try anything I'll say you tried to hit Shelley."

He smirked, pulled his hand away from his face, and looked down at the blood. "Should've known you two would stick together." He belched, scratched his bare stomach. "I don't know where the kid is, and I don't care."

Shelley turned away in disgust. "We'll go to her room," she said to Helen. "Maybe we can find something useful there." Behind them, as they went down a dim corridor, they heard Hef moving around in the living room, and there was a sudden burst of noise from the television set as he apparently switched channels. Shelly stopped outside a closed door and touched Helen's shoulder. "Sorry about that, I mean, the way I acted in there. I was totally out of line."

"Maybe," Helen acknowledged. "But as far as I can tell, you're the only person who seems to give a damn about her."

Helen could just make out the other woman's blush in the dim light. "Thanks for backing me up, anyway." With that she opened the door to the room before them.

Unlike the rest of the house, this room had some sense of personality. Posters lined the walls — mostly of currently popular rock stars, but one of the solar system and another of an advertisement for a planetarium in Los Angeles. Nick had kept her room scrupulously neat, almost too neat, as if making up for the rest of the house. The bed was carefully made, corners tucked in, pillows aligned at the head. "Nothing like my room when I was her age."

Helen nodded absently as she went to the windows and pulled the curtains aside. The windows faced west, and sunlight streamed in. Not a stray pair of shoes or a tossed aside shirt or a messy pile of schoolbooks was to be seen here. Helen headed for the closet, but had no luck there, either. Shoes lined up neatly on the floor, clothes folded and put on shelves, skirts and dresses hung next to pressed jeans on padded hangers — it seemed too perfect. "Maybe she was making up for how messy the rest of her life is. Especially her mother."

Shelley shrugged joined Helen at the closet. "Kinda sad, isn't it?" She ran her fingers over the maroon tunics hanging at the end of the closet. Helen recognized them as the same worn by maids at the Saddle. "She did odd jobs a lot at the casino, including cleaning and waitressing — mostly filling in for that stupid mother of hers when she was too strung out about the fine specimen of manhood in the living room to give a shit." Shelley's voice broke on the last words, and Helen saw her wipe a tear away from her cheek.

"Don't worry, Shelley. I know we'll find her. And Nick is tough. She's a survivor if I ever saw one. She probably just needed some time to sort things out on her own." Helen sat down next to Shelley on the bed.

"I knew," Shelley gasped, fighting back tears, "I knew it was a mistake for me to get so attached. But after my lover left me a few years back —" She sighed again and shook her head. "Robin just couldn't take it, when I came out. She wanted to stay closeted forever, and I refused to live that way. So I've been alone a long time, out here in the middle of nowhere. Then I met Nick. I tried not to hope for anything, but it sort of snuck up on me. I know, stupid, right?"

Helen decided that silence was better than any superficial words of comfort. She laid her own hand over Shelley's until the other woman's tears subsided, then went back to the closet. She flipped on the overhead light. There was something not quite right there, and she stood before the orderly rows of clothes and shoes before it struck her.

"Wait a minute." Helen got down on her hands and knees. No, it wasn't just a trick of the light — the carpeting did look slightly different here. "Take a look at this." She pointed at the back of the closet, where the nap of the ugly orange rug had a rougher look. Running her hands over the pile, Helen found the seam that edged the break in pattern and pulled hard. The carpeting came up without too much effort. "I'll be damned," she said as she tossed the square over her shoulder.

The manila folder lay precisely in the center of the plain wood floor where Nick had cut the carpet and made a hiding place for it. Shelley grabbed it before Helen could protest, and a thin pile of photographs slid out onto her lap.

"Holy shit," Shelley breathed. "What the hell was she doing with this crap?"

Helen recognized the work. She'd seen one of the same series of photos on Friday night, during her visit to Wilbur's shrine of paranoia. And the subject was the same, too. Here were Carmel and Hef in varying poses of intimacy, framed against the windows of the Saddle's unglamorous rooms. It still seemed unlikely that Carmel agreed to trysts in such unsophisticated surroundings. But maybe it wasn't so far-fetched after all, and the whole idea of being in such a place for such a meeting had a thrill of its own for her. The excitement of doing the unexpected, the mildly risky, probably did add a bit more spice to the encounter for her.

"I know where she got them," Helen said as she took the pictures Shelley proffered. "Carmel's brother, Wilbur." Shelley's face creased in puzzlement, then hardened as she realized who Helen was talking about. Without waiting for her to comment, Helen offered a brief description of Wilbur's intent to bring about his sister's ruin by means of his incriminating documentation. "And if he's had any contact at all with Nick beyond these photos, then maybe she figures his hideout in the desert is a good place to be right now."

Shelley scrambled up awkwardly from where she'd been kneeling on the floor next to Helen. "Let's go, then." She started to take the photograph Helen was holding, but Helen moved away.

"Wait a minute." Helen stared down at the black-and-white image, recalling the similar picture of Wilbur's she had stashed away at the motel with her luggage. "Now I can see who that is in the doorway. It's Sue."

Shelley peered over her shoulder. "Jesus, I think you're right. Do you think — I mean, maybe Sue's the one who —"

"Doesn't prove a thing." Helen got up and handed Shelley the photograph. "Let's get going."

She made Shelley wait long enough for her to place one more call to the motel from Sue's house. As the phone rang with still no answer from Alison, Helen decided not to leave another message. Maybe Alison had hooked up with Aunt Edna and Uncle Loy by now, or she was at the pool, or somewhere else. Surely Alison would understand that Helen had to see it through, especially when Nick was involved —

"Hello?"

"Alison. Jesus Christ, I've been trying to reach you all afternoon! Is everything okay?" Then, when there was only silence, "Alison, what's going on?"

"Helen, I — I can't explain over the phone. Just get back here."

"Is it Aunt Edna? Is she all right?"

"Yes, yes, your aunt and uncle are fine. Look, Mrs. Tilson is dead."

Helen froze. "How?"

"Looks like natural causes. I just think — I think you ought to be here. They found something."

"That she's not who she said she was," Helen said, remembering the newspaper clippings she'd found in Mrs. Tilson's handbag on Friday in Oatman, before Carmel was murdered.

"I'm not even going to ask you how you knew about that. I have had enough, and I need you to come back now."

"All right. I'll be there as soon as I can."

Shelley was waiting out in the truck. Helen got as far

as the living room, where Hef was slouched on the sofa watching an old black-and-white movie on the TV, a recently opened bottle of something in one hand and a remote in the other. Helen paused at the entrance to the living room. "We think we know where Nick is now. Will you be staying here, Hef?"

He swung the bottle vaguely in her direction in a kind of salute. "Don't know. As long as Sue's liquor holds out, I guess."

Helen ventured into the room and perched on the end of the sofa. Hef turned bleary red eyes to her, then fixed his gaze back on the pair of dancers — maybe it was Fred and Ginger — gliding around the screen to a tinny dance tune from the thirties. "You talked about Sue being crazy. Does that mean you think she killed Carmel?"

He laughed, more of a strangled snort, really, and took another swig from the bottle. "Hell, I figured she did it. I never told her, you know, that I loved her. Never did that. No, sir." He frowned as the dancers melted into a romantic embrace. "She was just a convenience when Carmel wasn't around, you know? And I never said different."

"How noble of you." Helen watched him as he set the bottle down on the floor and slouched deeper into the sofa. "So why the fuck are you here in her house, Hef?"

"Shit, I don't want to have to deal with her old man! Bastard should just go ahead and die — been hanging on for years with his fucking oxygen tanks and wheelchairs." He coughed and spat into a paper towel. "Way he operates, he probably knows every guy the bitch screwed since high school." As Helen got up to leave he called after her. "I didn't do it, you know? Didn't kill her. Wouldn't have done that."

Helen let the door slam on words and hurried down the steps to the truck. Shelley already had the engine running. "Look, Shelley, I can't go with you tonight. There's something I have to take care of. It's very important." Her stomach sank. She knew Shelley was disappointed, but Alison's words had felt like an ultimatum. "I don't think Nick is in danger. She's a grownup. The police would say the same thing I'm saying to you. Just go home, sit tight, and wait a little while."

"Tell me where this Wilbur guy is. I'll go find it myself."

Helen sighed. If Shelley had been angry enough to try to pick a fight with Hef, she had no business running off after a conspiracy nut armed with God knows what kind of firepower. She had some ability to control Wilbur with the threat of Romie Kittrick coming down on him. It would be much safer to persuade Shelley to calm down and wait a bit. "Look, if she hasn't shown up by tomorrow afternoon, I'll take you there myself. Then if nothing else turns up you can file a missing persons report."

Shelley drummed her fingers on the steering wheel a moment. "Okay. Fair enough. Like you said, Nick is a survivor. I just want to be sure she's safe."

"Me too." They sped away in a cloud of dust and gravel.

Chapter Fifteen

Mr. Tilson was waiting for her by the swimming pool when she left Alison. The sun was going down. Orange-red hues beamed into the impossibly bright blue water of the pool, where a few children, watched over by an exhausted mother, splashed and laughed in the shallow end. Mr. Tilson sat, impeccably dressed as usual, next to the diving board, moving his feet back and forth beneath the water. Pants legs rolled up, socks and shoes sitting neatly at his side, he looked like an executive taking a short break from the demands of business.

Without speaking Helen sat next to him, cross-legged on

the warm stones. Now and then a cool breeze from the hills, picking up speed as it crossed the river less than a mile away, blew through her hair. She reached down and, for lack of anything better to do with her hands, began plying her fingers in the water. Mr. Tilson glanced at her briefly then went back to his contemplation of his feet.

"Marla used to love to swim," he said in his usual soft voice. "She grew up in Pass Christian, on the gulf. Used to have a fishing shack, her old man did, take her out on his boat all the time. Me, I never did pick it up until she insisted we get a pool built in our backyard."

"Mr. Tilson, I'm so sorry. So sorry about your wife." Helen sighed. All she seemed to be doing lately was offering condolences for others' losses. Not much of a Thanksgiving weekend for anyone, as it turned out. She glanced up at the room where Alison waited for her. Only ten minutes ago she'd made hasty explanations to her, trying to get her to understand her concerns about Nick.

"You didn't answer the phone. I did try to call," Helen had said while Alison stood near the door, arms folded in what was becoming a very familiar sign of unhappiness.

"I was somewhat occupied," Alison said, her face and her voice equally stony. "Mrs. Tilson passed out downstairs, in the lobby. The ambulance took forever to get here, and until we found Mr. Tilson we didn't know how bad she was."

"Some kind of cancer?" Helen asked, flinging her jacket on the bed. "That would be my guess. All that pain medication I saw her carrying around — she had to be pretty near the end."

"Bone cancer." Alison had nodded, crossing the room and lying down on the bed. "Her husband refused to let them take her to a hospital, then the motel manager almost got into a fight with him, insisting — God, it was horrible, Helen. I think she must have died right there on the floor while they were fighting."

Looking at the man sitting next to her, Helen found it hard to believe that Tilson had stood fighting over his dying wife. He turned and saw her gaze.

"She told me you knew about us," he said. "That you saw the clippings in Oatman."

"She dropped her handbag when she was looking for her pills."

Abruptly he got up, shaking first one foot then the other. Helen followed him to one of the lounge chairs and waited while he put his shoes back on. "Let's go for a walk."

Helen looked at him in surprise. "Mr. Tilson, don't you think we should —"

"I know what I'm doing. We need to talk."

The casino strip was just lighting up. Neon flickered and flared in the dying sun, flashing bright primary colors against the soft beige and tan of the desert and deep purple brown of the hills. Tilson's eyes were red and swollen. How long had he been grieving? she wondered. Months? Years? Bone cancer moved quickly through the body, she knew, and apparently Marla Tilson had chosen not to undergo any extensive treatment.

As if reading her thoughts, Tilson sighed and said, "I didn't want her to die in any hospital. She said she'd had more than enough of hospitals and would rather go quick than be in a bed with a lot of tubes and machinery all around her."

"When was she diagnosed?"

"A year after our son was killed." Tilson coughed harshly and cleared his throat — hiding his emotion, Helen was sure. "It was like the last awful thing that could happen. I didn't think anything could hurt worse than my boy's death, but getting that news from the doctor just about did me in."

They walked in silence for a few minutes after that. Helen saw where they were headed but said nothing as they entered the walkway next to the river. Just ahead was the Silver Saddle.

She pulled her jacket closer around her and felt the folded white envelope crinkling in the inside pocket. "She sent those photographs, didn't she?" Helen asked. "The copies of that newspaper picture."

Tilson smiled at her. "Marla said you were smart. She was pretty sure you had it figured out, after you hung onto those clippings."

Helen shrugged. "Looked like they were from the same newspaper, that's all — and the date was the same as the story about your son."

Tilson and Helen sauntered onto the walkway. Other evening strollers were out, most of them smiling and laughing in groups, a few couples looking intensely at each other in either romantic obsession or argument mode. To them, Helen wondered if she and Tilson looked like another peaceful, calm couple taking a constitutional between gambling sessions. Not very likely, perhaps — Tilson was black and elderly and conservative, while Helen was anything but.

"Marla never quit blaming the Kittricks for his death. I think it was some of the kids on the other team, myself, but all she could see was that her baby, her one and only child — our one and only child — died at one of those damned fish places." He choked off his words and quickly went to stand by the railing, staring into the river. Helen joined him.

"Of course, we only got this trip," he went on at last, "because those damned Kittricks thought that would make us keep quiet about the whole thing. Family restaurant, right? Perfectly safe for kids, never any trouble."

"I did kind of wonder why you were there as guests, not winners."

He snorted in disgust. "Old Romie Kittrick had some idea, I guess, that he could make it up to us. He had his insurance people give us a settlement, kept sending sympathetic guys in suits to talk to us. Even helped with some of the medical bills for my wife. Marla had some notion of finding a way to get back at them, somehow, on this trip."

"Then they've watched you all this time?"

He shook his head. "They've been following us. Well, not exactly following. More like keeping tabs, especially since Marla tried to get into the Kittrick offices in Natchez. They let it go — didn't press charges, even when Marla outright accused the Kittricks of killing her child."

"You mean this whole contest thing was rigged?" Helen leaned over the railing with him. The sun had at last dropped behind the hills, and the river ran dark and silent below them.

"Why not? Call it a consolation prize," he said wearily. "I'm sure all their hotshot attorneys thought this was a lot better than being sued for damages."

Helen looked away from him, incredulous. Even given the sickening family dynamics she'd already witnessed among the Kittricks, the cold cruelty they showed to each other, she found it hard to believe this story. Possibly Tilson was telling himself this, just to get through the amazing series of bitter tragedies he'd suffered in the past few years — and now that was compounded by the death of his wife, literally in front of his eyes.

"Why do you find that so hard to believe?" She could no longer see his face in the darkness, but his voice rang out deep and bitter. "People with a lot of money, big companies with power — what's so strange about those kinds of people equating human life with dollar signs?"

"It's not that I find it hard to believe. I've just seen far too much of it on this holiday weekend." Helen felt for the envelope in her jacket and quietly pulled it out. Tilson didn't notice what she was doing — his face was turned toward the hills beyond. "Mr. Tilson, there's something I have to do, someplace I have to go."

He stiffened beside her and stood away from the railing. "The — the police?"

"What? No, no, not the police. Mr. Tilson, believe me, I have no intention of repeating anything you've told me." Helen put the envelope back into her jacket and reached out to take his hand. "I appreciate your honesty this evening. And I'm truly sorry about your wife."

He held her hand a moment, then shook it. "At least it's all finished, now. Marla, my boy — there's nothing left for me to lose. To hurt over."

"What will you do now?"

He dropped her hand. "Go home. What else is there?"

She left him standing at the railing. Helen went ahead on the walkway, past the lights of the casino, past the site where she'd seen Wilbur Kittrick two nights ago. She headed directly to the penthouse elevator of the Saddle.

"Excuse me." It wasn't Shelley, of course, not tonight. This was a man who looked to be about sixty. A heavy head of white hair bushed out over a weathered face. "I'm afraid you're not allowed up there, ma'am."

"Could you call up to Mr. Kittrick's suite and tell him Helen Black is here to see him?"

"Well —" He looked at her, puzzled, then led the way back to the registration desk. "Wait right here." Helen watched as the guard conferred with the desk clerk. The young woman glanced her way with recognition in her eyes, nodded and reached for a phone. The guard motioned her over as the woman completed her call. "Sorry to keep you waiting like that, miss," he said, escorting back across the lobby.

"Not a problem. I know you have rules to follow."

He smiled at her gratefully as she stepped into the elevator. Moments later she was striding alone down the hall to the Commodore Suite. One of the expensively suited Kittrick bodyguards opened the door for her.

She found Romie Kittrick sitting in his wheelchair on the patio. Far below the river was quiet and dark. Kittrick's chair whirred, and he turned to face her. "I take it you've decided to accept my offer?"

"Well, now, that's a bit of a problem." She leaned against the wall and studied his face in the dim light. The darkness was kinder to him than daylight. He looked relaxed, composed, almost well. Then she saw the plastic mask come up. "I'm afraid I'm not going to be able to deliver what you requested."

"What do you mean? That damn weasel Landry lied to the police, he lied to me — me, of all people."

"That may be, but he didn't send these photographs in the mail to your daughter." She tossed the white envelope into his lap. He fumbled for it briefly, then it slipped through his fingers onto the balcony. Helen bent over to retrieve it, then placed it into his hands. "It wasn't Landry," she repeated.

He moved the wheelchair so that he was sitting in the light from his rooms. With his face twisted in fury, he looked down at the envelope. "What the hell are you talking about?"

Helen shrugged. "I'm giving these back to you. They're of no use to you now."

"Then who did this? Who sent these to my little girl, if not that selfish monster Landry?" He threw the envelope back at Helen. It hit her in the face, and she awkwardly batted it away.

"The person who sent them . . . Believe me, Mr. Kittrick, it wasn't Marc Landry. It was a person who represents no danger to you." She picked up the envelope.

"Then who? Damn it, woman, I have a right to know!" He thumped on the armrests of the wheelchair and choked in his rage. "Talk to me," he gasped.

Helen groped for the oxygen tank, then shoved the

mask over his face and turned a valve that she hoped was the right one. A louder hiss of oxygen rewarded her efforts, and his breathing eased after a few moments.

"Should I call Louise, or one of the others?" Helen finally asked.

He shook his head. "No." He sighed, letting the mask fall to his chest. "No, I'll be all right."

Helen pulled up one of the lounge chairs on the balcony. "You're right, Mr. Kittrick. You do have a right to know about this." She looked down at the river. Was Mr. Tilson still down there?

Kittrick remained silent throughout her recitation of the facts she'd learned earlier that evening. "I knew that woman would make trouble for us one of these days," he said when she'd finished. "Why that whole terrible thing had to happen at a Romie's I'll never know. Of course," Kittrick went on, "it was a tragedy. But that's why we had to keep an eye on them. Marla Tilson was becoming such a nuisance, and the press loves to see a businessman accused of wrongdoing."

"Did you know Marla Tilson was dying?"

He shrugged. "What was there for us to do? The poor woman had terminal cancer. We'd managed to follow her movements after that time she tried to break into the offices —"

"Not to mention arranging for them to become guests of the Kittricks here in Laughlin. Right?"

His mouth twisted. "Poor old Tilson. The man must be crazy with grief." He tapped a finger on his chin. "Maybe we can do something for the man. Set up a grant or something in his son's name — I can get Louise on it right away —"

Suddenly the room felt overheated, in spite of the cool autumn air flowing in through the open doors. The closeness of the room, the lingering scent of the medicines Kittrick had splayed all over the suite, nauseated her.

"Ms. Black?" Kittrick was propelling his chair across the blue carpet. "We still have a deal, you and I."

"Not one I know of." Her hand was on the doorknob, but she waited to hear what he'd have to say.

To her surprise the old man chuckled. "You still want to set up shop as a private eye, and I still want to find out who killed my baby girl. Sounds to me like a match made in heaven."

"We're finished, Kittrick. I'm leaving tomorrow morning."

Tilson was nowhere to be seen when she made her way back to the walkway. There were only a few intrepid walkers and joggers on the pavement as she took the envelope in her hands. She took out the single picture of Kittrick surrounded by soldiers and put it in her pocket. No one paid her any attention as she took out the mangled photographs and tore them into small pieces. In small handfuls she let the fragments drop into the water and float away.

Chapter Sixteen

"See, I told you — there's nothing wrong with it."

Loy steered Edna through a cluster of people gathered at one of the gaming tables at the Silver Saddle. Helen and Alison followed close behind, threading their way around the edges of the small crowd.

"Now, tell me what this game is again?" Helen heard Edna say. The elderly woman's face was slightly flushed, and her lips pressed together grimly. But Helen could see, by the set of the woman's jaw, that her aunt was determined to prove to herself once and for all that her husband wasn't wasting his social security checks on wine, women and song. His arm protectively encircling his wife's plump shoulders, Loy gestured at the table and began to explain the rules of the card game being played out before them. During his monologue, Edna gave a couple of surreptitious glances at two women who leaned over the green felted table, then looked over at her husband. The pair were dressed in low-cut silky blouses, revealing a fair amount of cleavage, although the skin that showed was on the leathered side — too many hours at the hotel swimming pool, over a period of many years, Helen surmised. Their makeup, lacquered on as if with a trowel, was impeccable, although Helen feared a match lit nearby might send them both up in flames. Skin-tight spandex tights in vivid primary colors completed the look.

Edna pursed her lips and looked away. Was she about to expound on the temptations of painted trollops in this city of sin? Helen wondered. But she remained silent and turned her attention back to her husband. Loy showed no signs of wanting to play this particular game, Helen saw with relief — he was merely trying to show his wife the harmless fun to be had at the casino. And the two women who'd so engaged her aunt's attention took no notice of Loy or any other man at the gaming table. Their glistening eyes were fixed on the cards, their long, polished nails snicking softly on the polished wood that lined the table.

"Okay, now watch this —" Loy, absorbed in the drama unfolding before them, never saw the two women leaning so provocatively across the table. When she saw that her husband's eyes never strayed to the bountiful display of flesh right in front of him, Edna visibly relaxed and looked in the direction Loy pointed.

Helen sighed with relief. While she seriously doubted her aunt would ever feel completely happy about her husband's newfound interest in gambling, at least Aunt Edna seemed to have let go of the notion that Uncle Loy was frittering away the family's meager savings on a crap shoot. Watching them together, Helen was certain that Uncle Loy was much more taken with the spectacle of it all — the glowing lights, the sound of croupiers calling out their patter, the tinge of excitement and intrigue in the air. More than anything else, perhaps, a casino evoked the promise of possibilities, Helen decided. She leaned, watching and thinking, against one of the faux marble pillars that gave the illusion of grandeur to what was essentially no more than a big warehouse. Yes, perhaps that's what drew her uncle to this scene — that tantalizing hint of potential in the smoky air. The next roll of the dice, or the next play of cards, or one more quarter in the slot machine would bring the riches that would enable one of these people to create a whole new life.

"Looks like she's going to be okay," Alison murmured. She touched Helen gently on the shoulder. "I was worried there for a minute. Did you see those two women, the ones with peroxide hair?"

"I know, but see — Uncle Loy doesn't even know they exist." Now one of the women jumped up and down, sending her breasts into a lively jiggle, as her friend swept up a handful of tokens indicating a small victory. "And he's not trying to play. I think he just likes the excitement."

"You don't think he really has a problem with all this, do you?" Alison asked.

Helen shook her head and moved away from the pillar as her relatives backed away from the table. "No. Uncle Loy is fine. Besides, they're going back to Tupelo in a couple more days. He'll be surrounded by tractors and trucks and church on Sundays again. Not much of this kind of temptation around there."

Loy, his hand still on his wife's elbow, beamed at the two younger women as he guided Edna toward them. "We're going to go take a look at the slot machines for a few minutes." His hand emerged from his pocket with two rolls of coins — one of nickels, one of dimes. "Y'all want to come try it?"

Edna, a forced smile on her face, held her arms protectively to her chest and said nothing. "No, thanks, Loy."

You two need a chance to get away from it all, and you certainly don't need any chaperones," Helen said. "Why don't we meet you in — let's see — a couple of hours, over at the coffee shop at our motel?"

Loy nodded enthusiastically. "That'll be fine." He hugged his wife and planted a kiss on her cheek while Helen stared in amazement. Of course she knew her uncle loved her aunt dearly, but it was a bit of a shock to see him make such an open and public display of affection. She couldn't ever remember seeing him behave this way before in all the years she'd been close to them. No wonder Aunt Edna looked so surprised, and so worried.

"See you there." Loy began to unwrap the roll of dimes as the couple walked away, Edna glancing at him suspiciously as he gestured animatedly toward the nearest row of slot machines.

At Helen's side Alison chuckled. "I don't think they're going to need us baby-sitting them for a while," she said. "Maybe we should go back and pack up our things."

"Eager to get out of here? Why, Alison, dear heart, I can't imagine why," Helen said as they left the tables and headed for the doors leading to the river path. "That was sweet of you to offer the car to them. They act like they're going on a date, don't they?" One of the receptionists looked up with a brief smile of recognition as they walked by, then bent her head back to her computer monitor as she spoke into a telephone. "Besides, according to Detective Richardson, we aren't going to be able to leave until Wednesday. And this is only Monday afternoon."

Helen held the door open for Alison and caught the other woman grimacing in disgust. "Why the hell do we need to stick around that long?"

"Because, as he told us more than once, he needs to get a deposition from me tomorrow morning, and all the flights out are filled up until Wednesday morning. I just won't feel right if I don't at least wait until I see my aunt and uncle safely on that plane before we drive out of here." Helen's temper flared. "Alison, you're behaving as though I planned all this — from Carmel's murder to Bud Gilley behaving like a Neanderthal to Nick disappearing. What the hell is wrong with you?" Her voice dwindled to an intense whisper as the usual steady stream of people surged around them. "So I got partially involved, through no fault of my own. So what? I was in the wrong place at the wrong time to avoid this one. Enough already."

To Helen's chagrin a tear streaked across Alison's cheek. It glittered for a moment in the sunlight before Alison wiped it away and went to the railing on the path that overlooked the Colorado River. She turned with a rueful smile to Helen when she joined her at the railing.

"In spite of how it looks, Helen, I do know that. I guess I've just been so scared these last few days."

Helen resisted the urge to cover Alison's hands with her own. She stared out over the water, which sparkled as it tumbled down the narrow rocky passage that led a winding path to the mountains. "It's perfectly understandable, Alison. I mean, we've seen nothing but death and violence and terrible situations since we got here —"

"I know it's going to sound weird, or callous, but what I've really been scared of is losing you, Helen."

Helen's fingers closed around a pebble. She toyed with it for a moment — its surface, worn smooth by the elements, was hot on her skin from the hours of heat and light it was exposed to out here — then tossed it into the river below. "I'm not going anywhere. I'm here, right now, with you. Doesn't that count for anything anymore?"

Alison shrugged. "Maybe I'm still caught up in the way I used to live. When I was married, I mean."

"I don't understand."

She turned around so her back was against the railing and squinted up at the sun. "I was the model suburban housewife, remember? My world revolved around decorating our barn of a house and cleaning women and dinner parties for Bob's clients."

"Except for when your husband beat you." Helen spoke softly, trying to take the sting out of her words, but Alison flinched away from her. "Are you telling me that's part of the plan too? All that surface perfection covering up abuse?"

"No, it's not that. It's just — well, I'm trying so hard to live differently now. To not fall into the old patterns where getting hurt is normal."

"And you are." Helen finally took Alison's hand and held it tight. "Our lives have nothing to do with the way you lived before."

"Except for all the violence, Helen. No, you're not doing it — but it's around you. It's been around you ever since I've known you." The tears were gone, but there was pain in Alison's face as she withdrew her hand. "Helen, I really love you. You must believe that. But after all those years when even the sound of Bob's voice could terrify me — I just don't know if I can take dangerous situations again."

Helen shivered in spite of the heat. "If it's my work that bothers you, Alison, trust me that I'm eager to get back to that security guard's uniform and my nice dull life making rounds at a warehouse again. I've had more than enough excitement to last me a lifetime."

"No, you haven't." Alison shook her head and ran a hand through her hair as she searched for words. "From the moment everything started here, I could see it. You miss this kind of action in your life, Helen. It's what you want, what you need. You think I don't know how it tore you up inside, to give up your office and your career? To live quiet and afraid for the past year?"

"So now I'm some kind of drama queen. Is that it?" Helen spat the words out in bitterness and hurt. "Always in need of that adrenaline rush from other people's pain?"

"Helen, that's not what I'm talking about at all."

"Oh, isn't it?" Helen bit off a curse and struggled with the anger inside her. The last thing Alison needed — the last thing either one of them needed — was a tirade. "Look, I've been nothing but honest with you from day one. I've been working really hard to rebuild my life after being nearly killed while I was just doing my job. I've pulled away from the kind of work that made that disaster possible. I've given up everything to get my shit together. And I sure as hell didn't ask for anything that took place here."

"Helen, I'm not blaming you — oh, shit."

"Hey, guys! How are you?"

Shelley edged her way through the thin crowd taking a stroll during the noon hour. She looked happy and relaxed out of uniform, and Helen wondered if she often spent her off-duty time here at the casino. "Thought I'd missed you."

"Shelley, I'm not sure you ever met Alison Young." As the two women shook hands, Helen found herself watching Shelley closely. Had she been wrong all along about the security guard? From Shelley's open, eager manner, the solid handshake she offered Alison, she seemed as pleased to meet Helen's lover as she'd been to meet Helen herself. Helen smiled wryly as Alison nodded a greeting to the other woman. She must have deluded herself about Shelley, Helen realized. It wasn't a flirtation on the guard's part — the poor woman was probably just starved for others of her tribe and overjoyed to meet a lesbian couple in the depths of Laughlin, no matter what the circumstances.

"Oh, there's someone I'd like you to meet. Thea? Thea,

come on over here!" Shelley waved eagerly to a woman standing near the doors, and Helen recognized one of the women from the RV set that had arrived the night she'd met Carmel. It wasn't the one who'd befriended her aunt — that had been a no-nonsense butch type with a permanent.

Thea, however, was another matter. Long hair frizzed out in the heat, and her beads clanked together over her shapeless cotton shift. Helen picked up the scent of patchouli as she came closer, and a tattoo of a labyris symbol peeked out from under her sleeve.

"This is Thea Hawkwind. She's here visiting from Santa Cruz," Shelley said, beaming as she put an arm around Thea's shoulders.

A few moments were lost in introductions as Helen studied Thea. Shelley couldn't keep a shit-eating grin off her face, and Helen felt only a twinge of humiliation at the error of her own judgment. She was glad for the security guard, and hoped Thea would hang around for a while.

It took Helen a moment to realize that Alison was staring at her with a kind of desperation in her eyes. "Yes, it was Helen's aunt."

"I see." Thea cocked her head and smiled at Helen. "I don't suppose you or your aunt would be interested in a healing ritual in the hotel room where it happened?"

"Excuse me?"

Thea hurriedly explained that, with Shelley's help, they'd have access to the room for perhaps half an hour that very day. "In the next few minutes, actually, now that the police have cleared out." Thea leaned briefly against Shelley with a smile. "Nothing complicated — I just thought I'd burn a little sage and purify the room, you know, clear it of the negative energy from all that violence." She shuddered and closed her eyes. "It's important to do that, you know."

"Well —" Helen looked at Alison, who had that deer in

the headlights stare she'd seen before. "I can't speak for my aunt, but —"

"I'm afraid I have to get back to our motel," Alison murmured. "We have some packing to do."

"How about you, Helen? Please?"

Shelley's eyes were lit with happiness, and Helen hated to disappoint her. Besides, Helen had hoped for a chance to talk about Nick before they left. "I think I'll tag along with them, Alison," she said. "I can catch up with you at the motel in an hour or so. Okay?"

Alison smiled tensely and nodded. Helen knew she had to be relieved that at least she was not gallivanting off in search of death and danger. "Sure. Just remember, Loy and Edna will be looking for us there."

It wasn't until the three women were in the elevator that Helen asked Shelley about Nick. Shelley's face shadowed with a swift grimace of pain. "Not a thing."

Helen squeezed Shelley's arm. "I think I can get away for a little while this afternoon. If we don't find her with Wilbur we'll go to the police."

Shelley sighed and nodded as Thea opened a small leather pouch and took out a small smudge stick bound with blue string. Sage, maybe? Helen guessed. Silently Thea led them off the elevator as it softly chimed its arrival. With a start Helen realized, as she trooped out after the other two women, that the floor was empty of guests.

As if reading her thoughts, Shelley said, "Management will probably keep this floor cleared for a little while, until the excitement dies down and there's a whole new set of people staying." With one hand she flicked away a bit of yellow caution tape left by the police. Helen paused at the door while Thea murmured a few soft words, then calmly opened the door.

She and Helen stayed outside as Thea circled the room with the sage, leaving a trail of strong scent as she paced and gestured. Helen glanced down at the expanse of carpet where only a couple of days ago she'd seen death. The smooth pile under Thea's feet was fresh and clean — brand new. No doubt they'd replaced the carpet. Maybe even the furniture.

Shelley fidgeted nervously as a rattling clank sounded from the end of the hallway. "Damn, that's the maid," she muttered. "Hope Thea's going to finish up here, soon."

Sure enough, the heavy metal cart heaved around the corner as Shelley spoke. A small dark-haired woman in the casino's maroon vest appeared, pushing the cart and humming tunelessly. She waved at Shelley, pulled a huge ring of keys from the cart, and unlocked a door at the end of the hall.

Shelley shuddered. "Weird — I keep expecting to see Sue come around the corner. She usually did this floor, you know?"

"Yeah, I remember seeing her in that vest. So she held down two jobs, at least."

Shelley snorted. "Right. As if that asshole Hef would ever help her out. She probably took care of him, most of the time. Maybe the police think she killed Carmel Kittrick — she was in the room at the right time, after all."

Clearly the news about Bud Gilley hadn't gotten out yet. Helen remained silent as Thea stood in the center of the room, her sage stick upheld toward the ceiling. She glanced down the hall as the maid returned to her cart, rummaging around its contents. The maid gathered a stack of towels in her arms and went back into the room she'd been cleaning.

Next to her Shelley sighed with relief. "I think she's about done now. Hope that smoke alarm won't go off — should have thought of that before, I guess." Thea rejoined them at the doorway, taking a small ceramic bowl from the leather pouch. She placed the smudge stick, still smoldering, into the bowl and held it carefully. "Good timing," she said to Thea. "The maid's at the end of the hall, and — Helen, what are you doing?"

Helen, who'd taken a few running steps to the maid's cart, stopped when Shelley called her. She turned and stared at the two women, who stared back at her in surprise. "Sorry. I just remembered something. Shelley, I have a huge favor to ask you."

Shelley glanced at Thea, then back at Helen. "What is it?"

"I wonder if I could somehow take a look at the records here at the hotel, find out if Nick was really scheduled to clean this floor the day of Carmel's murder."

Shelley shrugged, and Thea, puzzled, edged closer to the security guard. "Don't have to look that up — I can tell you right now that she was. Nick was here."

Helen sighed as certainty knotted her stomach. What she'd figured out wasn't going to be easy to prove — maybe impossible. And it wasn't going to be any fun, either.

"Shit." Alison was waiting for her at the motel. Her aunt and uncle would be there soon, as well. "Then I need you to do me another favor."

"Does it have to do with Nick?" Shelley moved closer and whispered, as Thea hovered close behind. "What have you heard?"

"Right now, nothing. But I need you, and your truck."

Shelley pulled back in surprise. "Why?"

"We're going to pick up Alison, and then we're going for a ride into the desert."

Chapter Seventeen

"How long has he had this place?"

Shelley clambered down out of her truck and followed Helen down the slope that led to Wilbur Kittrick's desert hideout. The sun blazed down on their uncovered heads, and Helen gratefully took a sip from Shelley's bottle of water. With each step the women took dust puffed up from the dry, gritty floor of the basin where Wilbur had built his command post. "I don't know," Helen responded as she returned the bottle. "Long enough to turn it into some kind of fortress, apparently. His father must keep him supplied with enough cash to get all the equipment and provisions he needs."

"Needs? For what, an invasion? Jesus, it looks like some kind of World War Two bunker or something." Shelley stumbled on a clump of sharp rocks, muttered a curse and squinted down at the long, low barracks-like building. A hot breeze stirred over the mountain, flapping a screen door loudly against the metal siding. Helen stiffened at the noise, ready to run, but no one emerged with weapons armed and ready. There were no vehicles, either, except for Shelley's truck and Thea's rented car. Helen glanced over her shoulder to see Alison and Thea sitting in the car, staring blankly out at the desolate scene. Her heart sank as she realized they must be too late — Nick and Wilbur had already gotten away.

In daylight Helen saw details and features that had been hidden by darkness during her previous visit. A large propane tank nestled at the side of the building, with two thick pipelines extending across the sand and rock to the house. Green canvas tarp spread over a row of drums that held — Helen could hardly guess what. More fuel? Gasoline? Several empty wooden crates splayed across the ground near the edge of the slope where she and Shelley stood. Helen crouched down, sifted slowly through the broken wood with a careful eye watching for nails, but there was no indication of what these crates had contained.

"Something's not right. Something is out of place, or missing, or —"

"Helen." Alison had stepped out of the car. Shielding her eyes against the sun's glare, she peered down at them. "I think this is called trespassing. We shouldn't hang around here." From the way she stood Helen knew Alison was very pissed off. Thea seemed to be enjoying the intrigue, but Alison was far from thrilled at the hasty explanation she'd heard at the Saddle. If only Alison hadn't loaned her car out to Loy and Edna, or if only Shelley's truck could hold more than one passenger, she might not be standing next to a bunker with a furious girlfriend glaring at her.

Helen sighed. "I don't think anyone's at home, anyway. I'll go back and try to find Richardson. Maybe when he sees the photographs Shelley found in Sue's house they can try for a warrant to look for Nick."

Shelley shoved past Helen and Alison. "If you think Nick might be in there, I don't give a damn about warrants — I'm going in to look right now. Wilbur Kittrick can just deal with it." And she plodded down the slope toward the entrance.

Helen shouted after Shelley, trying to warn her that a person like Wilbur would probably have the whole place rigged with a variety of booby traps, just waiting for a chance to blow up some government operative who was hellbent on shutting down his investigations into conspiracies. But Shelley stormed up to the front door without incident and actually entered the building without setting off any explosions.

"Shelley!" Thea slammed the car door behind her and hurried down from the car, her long hair streaming behind her. Helen saw that her skin was beaded with sweat and her eyes wide and frightened. "Don't go in there. I have a terrible feeling about this place."

"Too late," Helen tossed over her shoulder as she ran after Shelley, with Alison close behind. When they got inside, Helen blinked and took a deep breath, startled by the gloom and chill in the building. Once her eyes had adjusted to the dim light seeping in from slivers venting the walls, she saw Shelley standing silently in the middle of the room.

"I don't fucking believe it," Shelley breathed. "Helen, are you sure he had all that shit in here Friday night?"

Helen, stunned, didn't bother to answer. Instead she gazed at the empty walls, the bare floors, the barren shelving. Where she'd seen reel-to-reel tapes and elaborate listening devices and a complex phone bank, Wilbur's makeshift lodgings now looked as simple and nondescript as a hunting lodge. The bed frame remained, but there was no sign of the lumpy mattress and filthy sheets. The cameras set against the wall were gone, and the narrow galley now held an open, empty food locker. Something rustled in the gloom, and Helen made out the furred outline of some small desert animal scurrying away from them into the shadows. A stray wind, hot and electric, blew across their faces as they turned as one, startled, to hear the door flap again with a loud bang.

"I don't understand it. Helen, you said he had this huge setup out here, filing cabinets and transmitters and satellite dishes. What the hell happened?"

Helen sighed and scuffed at the floor with her feet. Something glimmered by her toe in the light from the open door. She bent down and saw a thin strip of film lying brown and cracked on the dusty wood of the floor. "Yes, he did. I guess he figured out that sooner or later he'd have to haul ass and get away from here. I just didn't expect him to do it so quickly, that's all."

"All right, Helen. You got us out here — me, anyway — thinking we'd find Nick." Shelley strode across the floor and stuck her face up close to Helen's as Helen stood up. Helen could smell her anger and her fear. Thea stood nearby, uncertain, looking from Shelley to Helen and back again. "You mind giving me an explanation about why the fuck we're out here with our thumbs up our ass nosing around a deserted building?"

Helen twined the strip of film around her fingers. "Remember that scrapbook we found in Nick's closet?" she asked Shelley, ignoring for the moment the confused faces of Alison and Thea. "The picture of Sue, the one that looked like it had been cut out of something else? I figured out what was bugging me about it. It was one of Wilbur's photographs, like the one I took from him the other night. She'd cut away the part that didn't have her mother in it — who knows, maybe it had Hef's face in it."

"But why the hell would Nick come out here to be with Wilbur? Just because she had one of his pictures —"

"Not just that. Maybe Wilbur was trying to teach her his theories — hell, maybe trying to pass on the torch or something."

"To Nick." Shelley rolled her eyes in disgust and turned away, running her hands through her hair. "Look, Helen, it wasn't necessarily a bad idea, but quite obviously Nick isn't here. I mean, maybe Wilbur did befriend her, but I think we'd better get back."

"Shelley, I'm sorry. I swear, I wouldn't have dragged you out into the desert like this if I didn't think she was here."

"I know, I know. You're just trying to help —" Shelley's words caught in her throat as she struggled to keep away the tears. With Thea holding her hand she went outside.

"Fuck." Helen sank down to the floor and sat, cross-legged, amid scraps of paper and clumps of dust. "This was a really shitty idea, wasn't it?"

Alison crouched down on her heels next to Helen. "Not a bad idea, really. It's just — well, never mind."

"No, go ahead and say it."

Alison sighed and rubbed her hand across her eyes. "I think it gave Shelley false hopes. Helen, forget it. You meant well. This is one we'll just have to leave for the police to sort out. Nick is a very mixed-up young woman, and Shelley has a lot of love to give."

They left the building. Shelley had already revved up the engine on her truck. Thea walked over to them. "We'll both go back in the truck," she called out to Helen and Alison. "You two can take my car back —"

"Are you sure?"

Thea shrugged. "I trust you. We'll meet back up at the hotel." She glanced over her shoulder at Shelley, who stared down at her hands on the steering wheel. "I just don't want to leave her alone right now."

"I understand." Helen went to the truck. "Shelley, I'm more sorry than I can say. I wish I could have helped you more."

Shelley managed a small smile. "Like I said, I know you meant well. It's okay, Helen. Really." Thea climbed into the truck and backed it away, turned it around and pointed it toward the highway.

"Guess we'd better do the same." Alison jangled Thea's keys in her hand and walked to the rental car.

They drove in silence for a few minutes, then Helen cleared her throat and said, "So, you must be upset with me, too."

Alison shook her head but kept her eyes on the road as she drove. "Not upset, Helen, just tired and ready to get out of here. I've had all I can take of the Kittricks and Nick and the casino and your relatives. I need to get home." The sun sank quickly behind the mountains, and suddenly they were thrust into darkness. Alison fumbled for a moment with the unfamiliar controls before finding the switch that would turn on the headlights. The final rays of the sun mingled with the bright white beams from the car as they moved across the road. Far ahead Helen could make out the taillights of Shelley's truck. It looked like Shelley and Thea had just reached the turnoff.

"Me, too." Helen gazed out the window and watched heat shimmering off the asphalt in waves. They were coming up on that stretch of road where the abandoned car jutted out from the landscape like some rusted work of art in a vast and empty natural museum. God, she felt like such an ass — dragging poor Shelley into a wild-goose chase just because she wanted to be a private eye again. Would she ever learn? Would she ever get it through her head that those days were over, that —

"Stop! Stop the car, Alison!"

Alison slammed on the brakes. The tires screeched and Helen leapt out before the car had jerked to a complete halt.

"That's it," Helen breathed. "Look." She grabbed Alison by the arm and pulled her forward.

"What? What are you talking about?"

"That old junked-up car! I saw it the other night when I followed Wilbur out here."

"Yeah, and?" Alison asked, pulling free of Helen's grip.

"It was pointing the other way. I saw headlights facing me when I drove to Wilbur's place, and now they're facing us as we drive *away* from Wilbur's place." Helen stumbled over the edge of the road to the car. "It's been moved, Alison," she said, picking her way through the scrubby dry brush of the highway.

"So? What difference does that make, Helen?"

"So an old junked-up car doesn't move itself." Helen crept closer, watching her feet. God knew what sort of small animals might be hiding in the undergrowth.

The car, or what had once been a car, was now just a rusted shell. Although they hadn't been visible from the highway, Helen could now see that the remains of this vehicle were flanked by bits and pieces of what might have been two or three other cars — a bumper or two here, a fender there, whole doors lying under the sun as they disintegrated into metal fragments. There was no way of knowing how long they'd been there. The biggest portion, the shell that Helen had spied from the road, might have been anything from two to twenty years old. It looked to have been some type of four-door sedan, larger than a sports model, but not as big as a wagon or van. Helen moved around the brush and tumbleweeds, treading cautiously until she was opposite the front end of the heap. Yes, that's why she'd noticed it from the road, both the other night and just now. One of the headlights of the derelict car still retained a large sliver of chrome that, although heavily rusted, still glinted like a new coin in the light. Her own headlights had picked up that gleam as she'd rounded the bend while following Wilbur to his lair, and the headlights on Alison's rented car had just done the same thing.

"Goddamnit, Helen, you'd better have a really good reason to go wandering out in the desert," Alison spat out as she pulled herself free from some kind of prickly shrub and joined Helen.

"Wilbur as much as told me so, the other night. He was bragging about all the hidden places he'd fixed up here in the middle of nowhere, so he could get away from whoever might be chasing him down."

"Helen. You can't expect me to believe you paid any attention to that crap?" Alison folded her arms and shook her head. "This sounds like a tabloid telling us that Elvis is alive and well on Mars! I mean, really."

"It would be just his style. The man is convinced he's onto at least six different government conspiracies, right? From UFOs to military cover-ups — he had rations like those militant right-wing groups store for the apocalypse — and he laughed to me about how I'd be surprised at what I might find in his backyard. No, someone has moved these cars around, for some reason."

She strained her eyes, looking past the vehicular graveyard to a ridge just beyond. What had that prospector — the one with the fax machine — told them? The hills around Laughlin and the Colorado were riddled with caverns and caves, large and small. Not to mention all the abandoned mine shafts dug by prospective millionaires who'd broken into the rock long enough for money to run out or disappointment to overwhelm them. And the way Wilbur had mingled with the terrorist types at that gun show the morning of his sister's death — while Helen didn't credit him with the kind of fanaticism that encouraged right-wing militancy, she wondered how far a jump it was from being a conspiracy theorist to making fertilizer bombs in the garage. Or was she doing some kind of knee-jerk reaction simply because Wilbur gave her the creeps?

The first ping went almost unnoticed. Alison slapped at the air as if a bug had flown by her ear. The next one struck metal on one of the abandoned cars and ricocheted off into the sand. Helen's instincts kicked in at the sound of metal firing on metal.

"Get down!" Helen jerked Alison down into the sand next to her, ignoring her cry of pain. "Jesus fucking Christ, someone is shooting at us!" she hissed.

Alison froze in terror, her eyes wide and dark. Thankfully she remained silent, although she trembled next to Helen. Moments that felt like years passed slowly by, and the desert remained silent except for the faint rustle of wind and small animals in the dried shrubbery. Then there was another flurry of bullets. Helen, in spite of her fears, marveled at the silence surrounding them. What kind of weapons were being used here? Then she remembered the kind of camera and telephone equipment Wilbur had available to him. No telling how sophisticated his guns might be.

Finally Helen moved so that her mouth was right next to Alison's ear. "We have to try to crawl out of here. No way we're going to get stuck out here after the sun goes down." Alison nodded. Helen kept talking for a moment, as much to reassure herself as to comfort Alison. "I think those were just to warn us off. If they'd really wanted to hurt us, they would have hit us right away — we certainly gave them enough opportunity."

"Them?" Alison whispered shakily. "You mean it's not just Wilbur?"

"I don't know." Helen bit off further words and glanced up over the line of weeds where they'd fallen to the ground. "Come on, we have to move. Now."

But Helen's belief in the relative harmlessness of their

attackers' intent proved wrong. The second they began to wiggle backward, gaining distance from the junked cars, more shots thumped quietly through the undergrowth, some rattling against the automotive cemetery, most landing in the soil around them.

"My God, my God," Alison kept murmuring, but to Helen's relief she kept moving in spite of her terror. The more distance they gained, the fewer shots they heard. Once they made it to the highway, Alison tried to stand up and run for their car.

"No! Not yet!" Helen pulled her back down, forcing her to continue their slow, painful crawl. She cursed as she looked up and down the highway — not a single other vehicle in sight. Shelley and Thea were long gone, and there were no other headlights in the distance. Together Helen and Alison edged slowly to the rental car. It wasn't until they both reached the passenger side of the car that Helen allowed herself to lift her head.

"Now what?" Alison asked. Her face loomed large and white as she leaned close to Helen, the smell of fear on her breath.

"Now we climb in on the passenger side, get the fuck out of here and tell the police where Wilbur is holed up taking potshots at people."

"And if it isn't Wilbur? What about all those militia types you think he hangs out with?"

"All the more reason to find Richardson. And I still have a hunch that we'll find Nick with Wilbur." That discussion could wait for later, Helen thought as she carefully opened the car door.

One more shot spat out over their heads as they quickly climbed inside the car. With shaking fingers Alison handed Helen the keys. "Come on, come on, let's get out of here," she kept whispering over and over as Helen started the engine.

After a couple of false starts the engine roared to life.

Helen shoved the gears into cooperation and floored the gas pedal. Before they'd cleared the section of road next to the junked cars, however, the steering wheel jerked in her hands and the car slewed uncontrollably across the empty highway.

"Helen!" She heard one scream from Alison, who held on to the passenger door with both hands. Helen fought for control, her body going into reflexive moves to keep the car upright as she heard the metal rim of a flat tire whining on the road beneath them. Then another tire went out — it was both rear tires, by the feel of it.

The car lurched under her guidance to the shoulder of the road. Helen reached for Alison. "Are you hurt? Answer me!"

"No, no, just scared out of my fucking mind," Alison managed to mumble. "What happened? Did we hit something, run over something?"

There was sound outside the car now. It wasn't another car or truck — it sounded more like footsteps. Helen spared half a second to wish, in vain, that it was one of Wilbur's alien visitors come to abduct them.

"No, Alison. We didn't hit anything."

Helen sighed when she heard the tap on the window she knew was coming. She turned around in the seat, keeping one hand on Alison's arm, to see the barrel of a rifle pointed between her eyes.

Chapter Eighteen

The edge of a rusted car door bit into Helen's back, making a painful crease right below her left shoulder. She didn't dare move, though, with Wilbur's rifle aimed precisely at the bridge of her nose. Without glancing, Helen knew Alison was huddled silently against a shriveled leather seat from some long-abandoned luxury vehicle. Both to distract herself and to seek a possible way out of this situation, Helen let her eyes rove across the scene where she sat captive to Wilbur Kittrick.

It wasn't a cave exactly — more a protected area

beneath an overhanging shelf of rock that jutted out of the mountain behind the automobile graveyard. The top of the shelf was visible as far as the highway, but the ridge's lip hung down just far enough to conceal the movements of those who were careful in their activities. And the opening in the hill extended fairly deep, Helen was sure. Of course, there'd been no opportunities to explore, not with Wilbur keeping the rifle armed and ready with each step they'd taken across the field of dead cars. Under other circumstances Helen suspected she would have been amused at the way someone — Wilbur or other friends of his with the same interest in concealment — had furnished the cavern with odds and ends taken from the car parts strewn across the foot of the hills. Arranged around the rocks were an assortment of seats, ranging from cheap vinyl covers to cloth interior to expensive leather. The body of a smaller model, maybe an older Volkswagen bug, was in use as a storage cabinet. Helen could see cans and boxes stowed inside, piled high against the windows. Someone had even placed side panels from a station wagon or van lengthwise across two nearly level rock piles, creating a kind of desk or table near the mouth of the cavern.

That was where Nick sat now, spooning up something from a can. She stared at Helen silently while she ate, her jaw working vigorously. All around her, spread across the metal panels, cans and bottles littered the makeshift table. A kerosene lamp perched dangerously near the edge of the table. Although Helen knew they hadn't been holed up here for long, it looked as though they'd not left the area at all, judging by the number of empty ration tins. Except for the slight rustle of wind in the foliage outside, the scrape of Nick's spoon on the can was the only sound Helen heard.

Helen felt her legs tingle beneath the weight of her body. She had no idea how long she'd been crouched there, but her feet had gone to sleep. She shifted slightly, trying to find a more comfortable position.

Wilbur brought his rifle up with a quick snap of his arm. "I wouldn't do that if I were you."

"I'm just stretching my legs, Wilbur. That's all." Helen kept her eyes locked on his as she eased her legs out in front of her, forcing herself to move very slowly. She cursed herself for discounting the man as a harmless fool. He looked anything but harmless now. His sizable gut still swayed over his belt, stretching the fabric of his black T-shirt, but now his belly bulged above military-style fatigues in camouflage green. In addition to the rifle he carried, there was a shoulder holster strapped across his plump chest. She was pretty sure that at least some of the bulges in the numerous pockets were ammunition. He had laced his boots up over his ankles, tucking the pants legs inside. And in the lurid shadows his face sported a few ludicrous stripes of black. He must have seen one too many war movies, Helen decided. Right now, though, the gesture wasn't ridiculous. It was yet another indication of just how far he was gone in his fantasies of domination.

The only light in the hideout came from a couple of kerosene lamps turned down very low, casting weird shadows over everything. That only made things worse, Helen knew. It would be difficult for Wilbur or Nick to determine, in the gloom, whether or not Helen was stretching her legs or reaching for a weapon.

Not that there seemed to be any weapons at hand. Except for the firepower Wilbur flaunted, Helen guessed that any other guns were either well hidden in the rocks surrounding them or stashed inside the truncated Volkswagen at the other end of the cavern. From what she could make out, Nick didn't have a gun. But that empty stare coming from the woman at the makeshift table was as unnerving as Wilbur's newfound confidence.

Nick hadn't spoken a word since their arrival. Wilbur had prodded them forward, once slapping Alison as she stumbled and cried out in pain. Nick had been waiting for them at the mouth of the cavern, clearly unconcerned at their presence.

"Lookee what I found out there," Wilbur had chortled, shoving first Alison, then Helen, down onto the rough rock floor. Helen had bit back a yelp of pain as her palm bled from catching the force of her fall. With his rifle he'd waved them into positions that were neither close together nor very far apart — better for guarding them, of course. "Bet my daddy sent y'all out here, didn't he? Well, guess the old man is in for a surprise, ain't he?"

And Nick had merely opened up a can of something or other and started to eat.

Now, as she flexed her leg muscles, forcing the circulation back to normal, Helen stole a swift glance at Alison. Slumped against the rotted cushions, Alison was scarcely breathing, as if trying to be invisible. Helen looked back at Wilbur and fought down the emotions raging inside her. Now was no time for guilt or sorrow about getting them into this awful situation — if they had any chance at all it wouldn't be from bemoaning their fate.

Cradling his rifle in his arms, Wilbur peered into Helen's face. He stank of a variety of things — sweat, unwashed clothing, old food and cigarettes. "Did I say you could stretch anything, bitch? I don't recall giving you permission to do that." Suddenly he raised his rifle, preparing to slam it down on her legs. Alison's faint whimper stopped him. "What's that?" He grinned down at Helen. "Sounds like your little cunt over there don't want me to hurt you. Maybe I could get her to eat you out right now, go down into that stinking pussy of yours and lick it for me. How about that?" He giggled. The smile faded suddenly and his eyes glittered.

"We're not the enemy, Wilbur," she managed to croak, her throat constricted with fear.

"Is that right?" He lowered the gun and looked at her curiously. "The old fuck sent you out here to spy on me. Sounds like the enemy to me."

"He didn't, Wilbur. I swear it."

"Then why the hell did you come creeping out here?"

Helen glanced at Nick. She had finished her meager meal and now sat quietly, thin arms folded across thin chest, blank eyes taking in the scene as if she were at a school play. "I came looking for Nick," Helen went on. "There are a lot of people worried about her, you know."

"Like that bitch calling herself a mother?" Wilbur snorted. He stepped around Helen and bent protectively down over Nick. "I'm taking care of her, now. She's the sister I should have had — sweet and innocent and not spoiled rotten — not like Carmel." Helen watched with revulsion as he caressed Nick's shoulder. "Aren't you, honey?"

"Nick." Helen fixed her gaze on the young woman, longing for some kind of response in those blank eyes. "Shelley is worried about you. She wishes you'd come back."

"So the cops can put her away forever? Oh, yeah, they always say it's for your own good." Wilbur slammed a fist against the metal table, knocking over a couple of empty cans in the process. "Just like they kept telling me — 'This school will be better, Wilbur,' or 'Your mother would have wanted it this way, Wilbur.'" He stroked Nick's hair. "My little sister here ain't gonna get none of that shit, you hear me? No being locked away for things you didn't do."

"Then you don't know, Wilbur? You don't know what Nick did?"

He cackled again and approached Helen. "Hell, all she did was run away. Wish I'd had the guts to do that a long time ago. Don't matter now, though. We'll take off together for Mexico, or South America. Won't we, Nick? Someplace where no one will find us. Including the old fuck."

As he spoke he glanced over his shoulder, his grip on his rifle relaxed. She groped behind her for a better hold on the door frame that had been poking her in the back. By stretching her legs moments ago, Helen had shifted position just enough to ease the handle of the door farther to her side, where she stood a better chance of pulling it out. If she could just inch it a little more to her right, away from the rocks where it had been wedged, she might be able to grab the handle and fling it up at Wilbur's face, at least knock the gun from his hands...

Wilbur crouched beside her again. "All I got to worry about is you two bitches. Shit, if you hadn't screwed things up we'd already be out of the country."

"So, you got all that stuff packed up and put away? That was pretty fast work, Wilbur," Helen said, more in an effort to keep Wilbur talking and calm him down than to get any information.

"No shit, Sherlock. Minute you took off the other night I was getting ready. I knew sooner or later the old man would come down on me, quit letting me have my trust money. Hell, he's been talking to lawyers for weeks, now, making arrangements to lock me up for good before he dies. I had to make some fast plans, and there was no more time to wait for him to bite the big one." He frowned at her. "You really fucked things up for me, you know?"

"Why couldn't you just wait a while? Your father doesn't have long to live. When he's dead you'll get all his money and you can do anything you want."

"Yeah, that's a good one. He's got ex-presidents in his pocket, not to mention CIA friends who would assassinate me whenever he says so. Where do you think those death squads in Central America get their money from? Bake sales?"

For a moment Helen thought about the photograph in her pocket. She pushed the thought away as he paced, his rifle still pointed in her direction.

"If he finds out what I know about his ties with the feds, I'm a dead man," Wilbur pronounced solemnly.

"Sure doesn't look that way to me, Wilbur. Look around you — what do you see? I see a man in control. Hell, you don't need Kittrick to make it on your own. You've found your way out." Helen hoped she wasn't overdoing the admiration. She didn't know if playing his conspiracy theory game was helping or hurting their situation.

She needn't have worried. Wilbur actually looked pleased at her words. "I sure did! Hear that, Nick? We're going to be all right, you and me." The smile faded as he leveled the rifle at her face again. "Soon as I take care of you two, that is." He rose and went over to Alison, yanking her up by one arm and thrusting her down onto the rocks next to Helen. Fortunately Alison landed far enough away from the broken door frame to stay out of the line of attack Helen was counting on. In fact her sudden fall distracted Wilbur enough for Helen to work the frame loose from the rocks.

Helen took a deep breath, closed her eyes for a moment and decided to play the last card in her hand. "Sure you are, as long as no one finds out what Nick did."

Wilbur paused in lifting the rifle to his shoulder. Out of the corner of her eye Helen saw a flicker of movement from Nick, a gesture the girl quickly stilled. "What are you talking about?"

"Well, as long as you know, it doesn't matter if the police do. Isn't that right, Nick?"

Nick stood up. Her mouth opened, but no words came out. Wilbur sneered. "Nick didn't do anything. Stuff has been done to her, all her life — just like it was to me. Don't you worry, sweetheart. We'll be out of here soon, and it will all be a bad dream."

"Then you don't know, Wilbur? She didn't say anything

to you about Carmel and what happened in the casino?" Helen said, trying to keep the edge of desperation from her voice.

"Nick, go outside now. I'll be there for you in a minute." Wilbur watched as Nick hesitated. "I said, go on out. Now."

"Come on, Nick! Tell him how you killed his sister!" Helen said, gripping the handle at her side and gauging the distance between her and Wilbur's rifle. "Tell him how you were cleaning rooms at the Saddle for your mother that afternoon while she was out screwing around with Hef! Tell him how Carmel's face looked when it got smashed down on the edge of the sink! How you ran away to your mother only to find her stoned and not even knowing who you were." Helen paused, not knowing if she had the details right but not caring. Anything, anything at all to distract Wilbur from his intention.

Wilbur faltered, turned to look at Nick. The girl had moved to the side of the derelict Volkswagen. Her eyes flashed with fear, and Helen saw her hands tremble.

"But, but, Wilbur, you said you hated Carmel," she mumbled. "You were glad she was dead."

"Nick, did you do that? Those things she said?" He stared in amazement. His arms relaxed, and the rifle slipped in his grasp. He glanced down at Helen, then turned back to Nick. "I — I don't understand, Nick. You said you hadn't done anything wrong."

"But it was just Carmel, Wilbur." The high-pitched tone in her voice grated against the echoing walls of the cavern. "Remember how she always treated you? You told me yourself she acted like you were the dirt under her feet, that she —"

"Damn it, you lied to me!" He swiveled around, rifle pointed at the floor but still ready to fire. Nick quivered against the door of the Volkswagen. Helen saw two of the boxes inside the car topple from the top of the heap and disappear. "You made me believe that everyone was hurting you!"

"They were, Wilbur! Your sister most of all! She ruined my life, she ruined my mother's life, and I —"

"I thought you were pure. I thought you were honest." Wilbur's chest heaved as he towered over the terrified woman. "Now I come to find out you're like all the rest of the bitches out there." He took Nick's arm in a bruising grip and pulled her close to him. "I don't know which is worse — being a fucking queer like these two, or being a cunt like Carmel, or a liar. Huh? You want to tell me, Nick, which is worse?"

It was now or never. Putting all her energy into her shoulders and arms, Helen swung the door frame up by its handle and slammed it into Wilbur's back. Blood spattered as the jagged edge of the broken piece of metal grazed the back of his neck, and he gasped in pain and surprise.

Helen paused less than a second as he staggered on the rocks. Her arm swung up in a vicious arc and knocked the rifle out of his hands as he struggled for balance. She followed up with a knee to his groin when he spun around to face her.

"Ah, shit," he moaned, doubled over in pain. He made a feeble grab at Helen's ankle. Helen responded with another kick, this one landing on the side of his head. It wasn't enough to do more than stun him, but it bought her the time she needed.

"Alison! The rifle!"

Alison had already darted to the side of the cavern. Trembling she held the weapon out to Helen. Not familiar with this kind of weapon, Helen held it gingerly. She was certain it was locked and loaded and ready for business —

Wilbur's expression told her that much. He gaped up at her with wide eyes as she leveled the rifle at him.

"Get the gun in his holster," she said. Alison shook with fear but managed to pull the gun out and hold it in both hands. Nick still cowered by the Volkswagen, her arms thrown up over her face as if to ward off blows. "Alison, listen to me. I want you to take that gun and go back out on the highway to the car."

"Helen, no, I —"

"Listen to me, Alison." Helen kept her voice low and took a step closer to Alison, never letting her eyes stray from Wilbur. "We've got to get some help right away. I can hold them here with the rifle. You take the gun — no, take it — get back to the car and get it moving. I don't care if it has flat tires. Drive it until someone stops or you can flag down some help."

"Are you sure?"

Helen nodded with more conviction than she felt. "Go. Now."

The rustling sound at the mouth of the cavern told her that Alison had left and was making her way across the brush back to the road. Helen fought down a wave of fear and longing at Alison's departure and focused her attention on her two captives. Nick had lowered her arms and was now staring at her with that weird blank look she'd worn earlier. Wilbur jerked upright and made a sudden motion from the floor.

"Don't even think about it, asshole," Helen breathed. "My aim isn't all that good, you know. I tend to shoot low." She moved the rifle's barrel down into a line that ended at Wilbur's crotch. His face went white, and he pulled his knees up reflexively.

Helen wasn't sure how long she'd stood there, staring down at Wilbur, before she realized that Nick had crept into the shadows farther and farther from the broken body of the car. One of the kerosene lamps toppled over when Nick darted across the stone floor and made a run for it.

"Nick!" Wilbur screamed out and flailed an arm helplessly after her.

"Let her go, Wilbur!" The lamp flickered and died, casting strange shadows across the rocks and debris of the cave as the flame smoldered out. Now Wilbur was just a hulking shape of stinking tired flesh, sniveling in the dirt. Helen felt a surge of contempt for him.

That was when she heard the sirens. Had Alison been able to get help so quickly? Surely it hadn't been more than a few minutes. No, wait. It must have been Thea and Shelley. They would have wondered why they'd taken so long to get back to the Saddle, maybe even circled around and doubled back to find the rental car stranded by the side of the road and leaving a trail of skid marks behind it.

"That's it, Wilbur. Your little game of weekend warrior is up — for a good, long time."

"Fu-fuck you, queer!" He wept, sniffling loudly.

"Is that the best you can do? A trained terrorist like yourself, Wilbur? I'm ashamed of you."

A moment later Alison bounded into the cavern that was now lit by floodlights from a collection of police cruisers and vans. "Helen! Thank God!" She clung to her in a trembling embrace.

"Alison, Nick ran off. We've got to find her."

Exhausted, Helen leaned against the cavern wall as Wilbur was cuffed and led away, arrested for kidnapping and assault and a variety of other crimes. She could see a handful of uniformed state troopers armed with flashlights making a search of the surrounding flat expanse of scrubby bushes and weeds. She had no doubt that Nick would be found in just a few minutes. In this darkness, without light, she wouldn't have gotten far.

Then she heard the scream of brakes applied too hard,

too late, back on the highway, closer to Wilbur's command post. The eighteen-wheeler hadn't yet come close enough to the roadblock to slow down when Nick darted out of nowhere to the road. Later, Helen wondered if she'd done it on purpose, chasing down the escape from pain and loneliness and futility that had already marked her life. Did she think of Carmel before her own death came?

Chapter Nineteen

Helen didn't see Romie Kittrick until she and Alison had helped Aunt Edna and Uncle Loy check their luggage at the Las Vegas airport. She had just turned to one of the monitors that displayed flight information when she caught a glimpse of the wheelchair moving like an oversized insect through the stream of people coming and going.

Helen nudged Alison as they stood waiting for Loy and Edna, who moved slowly through the line threading its way to the airline counter. "What the hell is he doing here?" Helen muttered.

Before Alison could respond, Kittrick had spotted them

and was moving swiftly in their direction. Apparently he had only one retainer with him today. Helen made out the figure of a single bodyguard, muscular and bulky in his expensive dark suit, scurrying rather gracelessly behind the mechanical chair as it changed course and made a beeline toward them. The crowd parted as Kittrick waved one claw at them in either greeting or command.

"What a surprise," Helen said grimly, glancing at Alison. Her face was frozen in a blank smooth stare that Helen knew masked anger and resignation.

"Maybe he's leaving today too," Alison said as she locked her hands behind her back. Helen briefly wondered if the tight clasp of her hands was meant to prevent her from taking a swing at the old man.

"Afraid I'd missed you," Romie Kittrick wheezed. The chair whirred and clacked beneath him as he maneuvered it into a position that enabled him to see both their faces. "You didn't return my calls. Why not?"

Helen glanced at Alison, who blushed and turned away. "We've been very busy," she said with a quick flare of anger at Alison. She must have been getting the messages and not passing them on to Helen. "My aunt and uncle are leaving today, and we'll be leaving soon."

Edna and Loy joined the others as she finished her sentence. They looked in abashed awe at the gentleman who'd funded their excursion into Laughlin. "Mr. Kittrick, I don't believe y'all have met," Helen said, lapsing into a mild Southern accent and automatic manners in the face of being surrounded by so many others from her neck of the woods. Alison stood, a silent slender pillar, watching with a face that burned with anger and embarrassment. Her aunt and uncle were too confused at confronting Kittrick to say much of anything beyond a simple greeting.

Romie Kittrick sized up the situation quickly. "Alan, why don't you take these good folks — by the way, when does your flight leave? Not for another hour? My lord, yes, these delays are always so annoying. Yes, Alan, let's take these people over to the little diner they have over there and buy them some lunch." The cold blue eyes flickered back to Helen after this pronouncement was made. "I believe Ms. Black and I have some things to discuss in the lounge." He swiveled around to look at Alison. "Of course, Ms. — Young, is it? Ms. Young is most welcome to have a drink with me as well."

Alison stiffened at the invitation. "No, thanks. Helen, I'll stay with your aunt and uncle, if you don't mind."

"Of course not." She watched her lover stride impatiently ahead of the other three, then slow her steps to wait for Alan and the elderly couple to catch up with her.

"She's a real challenge to you, I suspect." Kittrick wheezed out a kind of chuckle while he swung the chair around to face the opposite direction. "The VIP lounge is right this way. They're expecting us."

"You don't want Alan to go with us?" Helen asked as they turned a corner and moved away from the noise of the airport crowd. The difference in sound level was astonishing. Helen was certain, as she followed Kittrick, that the corridor was deliberately designed to blot out the dull roar of the masses who milled through the echoing vault of the rest of the airport.

"Oh, Mr. Kittrick, Mr. Kittrick!" Helen turned to see Heather Gilley hurrying toward them as fast as her heels would allow. Her husband trailed behind her, loaded down with suitcases.

Heather grasped the arms of the wheelchair. "I just had to thank you before we left! You were our savior! Isn't that right, honey?"

Bud managed a smile. He glanced once at Helen then stared resolutely at the floor.

"I'm so glad Mr. Danvers could help you." Romie struggled to breathe as Heather leaned over him.

"Oh, he's the best lawyer in the world! He was right

there, all the time, until they dropped the charges and let Bud go. Didn't he, honey?"

"As I said, glad to be of service. Y'all have a safe flight home, now."

"Well, I was hoping to talk to you about the idea Bud and I had about the new gym we want to build over in Memphis. I thought you might be interested in getting in on the ground floor. Now, I have some information about the gym for you to look at. Honey, where is that folder?" She gestured impatiently at Bud, who sighed and unzipped one of the suitcases.

"Mrs. Gilley, my assistant Alan is over at the diner around the corner as we speak. Perhaps you could take him the folder, with my compliments?"

"Oh." Heather's face fell.

"I assure you, Alan handles all my most important business associates. He'll be able to help you."

After assurances from Kittrick that he'd be in touch with them, Bud and Heather trundled down the terminal and out of sight. "Poor pussy-whipped bastard," he said. "She'll definitely keep him on a very tight leash. And I'm afraid I haven't seen the last of her yet."

"You should have known after you sent her a lawyer that she'd stick around. That meant a lot to her."

"Anything to avoid an ugly lawsuit. People like the Gilleys would have sued me for ruining their Thanksgiving."

The chair whirred along the carpet, its mechanics muffled by thick carpet and paneled walls. "Thank God I sent Alan over to the diner with your folks. Contrary to popular opinion," Kittrick said, still chuckling, "I don't need a nursemaid twenty-four hours a day. Once in a while I'm permitted to go places on my own."

They reached the door of the VIP lounge. Above the heavy wood of the double doors a sign proclaimed this chamber to be the Lodge. Helen nodded at the pretty young blonde standing at a podium at the door. She nodded back, then smiled at Kittrick.

"We haven't seen you in a while, Mr. Kittrick," she cooed. With a silver pen she made a checkmark against some list on the podium. "Mr. Johnson is expecting you, and your guest," she added with a blatantly curious stare at Helen.

The doors swung silently open as he growled his thanks to Cindy, who must have pressed some sort of button hidden on the podium, Helen guessed, alerting the staff of the lounge to their presence. Under his breath, as he rolled inside, Kittrick muttered to Helen, "Little bitch can't wait to go out and gossip with everybody on her coffee break."

Helen shrugged. "Can't blame her. She probably doesn't see any real VIPs in her working day."

Kittrick grimaced in pain as he shifted in his chair, attempting to look up at her. "You mean, anyone who's got a murdered daughter and a son locked up in a mental institution." He turned away as two smiling young men, as blonde and pretty as Cindy, scurried up to them and arranged a table in a corner for Kittrick and companion. Helen allowed Kittrick to order drinks for both of them — bourbon and soda for her, bottled water for him — and surveyed the tweedy atmosphere of the lounge. A rack of pipes and tobacco jars ranged ostentatiously on a mantelpiece over a roaring fire that contained, she was sure, real live wood and real live flames. Paintings of hounds barking at dead foxes and birds loomed over leather-upholstered couches, and she even saw a smoking jacket sported by an elderly gent who chuffed and clucked and shook his head over the *New York Times* from a wing chair.

"I know," Kittrick said, grinning. "A bit out of place in the middle of Nevada, isn't it? At least they stopped short of hiring actors who could produce a passable English accent and wear a butler's uniform."

"Well," Helen answered after a sip of excellent bourbon, "that's kind of what a gambling resort is all about, I guess. Creating some sort of illusory world in the middle of a desert, letting people go places and do things they'd ordinarily have no chance at. Kind of like Hollywood, except you're not in a darkened theater — you're in a real, tangible environment."

"A real, tangible environment." Kittrick repeated her words thoughtfully and took a sip at his water, making a face at the glass as he set it down. "Like my son will be experiencing right now, courtesy of the police. A bit too real and tangible, I'm sure. I knew Wilbur was... excitable, but I never dreamed that — well, never mind."

"Do you know when they'll be transferring him to the hospital?" Helen asked. "All I heard was that he was being detained by the county."

He waved a gnarled hand. "Oh, that's already been done. All I have to do now is begin the whole paperwork process to get him from the institution in Nevada to the Jackson State Hospital. Shouldn't be more than a few weeks."

Not for the Kittrick family, at least, Helen thought. She shuddered at an old memory — driving with her grandfather in Jackson as a young child, going past the tall white stone walls behind barbed wire fences where in the distance, on the grounds of the hospital, a few forlorn figures in institutional white meandered aimlessly around straggling trees. She had no doubt that Romie Kittrick had more than enough pull on more than enough strings to get Wilbur moved out of Nevada back to Mississippi.

"I don't even think he knows who I am," Kittrick was saying with a quizzical tone in his voice. "He just rambles on at me about conspiracies and aliens. Looks like he's trying to write it all down, too. Guess his doctors thought it would be a good idea for him to keep journals, but from what he showed me so far it looks like he's just using pen and paper to make his manifesto. Maybe he thought I was somebody influential with the media."

Helen swallowed some more bourbon and leaned forward over their table. "You didn't drag yourself out here to the airport to talk about Wilbur, Mr. Kittrick."

"No, of course not." He took another sip of water, frowned and pushed his glass away. In the distance, their waiter looked anxiously in their direction but stayed in the background. "I need to know how you knew."

"About Nick." He nodded. Helen shook her head. "I've made numerous statements to the police, and of course when I'm called on to testify it will all come out soon enough —"

The table rattled as Kittrick slammed it, albeit weakly, with his fist. "Do I have to spell this out for you? I'll be lucky to make it past New Years', young woman. Tell me, now, before I go to my grave without knowing what happened to my children, to my family."

Studying his face, Helen saw only stubborn resignation — no anger, no shame, no sadness. "It was the towels."

"Excuse me?"

"That's what started me thinking about it. The room was all wrong. I was pretty sure that Carmel had used the room to meet with someone. Wilbur's pictures confirmed that she wasn't above doing that, using the hotel like her own mansion for being with lovers." She glanced up at him, worried about how he was taking this, but saw only grim determination. "And except for one bed not looking quite right, the room had definitely been cleaned by the maids. Bathroom spotless, carpet vacuumed, fresh mints on the table. There was just a pile of towels heaped on the end of the bed."

"Explain."

She shrugged. "This is speculation, but I'm guessing that Carmel would pay the maids on the sly to come in and clean up after her when she'd had one of her trysts. You know — straighten the room, change the sheets. What she didn't know that day, of course, was that Nick was filling in again for her mother. Like she used to do at the restaurant."

"So that girl" — he spat out the word as if it were a curse — "that girl came across Carmel alone, in the hotel room."

"That's what I think, anyway." Over and over again, during the last few hours, Helen had visualized the confrontation. Carmel, still flushed from sex, would perhaps have been preening in front of the mirror. She probably hadn't even known who Nick was, much less that Nick had been trying to meet with her. Maybe," Helen went on, "Nick tried to talk to her — introduce herself, explain who she was and how she knew Hef. After meeting Wilbur and seeing his photo album Nick might have thought she could blackmail Carmel and get enough money to get out of Laughlin."

Kittrick snorted. "She didn't know my daughter, then." He fumbled for his oxygen mask and waved at her to continue.

"Well," Helen said, looking at him closely. He now seemed to be breathing better, with the oxygen. "I think Carmel just laughed at Nick, maybe made fun of her or belittled her. Nick just lost it. She must have seen that Carmel wasn't going to listen, that Sue was just going to keep spiraling downward around Hef, that her own life was going to get worse and worse as her mother's did." Helen drained the last of her bourbon and looked down at the table, not wanting just then to meet Kittrick's eyes. "She probably took a swing at Carmel, they struggled, and in the fight Carmel struck her head."

"You mean she attacked my daughter."

Helen felt a wry smile stealing over her face. "Your daughter — her own mother, maybe, her whole miserable life. Carmel was just the figurehead, the person closest to hand she could blame for all her problems. Much easier than turning to her mother as the enemy, or facing down Hef, who was too big and too powerful, as well as allied to her mother."

The mask fell to Kittrick's side as he sighed, his color improved and his breathing easier. "Then why go to my son? He's another Kittrick, after all, no matter how sick and crazy he is."

"A psychologist would have to answer that one, but my guess is that she saw a kindred spirit. At least Wilbur had the same feelings toward you and Carmel that Nick did. He'd been hanging around the hotel a while, taking pictures. Nick would have had lots of opportunities to meet him at the Saddle. He's the one who supplied her with information about Carmel's lovers, remember? Not to mention that nothing would stand in the way of his inheriting the Kittrick millions, with Carmel out of the way. It must have seemed like her last chance, after seeing her mother die."

"And me without much longer to live," the old man whispered. "So, despite all the dysfunctional family bullshit it all boils down to money. She could get it through my son. And to think Wilbur showed her those photographs. Sickening."

Anger burned in her throat along with the bourbon. "What a fucking hypocrite you are," Helen said in a deceptively pleasant tone, with an eye toward the waiter who watched from the wings. "As long as it didn't besmirch the Kittrick family you couldn't give a flying shit whether or not Nick was exposed a few dirty pictures." She expected him to react with fury at her words, but she saw only surprise and even curiosity in his expression. "I have no doubt," she went on, "that if Nick weren't already dead, you'd be gathering wood to burn her at the stake."

His eyebrows lifted. "You can't even allow an old dying man the human capacity to pity this young woman, who saw her own mother die?" He smiled wearily. "Doesn't matter in the end, does it? At least she saw her mother go down in a kind of blaze of glory."

"A blaze of glory," Helen repeated. "As far as I'm concerned, anyone who can see tragedy as anything like a blaze of glory has lost all capacity to be human."

At first Helen thought he was having a seizure of some kind, but she soon realized that Kittrick was laughing at her. "Get the marble out of your ass, young lady," he wheezed once he'd caught his breath. "You're just as hypocritical and easily corrupted as the rest of the human race."

"Oh, really? I'm curious as to what makes you say that," she responded, leaning back and sipping at the bourbon.

In answer, he fumbled in his jacket and produced a slim envelope. "What makes me say that," he said, flipping the envelope across the table to her, "is this little experiment I've cooked up. An experiment that tells me you'll take what's in this envelope and use it."

"Why the hell should I take anything from you?"

"You could consider it a kind of payment for the picture of me you've been carrying around for a few days. Don't look so surprised. I told you Wilbur was writing his manifesto. Lots of details about what he believes is my own involvement in right-wing fascist movements."

Helen felt a chill run down her spine as she looked into his watery eyes. She wasn't sure how wise it would be to tell him she couldn't find the picture and assumed it had been lost in the scuffle at the cavern. "Are you telling me Wilbur is right?"

Kittrick managed a laugh. "My boy really got to you, didn't he? You don't know what to believe about me. Well, it doesn't matter if he's right or wrong. What matters is what's in the envelope I'm giving you."

"Kiss my ass, you piece of shit."

He folded his hands and cocked his head to one side, regarding her as if she were pinned down in a specimen jar. "We're a lot more alike than you might think. We both use people around us for our own ends. So did my children. Carmel used her lovers, and me, and her employees. Wilbur used Nick. Nick used Wilbur. The whole human race uses one another constantly, Ms. Black. Most of us just won't admit it. I am honest about my manipulations. That's the only difference between us."

"I certainly don't use people the way —"

"Oh, no? You might ask your lovely young girlfriend out there if she agrees with me."

"Fuck you, you old bastard." Furious, she shoved her chair back. "I won't let you drag Alison into your ugly hate, your contempt for the world and other people."

"I know you're dying to know what's in there," he said, still smiling, ignoring her anger.

In spite of her reluctance Helen picked it up, carefully opened the seal. The cashier's check, payable to her, was for more than she earned in six months. "I don't understand," she mumbled in amazement. "I've never contracted to work for you or your daughter. And what makes you think I'll take it, anyway?" She slid the check back into the envelope and laid the envelope on the table between them. Moisture from Kittrick's glass remained in small droplets next to the discarded cocktail napkin, and it seeped onto the edge of the envelope, spreading a pale stain on the creamy paper.

"I told you I wanted to know who killed my daughter. You did exactly that, whether working directly for me or not." He wheeled his chair backward, and the sudden motion signaled the blond waiter into action. He hurried to the doors and waited for Kittrick to exit. "I believe in paying a laborer his wages. And I know you need the money. You can't put up your shingle again without this cash. This is the best chance you'll get to go back into private investigation, and we both know it. And now," he said as he expertly wheeled his chair around and headed for the door, "if you'll excuse me, visiting hours at the county hospital will soon be over."

Helen shook her head and watched him as he wheeled away. She didn't get up until the waiter asked her if she'd like more bourbon.

"No, thanks." She sighed. "I've had more than enough."

The taste of the liquor still lingered in her mouth when, several hours later, she was behind the wheel of Alison's car heading west out of Nevada and back to Berkeley. Beside her, Alison slept, her mouth slightly open, her breathing deep and steady.

Helen turned onto the highway that would get them home, shifting gears. Kittrick's envelope crinkled inside her jacket pocket. Strangely, she didn't feel anything about it. Not right now. Maybe disgust would come later, or shame or guilt or grief or some other emotion that would keep her from going into the bank in a couple of days to deposit the check and start shopping for a new office. Or was her old one available? It was a good location, easy for prospective clients to find...

She shut those thoughts away and stared at the road. A couple of cars whizzed past, then a truck, then nothing for several miles. Alison shifted on the seat beside her. Just as clearly as Helen could see herself going to the bank and setting up her office on Shattuck, she could clearly see Alison fading out of her life over the next few months.

And who was to blame? Both of them? No one? Helen alone?

As much as she stared at the highway stretching out before her, it gave her no answers — just the dim glow of the stars, bathing the long dark road with soft light the color of pearl.

A few of the publications of
THE NAIAD PRESS, INC.
P.O. Box 10543   Tallahassee, Florida 32302
Phone (850) 539-5965
Toll-Free Order Number: 1-800-533-1973
Web Site: WWW.NAIADPRESS.COM
Mail orders welcome. Please include 15% postage.
Write or call for our free catalog which also features an incredible selection of lesbian videos.

WICKED GOOD TIME by Diana Tremain Braund. 224 pp. In charge at work, out of control in her heart.   ISBN 1-56280-241-0 $11.95

SNAKE EYES by Pat Welch. 256 pp. 7th Helen Black mystery.
ISBN 1-56280-242-9   11.95

CHANGE OF HEART by Linda Hill. 176 pp. High fashion and love in a glamorous world.   ISBN 1-56280-238-0   11.95

UNSTRUNG HEART by Robbi Sommers. 176 pp. Putting life in order again.   ISBN 1-56280-239-9   11.95

BIRDS OF A FEATHER by Jackie Calhoun. 240 pp. Life begins with love.   ISBN 1-56280-240-2   11.95

THE DRIVE by Trisha Todd. 176 pp. The star of *Claire of the Moon* tells all!   ISBN 1-56280-237-2   11.95

BOTH SIDES by Saxon Bennett. 240 pp. A community of women falling in and out of love.   ISBN 1-56280-236-4   11.95

WATERMARK by Karin Kallmaker. 256 pp. One burning question... how to lead her back to love?   ISBN 1-56280-235-6   11.95

THE OTHER WOMAN by Ann O'Leary. 240 pp. Her roguish way draws women like a magnet.   ISBN 1-56280-234-8   11.95

SILVER THREADS by Lyn Denison. 208 pp. Finding her way back to love...   ISBN 1-56280-231-3   11.95

CHIMNEY ROCK BLUES by Janet McClellan. 224 pp. 4th Tru North mystery.   ISBN 1-56280-233-X   11.95

These are just a few of the many Naiad Press titles — we are the oldest and largest lesbian/feminist publishing company in the world. We also offer an enormous selection of lesbian video products. Please request a complete catalog. We offer personal service; we encourage and welcome direct mail orders from individuals who have limited access to bookstores carrying our publications.